BIRD

WITH

THE

HEART

OF A

MOUNTAIN

BIRD
WITH
THE
HEART
OF A
MOUNTAIN

Barbara Mariconda

SKYSCAPE

SKYSCAPE

Text copyright © 2013 by Barbara Mariconda

Amazon Publishing
Attn: Amazon Children's Publishing
P.O. Box 400818
Las Vegas, NV 89140
www.amazon.com/amazonchildrenspublishing

Library of Congress Cataloging-in-Publication Data is available upon request.

ISBN-13: 9781477817339 (hardcover)
ISBN-10: 1477817336 (hardcover)
ISBN-13: 9781477867334 (eBook)
ISBN-10: 1477867333 (eBook)

Editor: Melanie Kroupa

Printed in The United States of America (R)
First edition
10 9 8 7 6 5 4 3 2 1

To Marissa –
may you always be
a bird with the heart of a mountain.

Spain, 1936—A country divided by war.

On the side of the moneyed classes and the Catholic Church are the Nationalists—who had help from Fascist governments like Hitler's Germany. In contrast, with support from the Soviet Union's Communist government, Republican loyalists champion the rights of the poor. In the midst of all this violence, mistrusted and slaughtered by both sides, stand the Gypsies. Sixteen-year-old Drina is one of them, yet she's also half Spaniard. She, too, is caught in the middle of this conflict.

This is Drina's story . . .

CHAPTER 1

Somewhere in Andalusia, Spain

MAY, 1936

The music seduces them.

I throw back my tumble of black hair, roll one bare shoulder forward, then the other. A wave of flesh, a flash of eyes. The stack of bangles on each wrist shimmies and slides as my hands rise like birds in flight. I sway my hips and my skirts billow and swirl.

At the outer fringe of this seacoast village, where the fairgrounds turn to nothing but dust and weeds, hungry men gather, drawn first by the driving rhythm, then hypnotized by the way my body moves.

Jascha sits off to the side, clawing the strings of his ancient guitar. His gnarly fingers strum in angry bursts, and the thumb and heel of his hand against the wood lay down the beat in between. On the ground, one tattered boot thumps a tambourine. He sings a raspy, wordless tune and, in turn, clicks a syncopated pattern with his tongue, all the while staring past the gathering crowd through his one crooked, sunken eye.

I know as well as anyone that, to these men, we Gypsies are no better than stray dogs. And that we, the Zaporatas, are even less than that.

But when the old man plays and I dance, I don't think.

I forget, for a time, who we are.

"Drina!" My mother calls from the tent. "Come in here." The sea breeze carries her voice. It lifts my hair from my forehead, whips the edges of my skirt around my ankles, fills the full sleeves of my blouse like the sails on a ship. I tilt my chin, throw back my head as Jascha furiously rakes the last bars of the tune.

"Drina!"

As the men disperse, she scowls, holds back the flap of the tent with one hand, her other hand on her hip. She steps out, fingering the gold and black pendant that rests at the hollow of her throat. I walk toward her, my bare feet shuffling the dust where our small *campagna* has set up camp.

"There will be another *feria* outside of Cadiz—time for you to earn a few *pesetas*. But turning tarot cards, reading palms, divining tea leaves—this takes practice!" She steers me by the elbow into the shade of the tent.

"But, the *feria* draws those who want to see us dance! I can—"

"No!"

Her face is a mask of stone, hard and steep as the limestone cliffs along the Arcos de la Frontera.

"But I do not see why . . ."

"You are right about this. You do not see why. You do not *need* to see why. I am telling you that dancing is not what you are to do."

"But—"

She pinches the soft underside of my arm.

"Ai!" It doesn't hurt much, but inside, my heart sinks.

My *daj* softens a bit, as she always does. "Come, we will share some tea before we begin."

She pours minty tea from a dented tin pot, aromatic steam rising from the cup. The sun filters through the tent cloth creating a golden glow. I am here with my *daj,* just the two of us.

Still, I wrap my hands around the cup and sip, refusing to meet her eyes. My resentment I wear like a heavy, oversized coat. But she pretends not to see.

We sit on the bright calico cushions that travel with us. The cloth from Granada, pieced, stitched, and sequined in Sevilla. She spreads a colorful woven scarf between us, fans the tarot cards, hands me the rest of the deck. I tap the rhythm of a *malagueña* against the stack of cards. Nod my head in time. This, she ignores.

She holds one card, facing away. "Here, the signifier? . . ."

"The card that represents someone, something. Asks a question we want answered." This I say in a flat voice. I look away. Try to hum a *rondeña.* Still, she is not put off. She flips the card. "Ah . . ." she says. Her dark eyes glint. "A powerful sign—the Empress . . ."

3

I hear Jascha's guitar outside. The sound of *jaleo* distracts me. My *daj* waits.

I inhale, then blow through puffed cheeks. "The Empress . . . she is pregnant. The creator—the womb where the primal spark grows." I recite from memory. "And like any new life, it is fragile. Requires patience and care."

"And what do you take from that?"

Outside, a seabird cries, its call soaring above Jascha's strumming.

"That it takes time to create a future."

"Yes." She looks away, touches the pendant again, running her fingers over its delicate black vines and cluster of grapes inlaid in gold. "The future unfolds . . ."

"What if my future is to be a dancer? Didn't Jascha say my father was a dancer?" This unknown father of mine—this dancer—surely he would see me, would recognize my need.

"Jascha says a lot of things." She gathers the deck in one sweep of her hand. Slaps the stack against her other palm. "For you, I want something better." Her voice has become brittle as glass.

I have pushed too far. Ruined the warm cocoon we could have shared here. I grasp at a way to reclaim it.

"Wait," I say. "I will turn one more card."

She nods, hands me the deck.

I shuffle, feel the cards fall in a wave between my fingers. I separate them in two piles, flip the edges with my thumbs, enjoy the sharp flutter like the roll of castanets. I repeat this several times, split the pile in two, and flip a card. My heart jumps.

"Nine of Cups!"

Forgetting that I am trying to make amends, I leap to my feet. I wave the card between us with a flourish. "Nine of Cups—the wish card! What you hunger for, you will receive!"

She stands, shaking her head slowly. Pauses. "Be careful what you wish for, Drina," she says in a hollow voice. "Your desire can be your undoing."

For a moment she looks through me, then wraps her arms around me in a sudden, crushing embrace. Standing stiffly, I stare over her shoulder. None of it makes sense. All of this I let go of as best I can and sink into the warmth of my mother's arms. She is all I have in this world, and though she maddens me, it is her approval that I seek.

And still, the Nine of Cups and the promise it holds remain with me.

Chapter 2

The day of the *feria* dawns gray and cool, sea mist swirling across the field and between our tents like wisps of smoke. A million teardrops of dew dampen the ground, weighing down the edges of my skirt and chilling my feet.

I slip away early to see what I can before joining my *daj* in her tent at the edge of the fairgrounds. The *Gadje* people—Spaniards and small groups of foreign *militares*—arrive as the sun begins to burn off the dew and chase away the mist.

There are many places here to lose yourself. A jumble of tents, booths, and tables form a ragged fringe around the festivities, housing sellers of food and vendors hawking trinkets, games, and curiosities of all kinds. I pause at a booth selling long strands of beaded necklaces. The fat woman behind the counter holds them to the light in her stubby, sausage fingers so the beads glitter and wink. She smiles and raises her eyebrows at me, then quickly shifts her attention to the next passer-by. Another tent displays combs carved from wood, etched with flowers and birds. I imagine pulling one through my hair a thousand times until it shines like silk. How I would like to be able to buy these things for my *daj* and me. Maybe, if I earn a *peseta* or two . . .

As people gather, our children run about, some clutching brightly painted boxes or small cloth bags, begging coins from the village men. They weave between the crowds with open hands and sorry faces. A few of the men toss them a *centimo* or two, and those who don't, give in spite of themselves when small, practiced fingers easily slip a *peseta* from the leather pouch hanging at a man's waist and skillfully lift a slender silver knife from the back pocket of another.

I move toward the center, where a small square of wooden planking covers the ground. Musicians assemble instruments, set chairs at the corner of the platform. I edge closer, see a *Gadje* man tightening the pegs on his guitar, tuning one string at a time, the tone sliding up, up, up until perfectly pitched. Another sets a tall drum between his knees, thumbs the drum skin, knocks at it with his knuckles. Two more guitars, another pair of drums, a stringed instrument like our *bari lavuta*, all of these being readied to play.

I find a rocky place off to one side and scramble up where I will be able to see over the heads of the gathering throng.

By the time the sun is almost directly overhead a pair of dancers appears. It is impossible to tear my eyes from the woman's scarlet, tight-fitting dress, sprinkled with black velvet dots, and the wide rows of black lace that flounce from ankle to knee. I imagine what it would be like to throw her fringed shawl across my shoulders, how I would let it slip, just so, to reveal the short, ruffled cap sleeves beneath it. On her head a black *mantilla* stands up on a red crown-like comb. Her partner is clad in tight black trousers and a short jacket embroidered in many hues. A flat-brimmed hat covers his head.

One strum of the guitar. Another. I edge through the crowd. Then her high-heeled black shoes strike the wooden floor like a roll of gunfire. She has the look of a sleek cat about to pounce. Suddenly she lunges, elbows raised like wings. Her shawl sails in rolling waves around her. She opens a fan, turns it round, snaps it shut. Her movements are sharp, deep. All the while, her partner edges closer. His feet pound against the floor, demanding, charging toward her and then retreating. He teases and tempts with his body, his eyes. Watching them makes me feel I should look away. But I cannot.

As they leave the stage, I am left with a longing that is like a deep thirst. I moisten my lips and return to myself, as I know I must. I push back through the crowd toward the tent. My *daj* will be waiting.

As I approach, a powerfully built yellow-haired man wearing the drab olive uniform of some militia emerges from my mother's make-shift lean-to. He shoves aside the canvas flap, pauses, spits, then hoists his dirty trousers higher on his waist. He smiles in a way that chills me. A moment later he's vanished into the crowd.

I run to the tent, rush inside.

I want to look away, but I can't.

My mother is sprawled on the ground, her skirts above her waist, her dress torn, breasts exposed. Her face is bloodied. She shakes her head, one forearm shielding a bruised and swollen eye.

"No . . ."

It's a moan more than a word.

"No . . ."

I catch my breath and kneel beside her. She winces, slowly props herself up on one elbow. Covers herself with her skirts. Yanks up the bodice of her dress. She's breathing hard, crying without tears.

I reach for her but she shoves my hand away.

"Leave me," she says through clenched teeth. She will not look at me.

"Just find Jascha and go."

"But . . ."

She raises a hand. "Now! I'll follow later . . . later."

I stand, heart pounding. She grabs my ankle. Her fingers dig in. She looks at me, finally. Her eyes are black coals.

"And tell *no* one. Do you hear me Drina? *No one!*"

I bite my lip and taste blood.

Outside, the bright light makes me squint. A sudden gust

of sea air lifts the edge of my skirt, and the word *Levante* swirls around the edges of my brain. Some say that when the wind they call *Levante* blows, it can cause every sort of madness.

I smooth my skirt and will myself to walk toward the wagon where Jascha waits.

"Where's Nadja?"

With his near-sightless eyes Jascha looks straight ahead over the bowed back of the mule, the reins slack in his hands.

I swallow, grateful he can't see my face, and take a deep breath to steady my voice.

"Another customer. She said for us to go on ahead."

The sound of the distant surf fills the silence between us. He glances over his shoulder at me. I feel him turning over my words, sensing some mystery between what my words say and my tone betrays.

He shrugs, then gives the reins a sluggish flip against the mule's flank. The cart jerks forward, its wheels throwing up a cloud of dust. I chance a look back at my mother's tent, at the bright colors just visible over the top of the hill. Now she's completely alone there. Sweat trickles from under my arms and snakes down my sides. The wind picks up again. I'm cold despite the lemony May sunshine. The brigade is camped just outside the fairgrounds. Will the yellow-haired soldier come back with his comrades? My skin ripples in a wave of gooseflesh. Would he? . . .

I grab Jascha's shoulder, yank his tunic. "Wait! Stop!"

"Whoa!" He pulls the mule to a halt. The beast stamps the ground impatiently and makes a flubbery sound blowing through his bit. Jascha turns. "What?"

I don't even think. The words come on their own.

"I'll wait for her. I've been wanting to tell fortunes. Read palms. Turn the tarot cards. I'll listen. Watch. We'll walk back together."

Jascha looks away and shrugs. I jump from the cart and run.

"Yah!" I hear the reins snap and the wheels rumble over the deeply rutted trail. I cut crossways through the field. My feet fly. My heart races. I don't stop until I'm there, out of breath, my chest heaving.

"Leave me. Find Jascha and go."

I hadn't thought about what I'd do when I got to the tent. She'll be angry I disobeyed.

I walk around the side, silently, placing one bare foot down, then the other. Stop. Stand against the tent, the sun before me so as not to cast my shadow against the cloth. I lean forward and look through a small gap between two sheets of fabric.

She's just as I left her, lying on the ground with her arm across her eyes. The sight steals my breath from me, because although I know she's alive—her chest rises and falls, her fingers twitch—the zest, the spirit that was Nadja must have trickled from her when that animal of a man spilled his seed inside her. I turn my eyes away. My fists are clenched and my nails press into the fleshy part of my hands. I need to *do* something. Break something. Maybe even kill something. Anything to release the sick churning inside me.

She groans. I peer through the slit in the tent. She's sitting up, her face blotchy. Her right eye swollen shut.

I hold my breath and hear her inhale, a long trembly sound.

She reaches for the scarf on the ground beside her, the *diklo* she always wraps around her dark hair, the one with gold specks that brings out the spark in her eyes. I cover my mouth with my hand, as she slowly lifts her skirt, spreads her knees apart, and begins to wipe away his filth.

I lower my eyes, wanting to erase what I've seen.

Now what?

I walk on silent feet back to the edge of the field and wait. Empty my brain, count to twenty . . . thirty . . . one hundred . . . If I can just hold steady, I might not explode. I might know what to do.

My heart begins to slow and I concentrate on the air around me, the way it blows through my hair, how it plays against my skin, how it whispers secrets through the trees, disturbing the leaves. . . . Shhhhh . . . I hear a bird, several birds in those trees beyond the field, their song suddenly loud in the silence, the lilting cheerfulness in contrast to everything else.

I tip my head back and take a deep, long breath. My feet begin to carry me forward.

"Mama," I call. "My *daj*, I've come back for you. And I'm coming in."

CHAPTER 3

It's six months before she starts to show. An extra shawl, a fuller skirt—that, and Jascha's dim sight and disregard, leave her secret with me alone. As the child grows in her, anxiety swells in me like a separate twin, a shadow sibling. When my eyes ask unspoken questions, her response is a dark glance, as if knowing is my fault.

From the day we silently walked back to camp, my mother and I have spoken, or not spoken, only in code. We both understand that my sudden desire to tell fortunes and turn tarot cards is my way to keep her from being alone. Yet what feels like gratitude at having me near one moment feels like resentment the next. I stay beside her, practice with the tarot, study the lines of palmistry. It seems I have some talent at reading Tarot.

But it is an unwanted gift. It does not make me long for dancing any less.

She told Jascha the two of us would be joining her sister's people for the next season. This to earn a better wage until Raul returns. To me Raul is nothing: Jascha's son, my mother's husband. He loves to remind me that my own father is an outsider—a *Gadje*. That he's not Romany, that he abandoned my mother when she became pregnant with me. I do not even know the name of this father of mine.

Yes, my mother is wise to leave before Raul tires of fighting the *fascistas*—the fascists. He left with a group of local peasants led by Russian *militares* to go off into the mountains with guns and explosives. Rumors fly—the latest that Raul's brigade had blown up a train and terrorized a town. Does he care for peasants and their politics? I doubt it. I think he sniffs out and hunts down any excuse to do violence. He has the heart of a jackal.

And now this. It is good we are leaving.

With rheumy eyes studying my mother, Jascha had nodded his agreement. There would be two fewer mouths to feed. Three, actually, is what I thought.

So each day we pass the time under a flimsy tent beside the dirt lane waiting for Aunt Luludja's clan to come through, as they always do in late autumn. We watch, too, with anxious eyes, for the troops—Republicans and Nationalists—who circle each other like rabid dogs itching for the war to erupt full force. And we know, firsthand, how they amuse themselves as they wait.

This day we sit, the Tarot deck spread face down across a

fringed shawl. I sweep the cards into a pile with one wave of my hand, slowly shuffle them, feel their worn, velvety edges against my palms. Glancing up, I see a flock of swallows winging their way south, as they do this time every year. Something like longing quickens in my heart at the sight of them returning, once again, to some distant shore. How good it must feel to fly free and still have a place to come home to. I sigh and wonder what this time away will bring.

The cards, I think, may tell.

I cut the deck several times, asking my questions: "What will this journey be like? What will happen to my *daj*? To this baby? To me? Who will we be when we return, *if* we return?"

I finger the top card, the signifier, close my eyes, and slowly turn it over. Open my eyes. Inhale sharply.

The Death Card—

Scorpion.

Serpent.

Eagle.

With trembling fingers I pick up the card and shove it back into the middle of the deck, out of my mother's view. I pluck the four edges of the shawl together around the cards and my few possessions and tie a quick knot.

In the distance I see a blur of color. They are nearly here. I shake my head to clear the dark images—scorpion, snake, eagle—and grab hold of my *daj*. Together we stand, our eyes fixed on the curve of the road. Looking straight ahead she squeezes my hand and, briefly, I rest my head against her shoulder. Perhaps, with her own people, she will find a way out of this darkness that has settled around us.

The line of *vardos* approach like a colorful bumping train, some of the wagons with curved wooden tops, their sides scrolled with carved swirls and curlicues. Curtained windows wink along the sides and backs. I am aware of all of this, but still I see scorpion . . . serpent . . . eagle.

Closer and closer they come. The horses snort, wheeze, and throw back their heads. The wooden-spoked wheels rumble and clank. We stare at this procession until the first of the *vardos* slows to a stop. Relief pours over me. Yes, I think, it will be better here in the midst of her clan. This hope I cling to like the last coin in my pocket.

My auntie jumps from one of the wagons, runs from the back of the caravan.

"Nadja! Drina!"

Holding my mother at arm's length she flashes a wide smile, then embraces her. My mother stands stiffly, her eyes dart to the side. Luludja shifts her gaze to me. I try to smile but my mouth doesn't yield.

A cool damp breeze lifts a strand of hair on my mother's forehead revealing deep furrows. In the November light her skin looks dull and lifeless. Aunt Luludja looks at me closely, I shrug, and drop my bag into the wagon. The old man driving the carriage, my great uncle, I think, pats the seat beside him and up I go. Wordlessly, Luludja takes my mother by the arm. I watch anxiously as they climb in back.

"You don't remember your old Uncle Hanzi," he says to me.

"No worry. Here we are now—plenty of time . . . and stories to tell . . ."

He smacks the backsides of the pair of sway-backed horses with a thin switch, and the wheels turn up a cloud of brown dust. He stares at me, and even though he's no longer smiling, the deep creases around his eyes and mouth hold the memory of it. I nod. No words come to mind. *"Kak* Hanzi," I say finally, staring straight ahead, using the respectful form of the word "uncle."

"Little Drina," he answers. I turn and look at him. He smiles again as we lurch forward, displaying one long white tooth, a gaping space, then a row of teeth like a crooked fence.

This is how our journey begins.

Chapter 4

One by one, they find excuses to come and sneak a look at me—the half-Gypsy, half-Spanish cousin / niece / curiosity—who they have, I am sure, heard something about. I suspect they know more of my origins than I do, which makes me want to protect the parts of me they don't know. I stay to myself, eyes lowered, chin tucked, shuffling my tarot cards, and pretend to concentrate on weaving a basket that should be round but is a lopsided oval instead.

Old Kak Hanzi provides commentary on each of the clan as they pass.

"Jofranka—the big one carrying the water bucket—her breasts hang down past her waist." He laughs silently, shoulders shaking. "Always smiling—like a fox, that one, or a snake. Watch out for her bite! Her husband, Tobar—as skinny as she is fat—there, with the drooping mustache and red cap— a tinkerer, he is—makes little tools and trinkets of tin."

I look in the direction Hanzi points and I recognize Tobar. "He can't hear, can he?"

Hanzi chuckles. "Just pretends he can't hear so he doesn't have to listen to Jofranka. Can't blame him, can you?"

I shake my head, smile. "What about him?" I stare through the wave of hair falling across my face.

Tall and barrel-chested, a young man walks slowly with his shoulders back, chin high. He has thick, muscular arms that bulge under his tunic. Black eyes shine beneath heavy brows. On his shoulder is a huge brown-feathered hawk wearing a leather mask-like helmet that covers its eyes like blinders on a horse. It occurs to me that the young man and the raptor are like brothers. They resemble each other—wild, only barely tame. Poised to fly. Ready to snatch up some careless creature as soon as the opportune moment presents itself.

He stares at me, through me. I glance up, and instead of looking away, his deep eyes bore into me until I turn, my face flushed.

"You don't need to know about him," Hanzi says.

"What's his name?"

Hanzi sighs. "No use," he says to himself, or to me, I'm not sure which. He clamps his mouth shut.

All afternoon I help the women prepare the evening meal, a meager vegetable stew, and listen to their banter. I watch, take it all in, keep my mouth shut. My mother sits beside me peeling a spotted potato. She's there but not there, drawn into herself, speaking only when spoken to. She is a stranger to me now, in the grips of this paralyzing sadness. Soon everyone will know her secret. Surely they suspect. BeeBee Luludja knows, of course she does. I've avoided my aunt these first days. I don't know what to say, or not to say.

Evenings, the *campagna* pulls into a circle around a roaring fire and the clan gathers. I stick by Kak Hanzi—not right alongside him—but near enough to meet his eyes. I have little appetite, and I play with the food in the tin dish passed along to me. Pushing the slices of vegetables around with a chunk of hard bread, I watch my mother stare into the fire. She sits forward and wraps her thin arms around her legs. Her face is vacant, her body a shell. I wonder where my *daj* has gone, and I am so absorbed in this that I scarcely notice the girl who sweeps in beside me and sits down, casting a look over her shoulder at another young woman who watches through narrowed eyes.

Once seated she smiles broadly and I'm taken aback by the stark contrast between her face and my mother's. This girl is as open as my mother is closed. She doesn't even try to conceal her interest in me as she looks me up and down. Her close-set eyes sparkle beneath arched brows, her nose a little too wide, her lips full. *"Kasko san?"* she asks, but doesn't wait for an answer. "Never mind," she smiles, "I already know where you come from. You're from Jascha's clan, and Nadja and Luludja are sisters."

I stare over my bowl at her, bread dripping, mouth open, then shift my gaze toward Kak Hanzi. He smiles. Nods. I glance back at her. "Drina," I say.

Her smile widens. "Kizzy . . ." She taps my shoulder. "You and I will be friends!" It comes from her lips as a fact, a certainty. The other girl, Jofranka's daughter—they both share the large breasts and squarish build—throws back her hair and pretends not to hear. I wonder, for a moment, if Kizzy's words are intended just for me or for this other girl's ears. Either way, something about this Kizzy draws me in, and the thought of a friend stirs the loneliness inside me with hope.

"Yes, friends . . ." I nod toward the necklace of gold coins hanging around her neck. "You're engaged."

"To Mihai." She waves to a young man tuning a violin. For a second he loves her with his eyes, then pulls the bow across the strings, listening, adjusting, tightening the tuning pegs and plucking each string with his index finger. Other musicians gather around him, guitars and violas, small drums, and tambourines, all readying to make music.

"What's wrong with your mother?" Kizzy asks.

I sigh, blowing a long, hollow whoosh of air through my lips, her directness rendering me mute. How to explain?

Kizzy touches my arm with her hand. "It's all right," she says, shaking her head. And that's that.

The music begins, a traditional *Gitano* tune. My heart thrills. I tap my feet. Like an itch, or a fever, it rises in me.

The buxom girl moves to the center and begins to dance. Kizzy snorts. "Florica," she says, shaking her head, "thinks she's something."

So do the young men, I watch the way they ogle her. Anyone can see she dances for them. For their eyes on her. As she spins, she casts haughty looks our way, seductive glances toward the men. A rivalry exists, surely, between Florica and Kizzy. And here I am in the middle of it.

The song ends and the next begins. This one, too, I recognize. Kak Hanzi peers at my *daj*, tips his head. "Nadja," he calls, a smile pulling at the edges of his mouth, "I remember how you turned heads . . ."

"And look where it got her!" Luludja glares at the old man, a reaction he seems to relish.

"You there, Drina," he calls, turning his attention to me, waving a hand toward the music. "Let's see if you're half the dancer your mother was."

My mother? A dancer? I look at my *daj*, the question tickling my tongue. She dismisses my silent query with a flick of her wrist, her mouth puckered as though tasting something bitter. Kak Hanzi jumps to his feet, knobby fingers curling and uncurling, gesturing for me to get up. "Drina," he insists, "You dance!"

Florica glowers. The focus of the crowd shifts from her to me. My face burns at their curiosity. Old Hanzi takes my hand, raises it in his. "*This* one has dance in her blood!"

Florica freezes. "*Gadje* blood!" She spits the words. Crosses her arms.

Hanzi ignores her, nudging me to the center. Kizzy whistles and claps. "Dance, Drina!" she shouts. "*Baila! Baila!*"

I hesitate, staring at the ground. Feel their eyes eating me up. The thought of my *daj* as a dancer . . . Perhaps, then, there is a way to appeal to her, to win her over, to draw her out of herself. The musicians pull back to just the heartbeat of bass guitar and drum.

Inhale. Exhale. Inhale.

I hold my breath, abruptly lift my chin, and throw back my shoulders.

The clan sits up in anticipation and falls silent.

I turn my head slowly, deliberately, scanning the mosaic of gaping faces and hanging mouths. Beside Luludja, my mother. My hands sweep upward with the melody, weave outward toward her. Palms up. Longing fingers. Begging hands. *Look Daj, look mother, I am here.* My desire burns. *See me, please.*

I roll up on my toes, rock to my heels, the backs of my calves tensing. My mother stares through me. The guitar enters, strumming furiously, driving forward, rippling through my thighs, my hips. Yes. The crowd knows it's about to begin. I have captured them. They are mine. All except one.

I give way to the ache that rushes through me. It fuels the dance, charges the night. Florica scowls, challenging me to misstep. I snap my head right, left, lower my chin, stare her down. Then back to my mother, the fixed point at the center of my whirling, hers the face I spot, again and again. Elbows bent, my hands beside my face, I clap *jaleo*. Demanding. Insisting.

Faster and harder I spin. My arms arc above me. My pulse and the music beat in time. My feet pummel the ground, kicking up a cloud of dust. Mihai's violin circles like an angry hornet, the sound of the *bari lavuta*, snakes below. They move. I move. We are one.

The song ends. I am exhausted, frustrated, and satiated all at once. Part of myself is left behind in the dance. My chest heaves, my head clears. Hanzi is grinning, his crooked teeth flashing, as though I'm the creation of his hands. Kizzy claps wildly and runs to Mihai. Turning on her heel, Florica walks off, glaring at me over her shoulder. I search for my mother.

There Nadja sits, nibbling the side of her thumb. Smoothing her skirt. She blinks at me. Invisible—still, I am invisible to her, blinded as she is by her own misfortune. Even a protest, an admonition against my desire to dance, would have been something. I long to be enough to draw her back to life—but clearly I am not.

Suddenly, I am so very tired. I've shown them all too much of me. And the one I yearn to see me couldn't.

The man with the hawk, whose name I do not know, stands to the side, staring. His lips are parted as though about to speak, or to invite a kiss.

I look down. When I sneak another glance, he is gone.

All that is left is the hawk circling the sky above the spot where he had been standing.

CHAPTER 5

Kizzy fingers the gold coins on her necklace. They jingle brightly.

I pick up the wooden brush. "Stay still, Kizzy, so I can work through these tangles!" She fidgets and grimaces as I brush her hair in long strokes until it glistens. "Ow!" she says good-naturedly. "Drina, don't be so rough!" She slaps my hand and I smile. Her exaggerated scolding warms me. Never have I had a friend like this, with whom teasing, talk, and even silence feels easy.

I carefully twist a fistful into a braid, weave small scarlet and yellow rock roses and some more gold coins into the thick column of plaited hair. It must look lovely today. It's the last time Kizzy will have her rich mane uncovered.

The *bandolier* is waiting to officiate. The wedding feast is prepared and the smell of the roasting meat makes our mouths water. The women have been busy for days with platters of herbed fried potatoes and savory boiled cabbage. All this scraped together and hoarded—good food a rarity since the war began.

"Stand up, Kizzy. Let me look at you!"

She is beautiful.

A pleated skirt in shades of ruby, violet, green, and gold sways with her, revealing strips of bright floral fabric beneath a layer of chiffon. Her mother and the aunties adjust her billowy red blouse, playfully loosening the satin drawstring at the neckline to reveal a little more bosom. Kizzy blushes and pretends to readjust it. The puffed sleeves are like large blossoms—peonies or hydrangeas—and her forearms look graceful beneath them. I, too, am feeling the specialness of this day in a full printed skirt the color of ripe pears and apples, cinched at the waist, and a gold, blousy shirt of Kizzy's that she insisted I wear.

The old woman—the one they call Catarina—enters the tent. The color drains from Kizzy's face for a moment, then returns, creeping from her chest to her neck and cheeks. Catarina is, no doubt, the *ajuntaora*, her arrival signaling my exit. The old aunties stay, of course, while Kizzy's mother, Shimza, steps outside with me. We stand side-by-side, saying nothing at all. The wedding guests elbow one another, waiting for the results of the *pañuelo*.

It must be done, I know, but I can't imagine leaning back, pulling up my skirts, that old crone examining me down there with the whole group of old Beebees watching. Every woman has to go through it, but lying there, spreading your legs . . . I press my eyes tight at the thought of that other tent, of my mother, her scarf in her hands, wiping . . . I shudder.

"Are you all right, dear one?"

Shimza touches my arm. I nod. "It's just a part of life, after all. Good girls like you and my Kizzy have nothing to worry about. Of course they'll find her intact."

I'm grateful the conversation is cut short. The flap on the tent is pushed open and Catarina appears, her triumphant smile revealing one gold tooth. She waves a cloth embroidered with three rose petals round and round in the air. The old Beebees march behind her, all of them singing, *"El Yeli! El Yeli!"* Kizzy emerges. She glances up, and I know she is searching for me. For a second our eyes meet. I see relief that this required indignity is over. The clan cheers, and as tradition dictates, the men tear their shirts, rush toward Kizzy. She laughs as they scoop her into the air and carry her on their shoulders toward the *bandolier*. Across the field I see Mihai being carried as well. I watch as their gaze connects them across the throng. Children, and a few stray dogs, run wildly around the edges of the festive group.

I follow the crowd, catch sight of Florica standing to the side with hands on hips. My mother, Luludja, and Jofranka sit with a group of women near the front. Luludja gestures for me. I pause. I feel the heat of someone's presence and turn.

He is smiling at me. Nods. Without the raptor on his shoulder he seems less fierce. I straighten the smile that teases my mouth, yet find myself nodding back. There is no way, unfortunately, to erase a nod. Immediately, I look away. Sneak a glance back. He nods again, an eyebrow raised. Kak Hanzi watches with pursed lips. Florica through narrowed eyes. Jofranka elbows Luludja. My mother stares. Others follow their gaze, making something of nothing. Something else to whisper about. Damn him! I'm aware that I'm scowling. He winks. I sweep away, quickly, toward my aunt and mother.

Kizzy and Mihai join hands in front of the *bandolier*. A tall man of wide girth, his importance in the clan is evident in his fine clothes. His neckerchief of bright satin stands out beside his richly ornamented tapestry vest. He brandishes a large gold ring as he waves us closer.

"Join hands," he says. "Mihai and Kizzy, do you promise to be true to one another?"

Hand in hand, face to face. "Yes!" they say.

The *bandolier* signals Catarina and the old Beebees. They come forward bearing a chunk of bread and a bowl of coarse salt. The men place chairs behind Kizzy and Mihai. They sit. The platter is set on Kizzy's lap. Mihai breaks a piece off, sprinkles on a pinch of salt, eats. Kizzy does the same. All to seal a harmonious future, with a little spice.

The music begins. Everyone is on their feet. A glass of ruby red wine is pressed into my hand. I take a swallow, feel its heat along my throat, its earthy fruit taste tingling on my tongue. Looking around, I am struck that I am a part of this, despite my mother's insistence on staying to herself. My heart suddenly swells toward Kizzy, who has pulled me in and kept me close. A tap on my arm and Jofranka passes me a plate of steaming fare. I realize I am becoming one of them. Included. Or perhaps it is the wine warming my view. Either way, my spirits are lifted as together we eat, ravenously after much war-time going without. Roasted pork, cabbage wrapped around rice and crumbled meat, vegetables in spicy sauce . . . Everyone is happy for this union, for this reason to celebrate. I try to eat slowly, fighting the urge to wolf down my plateful of food. I press my mother to take something, to nourish herself. "My dear *daj*, you must eat," I say. She is painfully thin, except for the bump beneath her skirt. Just as that *Gadje* soldier stole her life from her, his baby and this shortage of food are stealing what little fat Nadja has left on her bones.

Then Kizzy and Mihai open the dancing, Kizzy swirling her skirts, Mihai slapping ankles, knees. Clap, clap, stepstepstep, clap, clap, stepstepstep! In moments, everyone joins in, even the old Beebees circle one another, their movements small but true, stooped and shrunken shadows of their long-ago girlish selves. I see Kak Hanzi take up with one of them. Kizzy swings by, grabs my hand. I join in.

The tempo increases. Little by little the elders sit, leaving a small group of us whirling at a frenzied tempo. I spin, throw my head back just as the band drives home the final bar and abruptly flows into a *fandango*.

Sweat beads across my forehead. My chest heaves. I look up to discover his face, inches from mine. I back away. The crowd laughs and forms a circle around us. He moves, in time, toward me, in the traditional way of this courtship dance. Smooth and flirtatious, his hands grasp his lapels, his chest puffs out like a rooster—a cock strutting across the barnyard. I glare at him for putting me—us—in the center of things. This only serves to fuel the crowd, delighted at what they see as the feigned drama of the dance. He advances with the familiar crossover step, thumbs now latched to his belt buckle. As I step awkwardly away, Florica smirks. Kizzy yells, *"Baila* Drina!" Mihai whistles through his teeth and shouts. *"Baila* Boldo!"

Boldo.

He bears down toward me, his dark eyes never leaving my face. Swaggers to the beat. Challenges me.

Well then. We'll see if Boldo is as adept at the *fandango* as he is at falconry.

I know the steps by heart. Left over right. Step back. Shift weight. I raise my arms, arch them above me, fingers fluttering. Boldo mirrors my every step, but his upper body and arms are still, his muscles tense beneath his flowing cream-colored shirt. Advance. Retreat. Almost touching, an electric space between us. The crowd claps with cupped hands, echoing the rhythm. I circle in front of Boldo, shoot a glance over my shoulder. My hands weave circles in the air. They say, *Come.* They say, *Off with you. Come. Off with you.* Tempting and teasing.

I turn my head. Jofranka is nodding to the music, Luludja clapping. My mother suddenly straightens up—it's as though her spirit has returned, filling her body like wind in the sails of a ship. She stands, stares at me, and my heart thrills. She sees me? Dancing! She reaches out her hand. Points. Her eyes are wide.

But there is something not right about her face. All this I notice in the passing of a beat, in one single step. The moment hangs there and everything in my world slows. She isn't pointing at me, but past me. She looks through me, behind me, her face a frozen mask of hate, or maybe terror. A sound comes from her mouth, but her scream is swallowed by chaos.

I feel Boldo moving away even before I turn in the direction my mother points. And now bedlam is erupting all around me. Men are grabbing chairs, tent poles, knives—anything that can be used as a weapon. Women and children are running for the woods.

From over the hill, across the field, and now into the camp swarms a militia of maybe fifty men. Fifty of the yellow-haired man's brigade in their dirty olive trousers and *militar* shirts. My mother's nightmare multiplied. My heart has stopped, until Kizzy yanks my arm.

"Quick! Hurry!" Her face is white, hands frantic. My mother screams still, the sound lost in the din of tables and wagons being overturned, men shouting, the blunt thud of clubs, rifles hitting anything in their path. Shimza sweeps us on.

"Move!" she shouts, "Move!" She grabs. Pushes.

I pull away, take hold of my mother. Luludja has her other arm. She falls limp against us. We drag her toward the woods where we peek from behind the trees.

They are like a pack of mad dogs, starving and vicious. While some of them fight, others grab any food they find, devouring, shoving as much as they can into their mouths. They rip through the wagons, steal anything they can carry.

Boldo has moved to the back of the fray. I see what he's

trying to do—protect the food wagon. Chickens squawk and squabble as they're grabbed by their skinny feet, shoved under jackets and into sacks. One group of soldiers pile our food on an open cart—small but precious bags of grain and coffee, sacks of potatoes, jars of preserved fruit. Mihai, Cato, the men from the band—they punch, they kick. One swings a long piece of wood. Other *Gitanos* grab tools and implements, break bottles of wedding wine, handing off the crude glass weapons. A silver blade flashes, someone falls. Hanzi, the *bandolier*, and the elders, still in their wedding finery, grab what food they can, hustle it off to secret places. Another group fights over our horses. I gasp as one of our men is struck with the butt of a gun and drops to the ground.

My mother rocks back and forth. Crazed with rage, I take a step forward—to do what?

A gunshot, then two or three more, and the fight is over. The militia backs away, guns drawn, until they can run. They take two horses, two wagons, all the food they can carry.

As they retreat, Old Catarina steps into the open, her left hand extended toward them. Her chin trembles, her fingers shake. She crosses herself with her other hand. Her eyes are wild, then her lids droop, closing halfway. She lifts her wrinkled face. With a harsh call like a raven she shouts at them, *"Gadje* men! A curse upon your souls and the souls of your children!"

A shot rings out and Catarina falls.

A thought creeps in, uninvited. How I once saw a doe, shot through the heart with an arrow. The creature's legs crumpled beneath her. As she died, she extended her graceful neck, as though savoring her last breath.

Catarina does the same, tilting her face to the sky, lips parted. I glimpse her golden tooth, her head cloth slipping from her silver hair. I can almost hear her rasping, only it is not air but the curse that she tastes on her lips as she dies there in front of us.

ℭHAPTER 6

The body of Catarina is moved onto a make-shift stretcher beneath a canopy—the very spot where we danced just an hour ago. Shimza and the women move quickly, placing two silver coins over the old woman's eyes. Mirrors are covered. Water jugs emptied.

The lamentation begins. Jofranka and Florica, the Beebees and Luludja clasp their hands, fall to their knees, rock forward and back. Their faces, distorted masks in the late afternoon light. Eyes flash and roll white. The veins in their necks strain as they keen through taut, barely parted lips. Others join in. A wild sound, like a pack of wolves. It is chilling and right.

Kizzy stands just a few yards away like a column of stone, her back to me. I try to inhale deeply, but my breath comes fast and shallow. I shudder. I should go to her, but what is there to say or do?

She turns then, slowly, and faces me. Her wedding skirt is torn. Her eyes half closed, her face steel. Arms pressed tightly against her sides, fists clenched.

I am frightened. Where has my Kizzy gone?

I reach out. My fingers touch her cheek and push back loose tendrils of hair. Wipe away a smudge of dirt and sweat. Kizzy's bottom lip trembles, then quakes, and her face collapses. Her body heaves against mine. We cry for the wedding that died, and we cry for Catarina as well. Now all is *marime*—polluted, tainted.

The sun slips to twilight, twilight to evening. Kizzy and I watch the clan gather Catarina's belongings. Things useful to her for her soul's journey will be placed in her coffin. All her remaining earthly possessions are tossed into the bonfire. The flames dance, crackling and snapping as they lap at the old woman's ancient wedding portrait, the edges rolling up and disappearing in charred black curlicues. A carved wooden box, a fringed shawl, brown leather shoes with woven rope soles are consumed, sending sparks into the darkness.

Mihai, Boldo, and the younger men collect what can be salvaged. Women tend to those bleeding and broken. Kizzy circles about slowly, aimlessly. She runs her hand along the edge of a tipped table, steps gingerly between shattered bottles, spilt wine pooled like blood between shards of broken dishes. I step ahead of her, pushing aside trampled flowers, a torn table cover with a bloodied edge, a viola with a broken neck, sprung pegs, its strings coiling wildly. All of this I shield from her as best I can.

The older men construct a rough coffin, while others prepare the grave. This funeral must be quickly done, as nothing can happen—including the rest of the wedding ritual—until Catarina is buried.

"Ashen Devlesa, Romale," we say as Catarina is lowered into the earth, "May you remain with God."

Only then is the *divano* called, in a simple tent beside an overturned wagon. The elders sit on the ground in a half circle around a small fire, the *bandolier* in the middle on an upended wooden bucket. One by one the younger men join the outer circle. Kizzy and I mix with the shadows and slip around the back. It is not proper for the women to take part, but there is nothing to say we cannot overhear some words being thrown across the fire.

"What side were they on?"

"Who could know? They all wear the same uniforms, these small militias."

Their voices weave in and out, overlapping like the flickering flames we see illuminating the tent.

"Hungry, desperate men . . ."

"Fascists are winning . . . Fascist Nationalists. The ones with the fat pockets, land and property, German planes . . ."

I remember then, talk in the villages along the road of planes dropping many bombs on Barcelona. Talk of Nazis, of a Spaniard named Franco, of boats called submarines that swim beneath the sea. At the time, I paid it little mind. Barcelona and its war seemed far away, of no concern to me or to my people. We were used to abuse from both sides.

"The Republicans," a deep voice says. "Of course. The hands that stole from us were peasants' hands—calloused, strong. These Republican Loyalists have killed many Romany *Católicos*, burned churches. This I heard from another *campagna*."

Católica—we might be Catholic, I think. I see the cross hanging in some of the wagons, the pictures of the man Jesus with the glowing heart shooting sunrays, his mother with the sad eyes—Maria is her name. Kizzy crosses herself and I do the same. Yes, we must be Catholic.

The *bandolier* then, "True, but the Fascist Nationalists killed many of our *Rom* as well. They kill any who have helped the Republican peasants."

One of the men stands. His silhouette is distorted against the cloth of the tent, but still I recognize the broad chest and wide shoulders.

"So they fight, rich against poor, ruler against worker. But we only need to care about one thing: the clan. And never forget—in any *Gadje* war, both sides will use us to fight as easily as they will kill us for sport."

A rumble of assent.

Boldo goes on. "So, we do the same. Fight only when we need to. Support whatever side will leave us alone. Gain favor when we must, gather food, arms, horses, whatever has been taken from us."

I nod as the men shout their agreement.

"He is a leader, your Boldo," Kizzy whispers.

My Boldo. Something in me stirs again.

Kizzy and I remain while plans are made. We stare at one another and then into the darkness as the men plot and scheme. Without speaking, we both worry about what the clan will be called to do—venture into nearby towns, to farms, houses, shops. Our women distracting the villagers, telling fortunes, selling wares while the men carry out what they must. Barter and sell. Steal if necessary—take back a horse or two, then move on, quickly. Isn't it only right to get back some of what we've lost?

As the *divano* disperses and the clan gathers, there is a heaviness in the air, the pressing weight of responsibility to complete the wedding ritual properly, in spite of the attack. I am grateful for the darkness, as it shadows the expressions on our faces—slack and dumbstruck, pinched with bitterness, or glowing with anger. All of this I feel and push away. How else to carry on?

Shimza, Cato, and Kizzy's brothers and sisters "say goodbye." We circle them as they kiss her and weep. Shimza unplaits Kizzy's braids, and Mihai's mother carefully knots the *diklo* around her loosened hair. It is woven of colorful threads, mostly red, the color of luck and happiness. Mihai then takes his bride's hand and we follow them to the colorfully carved *vardo*, listing to one side above a broken wheel. They disappear inside. And so it is done. There are none of the traditional cheers—instead, sighs of deflated relief. And I wonder, now that Kizzy is married, if she too will be lost to me.

I am exhausted, my arms and legs thick with fatigue. My

mind, too, feels dull. I seek out my mother. She sits beside a pile of rubbish, waiting for I don't know what. Perhaps for the next bad thing to happen.

"Come my *daj*, come my mother," I say with effort, taking her by the hand. The hoot of an owl pierces the night and she flinches. Like a child I lead her toward our wagon. Luludja takes hold of her other arm and the three of us move as one.

Suddenly they are in front of us. Boldo and an old man, clearly his father—they are the same in build and countenance. We stop in a circle of moonlight, shadows playing about us. My heart pounds. Luludja's mouth twists in a stubborn way.

The old man addresses my mother.

"It is time for my son to take a bride." He extends a hand holding a bulging leather sack "I offer a generous *darro.*"

Boldo's steady gaze bores into me. I cannot breathe. I shift only my lowered eyes toward my mother. My mother shrugs and looks at Luludja.

"My sister is sorry," Luludja says. "But our Drina is spoken for."

"Spoken for!" I cry. I cannot believe what I have heard. "I have no suitor! There has been no *pliashka!* No engagement!"

Luludja stares past me. "The announcement would have been made at the wedding."

"But . . ." I feel the blood rush to my head.

Boldo's eyes blaze. "Who have you promised her to?"

"Luca," Luludja replies. "He can provide well for Drina. And for Nadja, as long as need be."

"Luca! Luca?" Tears pierce my eyes. Luca is Hanzi's friend,

39

an old man—nearly forty, stooped and gray, with a jowly face and perpetual phlegmy cough.

"It is done," Luludja says. The shadows across her face make her look even more severe.

"*Daj!* Mother!" I cry. "Tell me this is not so!"

Again my mother shrugs. I want to slap her. Wake her from her stupor.

Luludja shakes her head, glances from my *daj* to me. "This one is her mother's daughter, that is for certain. But no matter. As I said, it is done."

Boldo stares at me but speaks to my auntie.

"We will see," he says. "Nothing is done—until it is done."

He turns and walks away, his father following.

CHAPTER 7

JANUARY 1937

We are by the side of the river, Kizzy, Luludja, Jofranka, Florica, my mother, and me, scrubbing the laundry against flat stones in the rushing water. A heavy, colorless sky hangs against the earth, wrapping us in a bone-chilling mist. The water is icy cold and my hands are numb. I will not look at my auntie, will not acknowledge the arrangement she has made. They have agreed that Luca will come to call later this day, with a large dowry, no doubt. I stare at the threadbare fabric and do not see it, rub the harsh brick of soap against the grain with more vigor than necessary.

I feel a jab in my side. Kizzy elbows me again and I glance her way. She nods slightly—a quick uplifting of her chin. My eyes follow her line of vision to the far bank, and the soap slips from my hand.

The large raptor circles high above the trees. Below, Boldo stands in the clearing, watching.

Luludja pinches the tender underside of my arm, hard. "What are you sitting there for, doing nothing?" I do not allow the pain to show. I pretend she is a gnat, the rising welt a testament to my feelings for Boldo. She cannot make me look down. My jaw tightens. I am equal parts power and shame. The sound of their scrubbing slows as they gape at my insolence.

Everyone except my mother, who stands suddenly. She stares at the ground. Water trickles around her feet. Her shoes are wet.

It is not laundry water.

"*Daj?* . . ."

Her hands go to her belly and she groans. I forget about my smarting arm, about Luludja's anger. I forget about Boldo across the river.

The baby is coming.

It is too early and still the baby comes.

Luludja takes charge. "Florica and Kizzy—see to the laundry. Jofranka—gather your midwifery satchel. You, Drina— bring your mother to the birthing tent." There is a chill in her voice as she addresses me.

I take my mother by the arm and lead her away. Four steps and she doubles over. Her face is white, her lips thin with pain. She presses her eyes shut.

"Tsinvari," Luludja says. "The evil spirits know this child is *marime*, unclean. She is in their grasp! Quickly! Move her quickly!"

Scorpion . . . serpent . . . eagle . . . I shove the thought away. The vise seems to release its grip. My mother can walk again. I find a tent at the back of the camp. The women drape the doorway signaling the men to move away as the birthing begins.

I settle my mother on a straw mattress covered with blankets. Luludja props a large sack of grain and a pillow behind her back. My *daj* sits forward, her knees bent. Teardrops of sweat weep across her forehead, and her chest rises rapidly with each breath. Luludja swiftly snips the knots holding together my mother's clothing—this to ensure that the umbilical cord will not be twisted.

"Go bring some twigs and pine needles to make a small fire." Luludja's voice is a bit gentler, though she avoids my eyes. I go about it quickly, without chancing a glance back.

In minutes I return with a bundle of hastily gathered dried sticks and moss. We build the fire beneath a large ceiling flap to take away the winter chill and dampness. It smokes and sputters to life as another wave of agony grabs my mother.

She groans. The guttural sound rises and narrows into a scream. Wide-eyed, she clamps her jaw, leans forward. I move toward her, not sure what to do.

The curtained doorway opens and Jofranka fills it, a large embroidered leather satchel clasped beneath her huge breasts. "Step away, girl, and let me see her!"

My mother has fallen back against the sack. Perhaps she has fainted. I bite my bottom lip. Inch away.

Jofranka is surprisingly gentle. She lifts my mother's skirts, lowers her undergarment, and spreads her legs—all of this with a kindness that draws some inner calm from my mother.

"I'm going to see where the baby is," Jofranka says. She is on her knees staring into the privacy of my mother, one large, meaty hand probing inside, the other pressing on the great dome of her stomach. I see it all slowly—my mother's eyes and mouth, large matching Os, the crease pinching Jofranka's brow, the pursing of her lips.

Luludja bends forward and whispers, "What is it? What's wrong?"

Jofranka shakes her head, almost imperceptibly. She removes her hand from the dark place and runs both palms across the dome, her face raised, squinting. Her thick fingers knead and press as though divining the mysteries of an open palm.

Even I can see that what she reads is not good.

We wait, silent.

Then the pain returns, strangling my mother with invisible hands. Her panting and wailing, the mad clutching at her knees and writhing of her body seize my throat, cut off my breath.

"Help her!" I say, but the words are trapped inside. I am sweating and panting along with her now.

Jofranka stands, takes a thick, short length of braided rope from her bag. Hands it to my mother. "Nadja, dear one, take hold. Twist it. If you need to, bite it, if it helps." My mother stares through her. Jofranka places the rope on my mother's lap and rubs her shoulders until the front of pain retreats again. She continues to massage the tension from my mother's shoulders while speaking softly to me, her eyes never leaving her charge. "Prepare a kettle of water. We will make a medicinal tea. And my bag. Inside, a coral amulet on a red string. Walnuts and kernels of red corn. Bring them."

My hands tremble. Luludja takes the kettle from me, leaves to fill it. I search the bag, feel the silky strand and dangling talisman. Hand it to Jofranka. She waves it before my mother, whispers an incantation. Ties it around her neck beside the gold pendant.

I find the collection of small, calico pouches secured with string.

"Yes, those as well," Jofranka says. "Yarrow, nettle, and red raspberry leaf. Yes, we'll infuse them all."

Of course, for hemorrhage. I swallow hard. She anticipates a difficult birth. I inhale deeply, then arrange the herbs and plants on a wooden tray. When Luludja returns and hangs the kettle over the open flame, I reach for a chipped china cup. But as my mother screams, the dainty vessel falls from my shaking fingers . . . shatters against the edge of the kettle. A bad omen. Luludja rushes to sweep away the sharp pieces, as if removing them can reverse the fates.

"Wipe her forehead with a wet cloth," Jofranka orders. "Fill the bucket with cold water from the stream. Off!"

I approach the door, grateful for somewhere to go, yet terrified to leave. I glance back. My mother has reared up with crazed eyes, damp strands of hair hanging across her sweaty face. The image of a wild stallion comes to mind—the ones the

Gypsy men are so skilled at breaking. I rush through the door, thinking how men had so skillfully broken my mother's spirit as well.

I walk, looking neither right nor left. With each step the bucket bumps my shins. Around the tent, behind the wagons, along the stone wall at the edge of the clearing. Brown grass, gray pebbles, dust on the toes of my black boots. I watch my feet. Step, step. Step, step.

There is the snapping of a twig, a footfall beside me. I turn.

"Drina."

It is the first time he has called me by name. Hearing it on his lips brings color to my cheeks. I put the bucket down and face him. He carries three dead hares strung with rope, their bodies lean and limp. The large, masked hawk sits tethered on his shoulder, ruffling its feathers. Blood on its talons.

"Boldo."

"Your mother. How is she?"

I shrug. Tears come and I press my lids together.

He touches my arm. "Jofranka tends to her, yes?"

I nod.

"Then she is in good hands."

I sigh. "Yes, I suppose."

He smiles. "This baby wants us to be together. This is why he comes early. Surely Luca has been forced to stay away!"

"Yes. No. I mean, Luca cannot come with the dowry. I've been spared, at least until the baby comes." The tears pool again. One dangles from an eyelash. Boldo touches it with his finger. Pushes it away.

"Drina. We knew each other at first glance. We are to be together, and we will be."

"But, Luca . . . Luludja . . . Hanzi . . ."

"Yes, yes, they made a plan, but I have a plan as well. We elope."

My heart pounds with fear and something else.

"As soon as the baby is born and your mother is settled we'll leave in the night. Join my cousin's people for a season. Then return. Married. By that time you'll be carrying my son."

He smiles at the blush that creeps up my throat. "They'll accept us then."

My eyebrow lifts in a question.

"They *will*." He raises his fist, displaying the bloodied rabbits. "My aim is true—I *always* get what I am after." He runs his finger over the tawny hawk's breast and the bird tenses. "I'll make a stew of rabbit, wild mushroom, and wine. You need to eat, and so will your mother—afterward."

"Yes." I am not sure what I am agreeing to.

Boldo turns.

"But . . ." I begin. "Hanzi will be watching. And my Beebee."

"Don't worry," he says, and then he is gone.

I grab the bucket and walk to the stream, submerge it in the water, and drag it out, dripping.

Suddenly Kizzy appears, rushing toward me along the path.

"Hurry!" she says, breathless. "Hurry!"

I drop the bucket.

She grabs my hand and we run.

CHAPTER 8

My arms and legs go weak as I step inside the tent.
I want to go to my *daj*, but I cannot move. The sight of her
holds me prisoner where I stand.

A sea of red floods the mattress. She no longer screams. Her
eyes are narrow slits, her lips dry and colorless. The bodice of
her dress is dark with sweat. If not for the labored rise and fall
of her chest, I might believe her spirit had left her.

"Breech," Luludja whispers. "Baby is breech—feet first."

The air in the tent is, by turns, charged and sluggish. Jofranka
crouches on knees and elbows, her arm inside my mother halfway
to her elbow. She presses Nadja's abdomen with the other hand. I
am grateful for the groan from my mother's lips—she is alive.

"I feel the legs . . . there . . . the hips." Jofranka's voice is
quiet, flat. She is speaking to herself, perhaps for reassurance.

Twisting, probing, her face screwed up in kind. "Take hold above the tailbone." She pauses. Grimaces. Adjusts her arm. Sweat glistens on her large face and chest. She grasps, and my mother becomes rigid, leaning back, holding herself up on straightened arms, shoulders hunched. A stream of red leaks down Jofranka's arm.

"Stop!" I scream silently. "You're killing her!" The words are trapped on my tongue, leaving a bitter aftertaste.

In one slippery thrust Jofranka's fist emerges. She kneels back for a moment and I see a tiny scarlet foot, the size of a small river stone or a rabbit's foot. The second arrives carried on a gush of blood. Jofranka takes a deep breath, grasps the feet, presses above my mother's pelvic bone, pulls.

The small torso follows. Jofranka slips a finger in, hooks a spindly arm. More grappling and the second limp arm appears. She rotates the inert body, rests it on her forearm, and a shoulder emerges. She swivels the opposite way and in another spurt of red the second shoulder is spit out. I do not want to look at this headless thing swallowed up in the privacy of my mother, but I cannot tear my eyes away.

"Now, the jaw, the upper jaw," Jofranka whispers, probing again. Her words sound of a chant or a spell. She strains, tips the small, bloodied rag-doll upward, angling it so that the tiny creature's chin can slip through the canal.

My mother leans forward and opens her mouth. Her lips are moving. She grabs my arm, whispers.

"D . . . D . . ."

"I'm here, dear one—don't worry."

She is suddenly strong. Determined.

"Diego!"

Luludja goes to her. "You mean Drina. Dr—"

My mother silences her with a dark glare. "Diego—he said he would be back."

"You're gripped with fever. Delirious." Luludja wets my mother's face in a less than gentle way. Still, my *daj* is seeing something beyond Luludja, in this tent, this moment.

"Who, Mother?" My heart races. "Who is this Diego?" I persist.

She is still for a moment. Focused. Earnest.

"Diego—Honoria—Muentes!" Her eyes bore through me.

"But *who* . . ."

"Diego—my *husband!*"

She unravels. My heart turns over. I face Luludja who looks as though she has swallowed something vile.

"Auntie?"

"Her husband?" She laughs, rough-edged, sarcastic. "In her mind, perhaps . . ."

"Diego Honoria Muentes . . ." I repeat. "My fath—"

"Better you forget the name," Luludja says through clenched teeth. "He is dead to us."

I look to my mother.

"Diego Honoria Muentes?" I roll the sounds on my tongue, taste the syllables. But my *daj,* transported by pain, has returned from the place she just was.

Jofranka looks up. "Now, Nadja! *Now!* Push hard—hard!" My mother doesn't move.

50

"Bear down! Push!"

"Leave her be," I say. "She's too weak."

Jofranka turns to face me. "Then they will both die."

I am chilled. Frigid with fear. I nod. The words come of their own volition.

"Push Mother—for Diego, push!"

I ignore Luludja's glare.

"For Diego Honoria Muentes, Mother, push with everything you have."

Like a lightning strike, the name shocks her into consciousness. She hauls herself up, breathes deep, draws her knees high, pushes into the blood-steeped mattress with her fists. A low sound like a growl begins deep within and rumbles up in her throat. Her face reddens. Her fists open and fly to her knees, grasping, rearing back.

"Yes!" Jofranka says. "Yes, Nadja, good! Breathe! Breathe! Now again!"

She gulps air. Bears down. Her sound now a guttural rasping.

Finally, a release. The thin fragile thing is out, its hollow-cheeked bottom in one of Jofranka's hands, its slimy, pointed head in the other. A bluish cord dangles between the bloodied slit of my mother and the tiny slack body.

"Once more!" Jofranka instructs. "Push! You must push out the afterbirth."

My mother is reaching for the creature.

"A girl?" she asks.

Jofranka looks down. Up. "Yes, yes, a girl. Now push, dear one! Push!"

My mother implores with her arms. "Give her to me. Diego said we would call her Drina."

My throat closes.

"She is out of her mind with fever," Luludja says. "She is—"

"Drina," my mother whispers, reaching for the babe.

"I'll cut the cord," Jofranka says. "Luludja, tie it off." Kizzy holds the purplish body for a moment, and quickly they snip, tie, and pull. Jofranka grabs the baby by the feet, body dangling, head down. A clouded image teases my brain and then comes into focus— Boldo's hares, freshly killed. I blink and shake my head to erase the likeness. Jofranka taps the baby's chest, hard. The ribs stand out like chicken bones. She runs her finger inside the puckered mouth.

"Drina," my mother calls.

"Yes, *daj,*" I say, but she is staring at the infant.

A sputtering sound. A mewling cry.

My mother blesses herself: forehead, chest, shoulder, shoulder. Brings her gold pendant to her lips and closes her eyes.

Jofranka rights the child and hands her to my mother. Luludja has already loosened the bodice of her sister's dress. A sorry whimper of milk leaks from my mother's thin breast. As the sad little thing latches hold, my mother's eyelids droop.

I lean in to kiss my *daj* on the forehead and she grabs my arm.

"Promise me this—you will give my Drina a good life! "

"But—"

"Promise me!"

My insides shake at the intensity of this love for the one she thinks is me. I swallow the lump of resentment tinged with pity rising in my throat. When the fever lifts she will understand. But, for now, she needs peace.

"Yes, dear one," I whisper. "This I promise. Diego and I will keep Drina safe."

CHAPTER 9

Dusk falls when Jofranka leaves. An entire day has
passed. As she goes she orders Kizzy and me to take the baby,
clean her up, and swaddle her while Luludja stays by my
mother, wiping her down and urging her to sip her tea.

We draw from a kettle of warm water to wash the infant.
Her miniature arms flail, her spider fingers splay. She opens her
mouth to cry, chin trembling, sucks air and holds her breath. I
run water gently over her to rinse away the blood and mucous.

Just when I am afraid the shock of the water will kill her,
her voice catches the air and she wails. It isn't much of a sound.
Kizzy dries her with a soft cloth.

"So, what happens now?" she asks.

"I don't know." I am spent from not-knowing. Too tired to

think. Instead, I look at this child of the yellow-haired man and my mother—my half-sister. Unclean, *marime*. Who my hallucinating mother believes is me.

"What should we call her?" Kizzy asks. "We can't call her Drina, can we?"

"Just in front of my *daj*. Until her senses return."

The baby has exhausted herself. She shudders and her cries become quivering sighs. Her tiny lips and chin twitch at the memory of my mother's breast. I wrap the blanket around her snugly, in the usual way. This calms her. Her face stretches into a yawn.

"She'll sleep for a long time," Kizzy says. "Do you think she'll live? She's very weak and the birth was difficult."

My insides contract in a knot. *Scorpion . . . serpent . . . eagle . . .* What is it I hope for? I don't know. I shrug. Try not to think.

Instead, I hold her up. The sorry child's pointy head is covered in a thick cap of coarse, reddish hair that grows toward the middle from both sides into a pointed tuft. For a moment her lids flutter revealing two small, dark eyes. She has the pinched, wizened look of a little forest creature. A squirrel.

"Little Red Squirrel," I say.

Kizzy laughs. "Red Squirrel! She does look like a red squirrel!"

"That's what we'll call her for now."

Like a stray dog, I think, it is not good to give a real name. Once you give a real name you become attached. You start wanting to keep it. "That's her name—between us—Little Red Squirrel."

Red Squirrel sneezes, as though agreeing. We laugh, she startles, and then her eyelids droop crookedly.

"The rest will not call her anything at all. She is a banished, fatherless soul." As I say this, a heaviness weighs on my spirit.

"Enough," I say aloud, to myself, but I see that Kizzy understands.

"Speaking of names . . ." My voice trails off.

"Yes." Kizzy stares at me.

"Diego—Honoria—Muentes." He feels real to me, this stranger who is my father. I think, *Now I know my name. Not Zaporata. I have never been Drina Zaporata.*

"I am Drina Muentes," I say.

Kizzy nods. Touches my arm. "It seems everyone is becoming someone new today."

The cold winter rain turns the ground to mud, our spirits to despair. The days and nights run together as a week passes, then two. My mother is lost in the delirium of fever and infection they call childbed fever. Little Red Squirrel needs to be fed day and night. But my *daj* cannot nurse her. Even her milk is polluted from the infection. Luludja, who seems to have had a change of heart toward the infant, has sent me to a local farmer for goat's milk and a special dropper with a rubber nipple at the end. I sit and rock, and drip the milk into Little Red Squirrel's mouth. The thin liquid squirts in, and, with the sucking motion of her lips, it dribbles out again, trailing along her face and trickling into the creases of her skinny, sour-smelling neck.

Ah, evenings I hear the music of our *campagna*, but I cannot dance, chained to this insatiable Little Red Squirrel, and drawn with fear and love toward my *daj* who slowly spins further and further from life.

She groans. Her eyes dart furtively. They hunt about the tent until they fall on the baby.

"Here she is," I say. "Drina is here. No need to worry."

She nods and the tension runs out of her like the goat's milk from Little Red Squirrel's mouth. Pools up into something sour inside me. I have made a promise that weighs heavily. Is there nothing left of my *daj* for me?

I take her hand in mine, quietly sing an old *Gitano* tune she taught me when I was just a girl. She stares ahead for a bar or two, then turns her face toward me. Her lips mouth silent lyrics, her head nods the slightest bit in time. For a brief moment I see the light in her eyes that I once knew. My voice catches in my throat. I sing on, the notes wobbly, but true enough as reflected in her eyes.

The tent door parts. Luludja comes in, as she does each morning, goes to her sister. Wipes her brow. Urges her to take some tea, just a sip. Nadja clamps her lips shut, turns her face. She has the dank smell of death about her. Luludja sighs. My mother stares with wide, hollow eyes, the light dancing there a moment ago extinguished.

"Just keep that child alive," Luludja says to me.

"Yes, yes," I say, and again my mother is settled.

Little Red Squirrel smacks her tiny lips and yawns.

"At least as long as my *daj* lives," I whisper. Tears prick my eyes.

Luludja stops. Puts her face in front of mine. "Oh no," she says, shaking her head. "This baby will live all right. You will see to it. It is, after all, what you promised."

A dark, heavy feeling enfolds me, like I am sinking in murky water. "What do you mean?"

"You make sure the child is well cared for. That's all." Luludja eyes me through narrowed lids and leaves the tent.

Again, my mother moans. She is mumbling now—crazy fever-talk. A word here or there is all I can grab. I sigh, move close beside her. Lay Little Red Squirrel against her breast. My mother babbles, half in Spanish, half in Rom, words interspersed with a smile or a chuckle, an emphatic nod, or a disdainful twist of her lips. I can feel her heat radiate through her clothes and mine.

I lay back and stare at the ceiling of the tent.

"*Baila* Diego! *Baila!*" She shouts. Tries to sit up. Thrashes about. "*Mamioro!* Is it a ghost bringing this illness on me? It ties my arms, my feet. How can I dance without arms and legs?"

What is she saying? How can she *dance*? I sit up. Strain to make out her words. She has propped herself on one elbow. "Jerez de la Frontera, *si*". She furrows her brow. "Leave the *campagna? Marime!*" She falls back on the mattress and I rub her arms, push her damp hair from her face. "No, my *daj*," I say, wiping her brow with a wet rag. "You are not *marime*. You are my lovely *daj*."

"She is lovely—*rinkeni*—yes, our Drina . . . Drina . . ."

She doesn't hear me.

"Jerez, *si*, Jerez! I will go to Jerez."

"Jerez, Mother? What is in Jerez?"

She grabs my wrist. Her grasp is surprisingly strong. Her chest is concave and so still it appears she has stopped breathing altogether. Then her entire upper body heaves, gulping air. "Tell no one about Jerez! Do you hear me?" Her voice is all breath and effort. Her lips purplish and dry as leaves. "Tell no one! No one can know where I will be!"

My heart pummels the inside of my chest.

"Promise me!" Her eyes roll white for a moment and she wills them back. With effort she stares. Her eyes pierce me. I shrink away but she persists. "Promise! No one can find us!"

"Yes, my *daj*," I whisper. "I promise. I will not tell. No one will know." Suddenly there is a commotion outside the tent.

She stares off, sinks into herself, then whispers, "*Si*, Diego. *Vamanos.*"

I hear Kak Hanzi's voice outside and look toward the door. Jump up and strain to hear. Another voice—they speak together in hushed tones. I wring my memory to place the wheezy sound. My knees become weak when certainty sets in.

It is Luca. Hanzi and Luca.

I will convince my *daj* to refuse him. I tremble, sit back down to face her.

But, oh, sweet mother of the god of all, one look tells me that the spirit of my *daj* has departed forever.

CHAPTER 10

Three days later nothing of my *daj* remains, her few belongings tucked with her in the plain pine box—her tarot cards and head scarf, hair comb and teacup. At the last moment I remove the scarf, slipping it into my pocket. The gold pendant from her neck I place around my own—this I do with trepidation. In this world the small flash of gold and inlaid ebony never left the hollow of her throat, so perhaps it is bad luck to send her into the next world without it. But my need for something of hers is greater than this fear. My fingers fly to the smooth precious metal, knowing it touched her skin, and now it touches mine.

For three days I do not wash, do not comb my hair, do not change my clothing. I am unmoved by the lamentation and mourning. I refuse the strong coffee and even stronger spirits offered. I am as vacant as the water vessels that have been emptied, my heart as concealed as the shrouded mirrors. Somehow I walk behind Mihai and the small band playing a dirge on our way to the grave. Somehow I throw a handful of dirt and coins as the coffin of my mother is planted in the earth.

Through all of this Little Red Squirrel's constant needs hold me captive. I move through the motions of whatever is required of me. This I promised my *daj*. I feed, I clean, I burp, I change, I rock, then feed, burp, rock, clean, change. . . . There is no end to it. I do all this without seeing, without feeling.

Kizzy has shown me how to swaddle the baby and strap her to my chest. On the floor of my tent I place my mother's colorful cotton scarf—the one she'd always spread beneath her tarot cards. I push the memory of this aside, take Little Red Squirrel, and lay her across the large diamond of cloth woven in shades of red, gold, and indigo. I fold up the bottom point, capturing her feet, then pull the right corner snugly over to her left, tuck, then the left corner across to the right. Pull, wrap, tuck. Little Red Squirrel flails her arms and legs at first; then, once she is tightly swathed, she quiets.

I bend and look at her. She is like a colorful butterfly, just emerged from the chrysalis, wings not yet spread.

Her eyelids flutter open. I begin to look away, but it seems she is staring at me. Her gaze is like that of a very old soul, one that feels familiar to me.

I look away, then back. Still she gazes. My pulse quickens and my hands shake—my mother's eyes, and mine, I see in hers.

Something inside me shifts. Like the steep sides of a riverbank during the spring floods, it slips, breaks away, and there is no way to stop it. I scoop the bundle of her up and press her tightly to me. Her tiny head fits in the curve of my neck. I feel her moist breath against my throat, the warmth of her small body against my chest. I will banish the yellow-haired man from my memory. He will no longer exist. No longer taint my Little Red Squirrel.

I stand like this for a long time before I begin to sing in a trembling voice, then dance with her to the lamenting melody of a *petenera* song.

"Drina."

It is Kizzy. She pushes aside the flap of the tent and comes inside.

"You must rest now." I begin to protest, but she takes Little Red Squirrel and places her in the *zelfya* she has fashioned, hanging from the top of the tent post. "Little Red Squirrel will sleep and so will you," she says, bringing me to a fresh mattress beside the hammock-like cradle.

"But if she wakes . . ."

"You'll hear her. And it is sometimes good for a baby to cry." She looks at me, her eyes wide with tenderness. "It is sometimes good for you to cry as well."

My insides quake and the stone that is my heart begins to move. But I cannot do this now. I inhale. Hold my trembling breath. Wait. Wait. There—all is still.

Heavy with grief and fatigue, I nod. I lie down and Kizzy shields me from the chill with a worn, soft, patchwork quilt.

"Tomorrow, my friend," she whispers and kisses me on the forehead.

"Tomorrow."

I lie there watching the tent change color as the winter light wanes. Little Red Squirrel snores softly, the cloth *zelfya* breathing with her. My throat swells and I push the feeling away. What *is* this feeling? It rises again no matter how I try to swallow it—it is not this, it is not that.

If not for Little Red Squirrel, my *daj* would yet be in this world. I would not have become invisible to my mother, except in memory, stirred up by the presence of this child of rape and violence. I *hate* the seed of the yellow-haired man, *hate* the tragedy he placed on my mother. I *hate* . . .

But no. Little Red Squirrel has become a reluctant part of me. And yet . . .

Circles . . . just maddening circles. My thoughts follow one another like mad dogs chasing their tails, nipping, snapping.

The day is spent; night creeps in. The drape of the tent, black velvet. A sigh shudders through me and I turn on my side, knees tucked, hands clasped beneath my chin. I pull the quilt over my nose and feel the warmth of my own breath. I begin to let myself slip away.

Something stirs outside. A light footfall, a rustling of dried pine needles and leaves. The flap of the tent opens and there is Luludja, framed in moonlight.

"You're asleep?"

Her voice is edged in disappointment. I prop myself on an elbow.

"No."

She kneels beside me.

"I've brought you some tea. It will help you sleep. Calm you."

"But, Lit—the baby might wake."

She places the steaming cup before me and I take it. It warms my hands and I bury my face in the pungent steam.

"Don't trouble yourself with that," she says. "I'll come to check on you both. And, besides, the spirit of Nadja will, no doubt, wake you when her baby *Drina* cries."

I sip from the cup uneasily. There is something unkind in her tone. But the tea is sweet. It heats my throat and then my chest.

"That's it . . ." she encourages.

I put the cup down, rub my eyes.

"A little more," Luludja urges. "We don't waste. Not enough of anything these days to waste."

I sigh, pick up the cup, and gulp the rest. Then perhaps she will leave me.

"Good!" she says. "Now sleep, dear one."

Back in my cocoon, I am deadly tired. I scarcely hear the swish of the tent flap and the quiet sound of her retreating steps.

It is a night of unsettling dreams and visions: Boldo's hawk carrying Little Red Squirrel in its talons. My *daj* appearing as she once was, eyes flashing, tossing back her head, laughing. She turns my way and looks at me kindly. But when she smiles, her teeth are decayed and rotten. A serpent crawls from her mouth, a snake slithers around her feet. Her face becomes Luludja's and she wags a finger, *"Forget the name! He is dead to us. Dead to us!"* And then, I am dancing with Boldo. The *fandango*.

He circles about, places his arm around my waist. My insides heat up. I feel his breath on my neck and turn. It is not Boldo, but Luca! He presses up against me. I recoil.

Someone shakes me, hard. Will this nightmare never end? My name . . . over . . . and over . . . I am shaking, soaked in sweat.

"Drina!"

I think I am awake, though I'm not certain. But I am upright—how, I do not know. I try to open my eyes, but my lids are cement.

I am lifted to my feet. My knees are jelly, my arms useless. I groan.

"Shhh! Drina—be still!" The whispered words buzz in my ear. I strain toward the voice. My eyes slip across the darkened tent, adjusting, willing myself to make sense of the shapes, the sounds, the edges of the nightmare. There, my bed, there, the quilt. But *ow . . . ow . . .* Who is pressing their thumbs under my arms, forcing me up? Focus, Drina. *Focus!* There, a leg, a boot inching beside me, somehow connected to the hands propping me up. There, the teapot, there, the cup. There, the *zelfya,* there the—

Wait.

Wait.

Something is wrong. My brain is muddled, but my heart races. The *zelfya*—A sound comes from my mouth that I do not recognize.

"Shh! Not a sound!"

It is an effort to turn toward the voice. I force the face into view. Squint. My head pounds. I blink many times to capture the blurred, moving features.

"Boldo? Why? . . . wha? . . ." My tongue is thick, my words fuzzy-edged and slurred.

He is shaking his head. I open my mouth and he presses his against mine until I am stunned silent. He backs away only an inch or two.

"No words! We have to leave! Now!"

I stare at the *zelfya,* slack. Swinging slightly. Then at Boldo.

"There's a brigade in the hills outside of town. Fascists. I tracked them, watching, making sure our *campagna* was safe."

I struggle to follow.

"On the road I saw Luludja."

What is he saying? "Lulud—"

"Shh! Just listen! She was walking in the shadows carrying a sack of some kind. I followed her, out of sight. She made her way to the edge of town and met a *Gadje* woman. I realized it wasn't a sack; it was something bundled in a blanket. She spoke to the woman, turned back the edge of the blanket, and I heard a baby whimper."

I am crying now inside. Tasting the bitter truth I cannot digest.

He lifts me then, like a babe, carries me out of the tent, swiftly, around behind the *campagna,* into the woods, then up, up, onto the back of a fine, tall horse. I feel Boldo's sturdy body behind me, feel him dig his heels into the side of the animal, the ground moving beneath us. All this I feel, and don't feel. I shiver, crying without tears. He speaks softly, his breath tickling my hair.

"Gold coins. The *Gadje* woman traded them for the baby. I watched Luludja count them, one by one, into her apron."

I sink into him, my head flopping against his chest.

"I followed her—the *Gadje* woman—to a large manor set on a hillside. Then I came back another way, leaving signs—*patrin* signs."

Patrin—my mind raced.

"We can find her, Drina . . ."

My head begins to clear enough for me to sit forward. But my stomach clenches. Acid burns my throat. Oh God, then I retch, right there—unclean, *marime!* My face burns in humiliation. Boldo draws up the reins, stops the horse.

"Oh, dear one," he says, wiping my face. "Here, wash your mouth . . ."

He hands me a metal canteen, military issue, surely stolen along with the steed. I swish and spit, sickened by my own smell. I am crying real tears now, my face watered with them and soaked in sweat, spittle, shame.

He is not repulsed. Instead he hands me a moistened cloth, rubs my shoulder with one hand, moves the stallion forward with the other.

"When I got back I couldn't rouse you—thought you were—well, until I found the tea. . . . You wouldn't have awakened if the entire Nationalist Army raided the *campagna* and carried you off."

Luludja. I am black with rage. I sit up even straighter, spit on the ground.

"Yes," he agrees. "Yes."

"We will get my baby back!" I say.

His arm curves around my waist, his hand cups mine. I feel his chin in my hair, nodding.

"Yes. We will get her back. For your mother." He gives the horse a kick. "And for you."

Chapter 11

He speaks softly as we ride in the dark, his words barely rising and falling, their meaning so different from the tone in which he delivers them. "There's fighting in the hill country. The Republicans have massacred a small unit of Nationalists—some from Portugal, others from Germany and Italy." He reins in the horse from time to time, holding the beast motionless for slow-moving minutes, both of us grasping at the forest sounds to ensure that . . . what? We are not being followed? The squadron from whom he stole the horse is not in pursuit? That we will not be shot by a rogue soldier? Or beaten by local peasants?

All the while, none of this is my real concern. Instead, I imagine Little Red Squirrel crying for me in that *Gadje* house, wailing for her small bottle of goat's milk—and oh no! I do not have her bottle! I left with none of her things—no blanket, no diaper cloths, no baby clothes. How will I? . . .

"Boldo, I have none of Little Red Squirrel's things. And your hawks, what about—"

"Wait." I feel Boldo's body tense. He points left. "Do you hear that?"

I am about to say no when I detect something—a rustling of underbrush.

"What do you th—"

"Sh! Don't move. Don't breathe."

A distant, crisp, ratcheting sound. In response, a low-pitched, stomach-thumping boom.

"A *maquina*," Boldo whispers. "A gun that fires many times with one pull of the trigger. And grenades. Bombs. The fighting is close."

The rustling becomes a footfall—no—the quadruple meter of hooves.

Boldo backs our mount into the cover of a low-hanging pine. The astringent evergreen smell sharpens my senses. The needles prick my arms and legs. The hoof-beats grow closer, then slow. I can make out the silhouette of a war horse with a large pack slung across its back—but there is no rider. He faces us, standing like a sentinel, a granite statue in the town square.

"Stay here," Boldo says. He gives me the reins and slips to the ground, approaches the stallion. The horse rears slightly, circles back. Boldo takes the halter, quiets the beast with his

70

hands, outlining its curved muscular neck with open palms, cupping its muzzle and jowls, stroking its forehead.

"Dismount and come forward, slowly."

I hesitate.

"Drina . . ."

I swing my leg over and, hanging onto the reins, lower myself clumsily. "Tether him and walk to me . . . calm . . . calm . . ."

I tie our horse to a sapling and step closer.

"Now, I'm going to hand you these reins. Hold steady."

I step forward and gasp. Smother a scream with my open palm.

"It's all right," Boldo says.

The pack across the horse's back is not a pack at all. It is the bloodied body of a man, slumped over the saddle. Death has preserved his expression of horror—his bulbous eyes and gaping mouth frozen in a hideous mask, blood dried like spilled gravy in the hollow of his cheek. A black hole above one ear, scarlet matted hair.

"Don't touch!" I whisper. "He is *marime!*"

Boldo grabs the man's jacket and shifts the dead weight off center.

"He may be unclean, but his belongings shouldn't go to waste. You don't have to touch him. Just mind the horses."

The corpse hits the ground with a thud and both horses startle. I hold on tightly, as much for myself as to secure the skittish beasts. Boldo scavenges through the man's clothing, stripping off the wool jacket, tugging the leather boots from his stiffened feet, peeling away the heavy socks, pocketing a gold ring, a silver watch. Beside the corpse is a knapsack that Boldo empties. A canteen and rations, a blanket, a knife, and a pistol all carried in the vain hope of warding off danger. All of it ours now.

He rolls the lifeless form into a shallow gully and covers it with pine branches and debris. Nothing is left of him except his horse and his useful belongings. I resist when Boldo drapes the drab olive jacket around my shoulders. It is *marime* to wear the clothing of a *Gadje*, even worse, the clothing of a dead *Gadje*.

"But, sweet one, it is winter, and we have nothing else. When we get to my people we will burn it. It will be as if it never existed." I grudgingly shrug into the rough wool while Boldo puts everything else in our horse's pack. The faint rat-a-tat-tat-tat of gunfire in the distance grows louder.

"We'll travel a ways south, away from town. Find an out-of-the-way place to spend the night. Keep the horses out of sight. I know such a place, a kilometer or so from the big pink house where the *Gadje* woman has the baby."

He helps me onto his horse, mounts behind me, and we start off, leading the dead man's mount behind us. I nod off, awaken as he eases me to the ground. I glance around in the darkness. We are surrounded by pines. "Where is this house where my Little Red Squirrel is being kept?"

"To the east," he points through the trees, "and up a hill." I try to imagine her there, but I cannot form a picture in my mind. Boldo spreads a blanket over a bed of evergreen boughs. "In the morning we'll find her. Come," he says. "Rest."

I hesitate. Now what?

He sees my thoughts. "We must stay close to keep warm. That's all."

I am too tired to protest. I lie down and he lies at my back. "Winter nights are cold," he whispers, as he folds the length of his body against mine, his chest against my back, knees tucked behind mine, in tandem.

For so long I have been alone. I begin to drift into the warmth, the closeness of him. Something in me says, "Don't," and I remain rigid. He drapes an arm over my shoulder. I start to slip, to slide into him, and then try to regain some kind of hold on myself before I dissolve into his sleepy embrace.

We stay this way until his breath steadies. His chest rises and falls in the rhythmic waves of sleep. I roll onto my back, his arm splayed across my chest. His face illuminated by moonlight, his high cheekbones and strong jaw in silhouette. I stare at him freely. He cannot observe my interest, so I indulge. Thick brows, a furrow between them, long black lashes, the wide, straight nose.

I look so intently that the familiar features become foreign to me. I realize I don't really know this man at all. Who is he? Do I love him?

I don't know.

A chill runs through my veins. I am lying with a stranger.

Yet, I am drawn to him in a mysterious way, as he surely is to me. It is alchemy—me, a battered tin cup, something cast aside by the tinkerer—yet in his eyes I become a golden goblet. This, a miracle.

He is a stranger to me, and not. Familiar, and not. But who else in this world do I have?

My thoughts fly to Kizzy. Surely she was unaware of my Bee-bee's treachery. But by defying Luludja, Boldo and I forfeit our place in the clan. I will not be welcomed back. At that thought my eyes well up. I have lost my *daj*, my Little Red Squirrel, and now my good friend who sought me out and knows me best.

My throat becomes thick with loss upon loss.

But this man, whose arm is draped so gently around me—this I have not lost. And he will help me get my baby back.

For this, I do love him.

My eyes close and we sleep.

An explosion rips us out of slumber. The horses whinny, pull on their tethers. Their hooves thrash the earth.

We are on our feet. Percussive shots. Staccato flashes of light. Another boom. The cries of battling men.

"Quickly!" Boldo jolts me from my stupor, unties our horses. In a scant second we've mounted. I dig in my heels. The horses run from the battle, ears pinned against their heads, hindquarters pumping, hooves beating the ground in a gallop. Boldo first, my horse in pursuit.

"Hang on tight!" he shouts, glancing back.

He doesn't need to tell me. My hands are clenched around the reins. My legs tremble from the pressure, my body pitched forward. The mane whips across my face.

Up, up we climb, into a pine-studded, rocky hillside. The horses ease up on the incline, picking their way carefully between stony outcroppings. The battle now rages in the place where we slept only moments ago. Men, some on horseback, others on foot, take cover where they can, firing from behind trees or rocks. I gasp when I glimpse the road, far below. It is lined with trucks and artillery. Scores of soldiers pour from the vehicles like ants from an anthill.

"Whoa. Easy now . . ." Boldo's horse comes to a halt, tail flicking. Mine follows. He jumps down, grabs the reins from me so I can dismount.

"We need to stay out of sight. That brigade will drive the little militia into these hills, corner them and force them out."

I sweat and shiver. We are in danger from both sides. He reads my face. "Not to worry. We have a gun and a place to wait this out. I'll kill if I need to."

I follow him around a bend to a sheer wall of rock. In the pink-gray light of dawn I see a small crevice. As we circle around, Boldo points to an opening near the ground, mostly concealed by tall dried grasses.

"I'll hide the horses. We'll take cover in this cave. Go inside and wait for me." I edge toward the opening and pause. He is already leading the horses away. I am frightened to be outside, exposed, yet afraid to be swallowed up by the darkness inside the cave. I wait, anxious, skittish as a hare. I flinch with each shot. My stomach quakes with every detonation. Minutes stretch endlessly. The roar of the fighting grows ever closer.

Where is he? What is taking so long? Sweat trickles down my back. I stare at the place where I expect him to appear until my eyes and forehead ache.

The voices of warring men rise to a fever pitch. The gunfire, incessant, closes in. I cannot breathe. Cannot move. Flashes now, through the trees, the whizzing sound of flying bullets. Screams. Curses.

I drag my legs from where they're planted and command them to move, one, then the other, into the cavern. I slip, fall on my side, and slide into inky blackness. Down a pebbly slope, a tunnel of dank air. I cough. Feel the webs, the dampness, the chill of the underworld on my skin. Finally, I skid to a stop, pawing the darkness, frantic for some sense of orientation. There, an edge of rock, there the small circle of gray sky. I crawl back up so I can watch for Boldo, so I can breathe a wisp of outside air.

The fighting seems to be right above me. I cower with each violent eruption but keep my eyes trained on the circle of dawn at the mouth of the cave.

Oh, praise God, I catch a glimpse of his black boots pummeling the ground, his brown pants, a blur of movement.

And then, Mother of God, I see other boots, hear the voices of other men, the crackle of gunfire, groans and screams of injured soldiers.

Then an enormous blast. The earth trembles. I squat. Cover my head with my hands. A rain of pebbles and small stones sting my skin. They skitter and roll into the jaws of this wretched underground tomb.

I claw the ground, scrambling toward the light. My feet

shuffle and skid on debris, the acrid stench of explosives burns my throat. I approach the opening. Peer out into this sorry day dawning. All around is a hell of burning brush, of cratered earth, of broken, bleeding bodies.

Amid birdsong, I watch two soldiers drag Boldo off, a third behind them with a gun to his head.

CHAPTER 12

If I lie still long enough in this dark, underground crypt, perhaps I will die and it will be over.

This is what I attempt to do, but even this I cannot accomplish.

Worry squirms in my head. Where have they taken him? Have they killed him?

I drag myself up, and like a denned creature, crawl to a corner to relieve myself. My fear has turned to stone. What else can hurt me? What else can be taken from me? My terror and longing have become something new—blank, and untouchable. I will not think or feel. I will only do the next thing that needs to be done.

"Get up."

The hollow sound of my voice in the cave startles me. I

am suddenly aware of myself as something beyond this tight-wound twist of fear and anger.

"I am here," I say aloud.

Hesitate. Swallow.

"I am me."

Somehow, this bolsters me.

I force myself to think. When we were down near the pines, I'd asked where my baby was being kept. Boldo had pointed through the trees. "Up this hill and to the east."

Could I find the spot where we'd slept? Would I recognize it in daylight?

"A pink house, a manor house, just a kilometer away," he had said. How hard could it be?

But wait, I remember more. He said he'd left *patrin,* runic signs—twigs placed in the prescribed way, a stone or a feather, twine, a colorful rag, a clump of leaves. All this he has done for me! And now he is gone. My heart swells with gratitude and longing. I will head down the way we came and search for the markers. Go due east, where the pale winter sun had risen.

Boldo will know where I'm going. Surely he will escape. Surely he will find a way to come after me.

But I cannot afford to hope. No. I must get my baby back and that is all.

I pull myself from the cave and am blinded by the light of this white-sky day. The litter of war desecrates the ground—here a bloodied cap, there a tattered boot—the earth cratered and torn by explosives, underbrush scorched and trampled. I pick my way gingerly over the spent brass sleeves of bullets, around a drab green canvas bag.

I stop. Crouch. Stare. Should I open it? Might there be something useful? Perhaps a small blanket or a bite to eat? Something for my Little Red Squirrel? I cringe as I finger the buckle—*marime!*—lift the flap between thumb and index finger, stretch its mouth wide and peer inside.

I pull out a small parcel wrapped in parchment paper. A dull wave of pain fills the void in my gut. My mouth waters at the hunk of cheese before I even unwrap it. When was my last meal? At the funeral of my *daj*. I break the sharp, crumbling wedge with trembling hands, shove large chunks in my mouth, gulp, lick my fingers clean. Sitting back, I breathe heavily, the salty meal awakening a great thirst.

I rummage through the rucksack, thinking of the canteen in the pack on our horse. But no. A knife in a leather case, a photograph of a young woman, a pair of socks—these I lay aside. The bag is still weighty and I reach to the bottom. A large, turtle-like, egg-shaped object, heavy in my palm. Made of green-gray grooved metal, with a cap and a handle. A thin silver ring hangs from it. I don't know what this is, but perhaps it has value. I will keep the rucksack and its contents—the knife, socks, and this metal egg. I look at the photograph. She stares through me, searching for her soldier. Without thinking I say, "I, too, worry after one I love."

I shove the photograph of the woman into the bag, slip the strap across my body and over my shoulder, and set off.

A stream trickles through the wood. I cup my hands, drink deeply. I would like to strip off my week-old clothing and launder it in this running water. Wade in and feel it washing me clean. If the sun was warm, if I was not alone, if I had a change of clothing . . . if, if, if . . .

There isn't time.

I scan the terrain looking for the grove of pines where we slept, but there are many. I cannot distinguish one from another. I stand, perplexed. Sweep my eyes across the landscape again and again.

Nothing. No, wait. There—a cluster of twigs tied to the trunk of a tree with twine. My heart thrills. I rush toward this first sign. Check the sky to determine the easterly direction. But with the clouds I cannot tell where the sun hides. My faint shadow falls behind me. Perhaps, then, east is before me? This is how I proceed, with my shadow trailing.

A lone tree in the distance, something red flickering from a low-hanging branch. I nearly run, the dead man's oversized wool jacket flapping about me. The rucksack bumps against my hip. Yes, a scrap of scarlet cloth held by a rusted nail.

Fewer trees here, an open field. A branch speared in the ground, a long reddish-brown feather tied on top by a bright blue strand of yarn dancing in the breeze. My throat swells. I slip the feather from its string. The tail feather of a hawk—a talisman he's left for me. I gently place the pointed hollow end through a buttonhole of my jacket, so I can feel the smooth, cool fibers caress my neck. This sign Boldo left behind feels like one more gift—a gift full of his presence. For this, I silently thank him.

A rise of land grows into a hill. I rush forward. Sweat chills my back, dampens my dress. Calf muscles throb. I breathe hungrily, open-mouthed. Climb, run, climb. There, beyond a fringe of tall winter grass, a sliver of pink.

I stop.

Think. Gaze about.

To the left, some tall dense bushes, a grove of saplings. Rocks and vines. I step quickly, slip into the cover of leaves, branches, stones, and stems. Up, up, fighting tendrils and roots, I train my eyes on the growing strip of pink. The graceful roofline of scalloped red tile, windows guarded with swirling iron grates, an expansive terrace high above the ground, a grand oak door secured with a heavy, wrought iron latch.

My hands tremble. It looks impenetrable. A fortress.

I inch closer. My arms swim through foliage; my feet overtake shrubbery. I find a boulder tucked inside a tent of greenery formed by the branches of a large drooping bush. I scramble up and sit. From here I will watch and make a plan.

I must have dozed off. I awake feeling warm. The morning clouds have burned off. It is near noon, the sun directly overhead. I blink, rub my eyes, peer out of my leafy sanctuary. My throat catches.

I see a tall, stately woman, with upswept black hair, glide across the terrace. In her arms is something small wrapped in a blanket the color of wild heather. My Little Red Squirrel! The woman walks one way, then the other, patting and jostling my baby. Snippets of a melody float in and out of hearing. She is singing a *Gadje* tune to soothe her. I want to look away, to erase her mothering, but I cannot.

She sits, then, on the terrace wall, rocking forward and back, forward and back. Beside her a bottle of milk. I press my eyes shut as the woman takes the bottle, leans in, and eases it toward my Little Red Squirrel. Behind my lids I see many things—my mother's thin breasts, leaking at first sight of her babe; Little Red Squirrel's delicate pursed lips, twitching in her sleep; the small bottle of goat's milk I fashioned and coaxed into her.

At least she is not hungry. At least she is not cold. I am thankful for this, but a hard shaft of anger pierces my heart.

I creep to the edge of the brush and crouch there. I wait. Watch the *Gadje* woman lift the blanketed bundle to her shoulder, pat the little back, dab at the face I see only in my mind's eye. My legs are all pins and needles before she slips back inside.

Finally I cross myself—forehead, chest, shoulder, shoulder— lift my mother's pendant to my lips, and run across the open space, head lowered, clutching my jacket and bag to prevent any sound.

I slip between the palms and bushes lining the side of the house, duck beneath the window there, hopefully out of view. Panting, I wait for the knowledge of what to do next.

I sit this way for a very long time, but an answer does not come. Longing for comfort, I turn my face toward the feather on my lapel, to the velvety smoothness against my cheek. But it is gone. Lost, no doubt, as I ran across the lawn.

Out of nowhere an assault of tears. I shove my fists to my mouth. All this for a feather?

A sound. The creak of a door. Footsteps.

A woman—a servant, judging by her clothing—appears, frowns. She is only a stone's throw from where I hide. In her hands, a towel-full of table scraps. She scans the path. "Who's there?" she calls. "Emilio, is that you?"

I hold my breath, slump against the wall. Shuffling, then the rhythmic shush of shoes on steps, the groan of hinges, and quiet thud of the door.

I open my eyes, amazed I am still undiscovered.

Then a movement on the terrace—the servant woman. She has a basket balanced on her hip. Stretches an arm to a line I hadn't noticed, reaches in the basket, retrieves a white cloth, clips it to the line.

Diaper cloths. She is drying clean diaper cloths for my Little Red Squirrel.

Good. These I will steal as well. From here I see a staircase leading to the terrace. I see a wooden cradle and some chairs fashioned from woven willow. Glass doors that lead into the main house.

The servant leaves the basket behind and goes inside. In moments the *Gadje* woman comes out with Little Red Squirrel, sits in the willow chair and rocks. Each back and forth movement makes me more determined. I count her rocking—one, two . . . five . . . ten . . . At one hundred I start again—one, two, three . . . She stops at fifty-three, stands, and walks to the cradle.

Eases the bundle from her shoulder and into the small wooden bed, tucking, tucking. She calls out, "Maria, bring me the woolen blanket." Waits. Shrugs. Strolls to the door and disappears inside.

I do not think.

I run.

Out from my hiding place, across the grass, up the stairs, one, two, three, ten, sixteen. Dip my arms into the cradle, sweep her up. Run! Rip one white diaper cloth from the line, then another. Fly to the stairs. Down, down, I am halfway down before the door opens, three quarters of the way down before the woman screams.

I do not look back. Along the edge of the house where she cannot see me, across the lawn, hurry, hurry, into the underbrush. I bend into my precious bundle as the branches whip across us, hold her tight against my chest until my arms ache. Their frantic voices, their frenzied footsteps fade. I inhale the green of this haven. There the weeping bush, the tent of leaves.

I duck under and catch my breath.

I fold down the soft heather blanket.

She is fussing a little, her tiny fingers splayed. I place my face beside hers to feel her soft skin. Her tuft of orange hair smells of rose water. Her tiny body is cloaked in a pale pink gown, little knit socks tied with ribbons on her delicate feet. All this they have given her.

What can I give her besides nothing? The thought rises in my throat like acid.

Still, I have done what I promised.

A crazy thought barges in behind the last: I could always bring her back. Wait until dark, creep up the stairs, set her on the terrace.

Footfalls suddenly, frantic cries. Maria, the servant, a man, and several others, start down the hill, spreading out in all directions.

No more thoughts. I take my Little Red Squirrel and run.

CHAPTER 13

I hear their angry, frantic voices closing in.

A barking dog. Maybe two.

Hurry!

I stumble. Try to shield her. Hold her too tight. Fall.

Get up! Up! Move!

She cries and I cannot comfort her.

Which way to go?

Down, down the hill. There is a shout. Someone else calls out. Do they hear her? I cover Little Red Squirrel's face with the blanket.

The slope drops steeply and my feet slip from under me. I fall back. Hit the ground hard. Slide down in a rush of pebbles and dirt. A pain shoots through my leg. Still, I get up and hobble on. And still Little Red Squirrel whimpers beneath her blanket.

The battlefield is ahead of me. I limp around the craters. Turn an ankle in a ditch. Bloody my knee. Get up! Up!

The blanket falls away. Little Red Squirrel's brow is furrowed, her tiny mouth pulled back, her face scarlet. Her arms escape, trembling, the whole of her tensed in a spasm.

I see the cave.

Around the tall grass, the black cavern mouth gapes. I slide into the darkness and sink against the damp wall. I cradle a sobbing Little Red Squirrel in my lap. "We are safe, my little one," I whisper.

I rock her, hum a *Gitano* tune, rub my face against hers. Her crying slows to a quivering sigh.

I tip my head back against the uneven stone wall. Let the chill of the wet rock refresh me. She shudders and finally relaxes in my arms.

I long to look at her, but the darkness is too thick. I run my fingers along the soft velvet of her cheek, trace the upturned nose, gently touch the tiny pursed lips.

I must think, find food or milk, and in time, find a way to live. But I am too tired, frightened, shocked at my own actions. I must rest.

A thought creeps in. I have come back to the place where Boldo left me. Maybe he has escaped. Maybe at this moment he is coming back here. Maybe he will save us, as he did before.

What other hope do I have? I sink toward sleep, clinging to this. When he returns we can go on and join his cousin's people as he planned. We can be married. I will wear a colorful skirt and weave flowers and coins in my hair. My Little Red Squirrel will have a real home. I will dance and he will raise his hawks.

After a while, our clans could join together—his people and Luludja's people. (I spit at her name.) Time can make them forget. I will see Kizzy again!

Is this any less possible than what has already taken place? No. In fact, it is more likely. It *can* end well. Isn't it time for something to end well?

On these sweet hopes I drift to sleep.

A sound awakens me.

Am I dreaming? I am sure I hear his footsteps! I carry my Little Red Squirrel toward the thin shaft of light at the mouth of the cave.

His voice is soft, intense. *"Beng tori."*

I must hear wrong—*the devil comes?*

"What?" I scramble toward his voice.

Another word . . . *"jostumal . . ."*

What is he saying? . . . *wishes me harm?*

I hold Little Red Squirrel in one arm, pull myself up with the other. I see his boots! The cuffs of his brown trousers! He grabs my hand. I am weak with relief.

Then a vice-grip on my wrist, a violent thrust. I cry out. Raise my eyes.

Oh God, he is not alone. His face is contorted, the veins in his neck bulge.

They drag him back, yank me forward.

"We have them!" the man wrenching my arm shouts.

Boldo thrashes and kicks. They snatch my baby. In shock, I do not resist. They pass her between them, away, away from me. The soldier in charge draws a pistol, points it in the air, fires twice. I scream and keep screaming. Boldo lunges, twists away. The gunman laughs, slams the butt of the gun down on Boldo's head. He crumples. And I go down with him.

CHAPTER 14

We are thrown into the back of a truck alongside tattered soldiers, bleeding, unconscious, or both. Some of the ones in charge have the fair complexion of the yellow-haired man. They glare and bark orders. The other prisoners are Spanish peasants—Republicans. They mutter and spit, but still hold their chins high.

The one in charge had ripped the dead soldier's jacket and rucksack from me, made a fuss over the knife—but the green metal egg caused an even greater stir.

Boldo has come to his senses. The large gash and lump on his head make a map of blood along the side of his face. We sit shoulder to shoulder with the other prisoners and three guards. Late afternoon light casts deep shadows, slicing their faces into sharp angles. The metal of their guns, deep blue and cold.

"That Gyp who stole the baby . . ."

I hear them speaking, nodding toward me. " . . . wearing the lieutenant's jacket . . . his knife and grenade!"

They shake their heads, the edges of their mouths drawn down. "Goddam baby stealers . . . no respect for decent people . . ."

My Little Red Squirrel rides up front, in the enclosed part of the truck, with the driver and two more soldiers—the ones who allowed Boldo to escape, then followed him to the cave. This he explains in hushed tones as we ride. When the word got out that a *Gitano* woman had stolen a baby, and that a *Gitano* man was found nearby with the horses of two dead officers . . .

"But why steal the baby?"

I want to scream, want to tell them it was the *Gadje* woman, the *Gadje* woman and Luludja, buying and selling my baby!

" . . . can smell her from here . . . doesn't even wash . . ."

I am ashamed, suddenly aware of my filthy clothes covered in sweat, vomit, and dirt. My cheeks burn. *Marime*, I think.

" . . . fascist pigs . . ."

"Don't listen to them," Boldo says through clenched teeth. "Don't listen!"

"Shut up!" One of the guards pokes the barrel of his rifle into Boldo's neck, then levels it at his temple. "Want me to blow your brains all over your dirty little whore?"

Boldo jerks forward, nostrils flaring, hands chained behind him.

"This one's pretty feisty," the guard chuckles. "Wonder what he'll do if I touch his little Gyp woman?" He touches my ankle. I pull away, trying to tuck my feet beneath me. I yank my skirt over my curled toes. Inch as far as I can into the corner.

They snicker.

Boldo struggles against the shackles. The guards laugh. Prisoners smile. They are suddenly allies in ridiculing us. The guard who touched me cocks his rifle, still aimed at Boldo. "Always a good day for a Gyp to die . . ."

I pull myself up, lean forward. Every muscle tensed. I fix the guard in my stare—hatred shoots from my eyes like the fire from their guns.

They fall silent.

I raise my arm, point my thumb and two fingers toward my captor, "*Gadje* men! A curse upon your souls and the souls of your children!"

"I should kill you right now, you dirty bitch . . ." He points the gun at my forehead. I stare back, the spirit of Caterina and my mother flowing through me. I clench my jaw, breathing heavily, my hand still raised in the curse.

No one is laughing now. The moment stretches between us.

A second guard pushes the gun away. "Don't kill her," he says. "Gypsy magic is powerful. She'll be dead, but her spell will follow you."

I remain fixed, arm extended, fingers trembling.

"Instead, make her take it back. Take it back, Gyp!"

I slowly lower my arm, but my eyes never leave him. In Spanish I say, "Harm us or my baby, and this curse will follow you and your offspring to your graves."

I do not know if this is true, but it is only important for them to believe it. The gunman looks away. No one will meet my eyes, except Boldo. His eyes tell me he is pleased. For an instant I bask in this. Then I sit back.

The truck bumps over the road. Our shoulders bounce. My back aches. I rest my head on my knees, glance sideways through the back window of the cab for a glimpse of Little Red Squirrel. I cannot hear her, but I know she is crying.

Our captors tip their heads together, talking in hushed tones. "... split them up ... the Germans ... a Portuguese ... Gitanos ..." Boldo nods slightly. Mouths the words, "Don't worry."

The cursed guard kicks Boldo's foot. "Shut up!"

"... questioning there ..." I listen intently, eyes cast down. "... Sevilla ... some to Jerez ..."

Jerez. My throat swells. The place my mother longed to be ...

In the distance a city appears. Its red rooftops shine in the last of the day's sun. The road weaves though vineyards and fields. In the distance many spires and minarets pierce the sky. The fanlike leaves of palm trees and wide-topped, bristly *pino pinioneros* stand beside whitewashed and sand-colored buildings, one upon the next. An ancient fortress wall runs around and between buildings and *bodegas,* its lookout towers and rooftop walkways like a row of square teeth. The closer we come to the outlying margins of this city, the more I feel pressed in by its confines of concrete and brick.

Street after street, one the same as another, and yet different. *Tavernas* and *cafeterias* with outdoor tables, cobbled streets, a grand church with towers and bridge-like buttresses, massive wooden doors. All this I see, and do not see.

We jerk to a stop outside a brick and concrete building. The doors creak. Two in the cab jump to the ground and take my Little Red Squirrel from the truck. Without thinking, I stand, so I can see where they're taking her.

"Sit down!" The guard shoves me to my knees. I peer over the rails. A dark car pulls in beside our truck. The driver gets out, opens the back door. A woman rushes out—the black-haired *Gadje* woman. She sweeps toward the guards, sobbing, reaching out for Little Red Squirrel. What a show she puts on for them! She barely knows this baby. My insides churn as I watch.

They yank me from the truck, nudging me with the ends of their rifles. "Is this her?"

She stares at me, eyes narrowed. "Yes, I think so. It must be her—the one who stole my sweet little Paloma!"

I rush at her. They grab my arms, restrain me. I spit. Spit again. She steps away, hugging Little Red Squirrel against her beautiful brown silk dress. They yank my wrist behind my back, pulling me away from her.

I am so angry that I do not recognize the grinding roar of the engine as the truck pulls away. I crane my neck, this way, that. I struggle for a glimpse of Boldo, as though holding him in my sight could keep us together.

The truck rumbles toward the corner. My body strains in that direction. I hear a gentle voice speaking. But not to me. "Not to worry, Señora Castillo. It is over now."

When I look back, the truck is gone.

There is a strange keening—the sound of a wild, wounded animal. My legs give way. The sound pours from me. The guards grab me under my arms. Their fingers press and bruise the soft hollows. "Get up! Move!"

No. I am dead.

Lost.

My feet hang. Arms dangle. Between them they drag me up the stairs, through the door, down the corridor. My skirts mop the floor. My head falls onto my chest, then flops back against my shoulders. Yellow bulbs hanging from the ceiling flash behind my eyelids. I press them, tight, then open them. Searching, still, for Little Red Squirrel. They jostle me around a corner into a dim room.

"This is the savage who stole Señora Castillo's baby . . ." The guards push and prod. One of them pokes me with his gun for emphasis.

A man sits behind the desk. The light reflects off the balding dome of his head. His mouth moves slightly beneath a thick, graying mustache. He looks at my face covered in tears and dirt and snot. Sighs. "Jesus, Mary, and Joseph," he says quietly, shaking his head. "Sit, now, please . . ." He gestures toward a chair.

I slump into the wooden seat.

"You've done your duty," the man behind the desk says. "Leave us now. Go." As the soldiers depart he turns to me. "Now it is your time to speak."

He waits. I wait.

96

He sighs again, more deeply. "You people do not make it easy. I have a statement from Señora Castillo." He pushes a paper across the desk. I do not look—the marks on the page mean nothing to me. I slide it back with my index finger. The black crescent of dirt lining the underside of my nail shouts against the white sheet. I curl my fingers, pull away.

He picks it up. Clears his throat. "I'll read it to you."

I hear the words—how I took Little Red Squirrel— "Paloma"—and ran down the steps, into the woods, how they found me in the cave . . .

"Now, can you tell me your side of the story?"

"What difference would it make?" I spit the words.

He raises his bushy gray and white eyebrows. "You can speak! That is good. A first step." I glare into my lap. Grip the arms of the chair with white knuckles.

"Look at me. Please." His words lack the sharp edge I've come to expect. I want to look up, to examine this face, but I do not.

He sits patiently. The clock on the wall ticks.

Then quietly, "I read hearts. See what's behind the eyes. Hear beyond the words. To read the human psyche is my gift and my curse. I might not be able to help you—and you might not deserve my help—but why not tell your story? What else do you have to lose?"

He is right about that. There is nothing left to lose. I look up. Meet his eyes. His chin is propped on folded hands. I take a trembling breath.

"The baby is—was— my mother's. My *daj* was raped by

97

a yellow-haired *militar*, of the type in the truck with us. She carried his seed, lost herself in a deep sadness, gave birth too early. She died of childbed fever." I rub my eyes with the backs of my hands. He hands me his handkerchief. I catch my breath, wipe my face.

"I promised my mother I'd take care of Little Red Squirrel—that's what I called her." I am saying too much, but I go on. "My aunt took her away. The baby was *marime,* unclean, because of the vile act of that soldier, and this *Gadje* woman—Señora Castillo—bought her for a handful of gold coins! Boldo . . ." The tears come again. "Boldo saw the whole thing, followed her, discovered where she lived. We went there and I took back what was—what is—mine! Why don't you ask her where she got the baby? Ask her! And now they are taking Boldo away . . ."

"You have suffered much, I can see that. Have you had anything to eat?"

I shake my head.

"Or drink? No place safe to stay? Your family?"

His kindness unravels me. "I have nothing left . . ."

"You haven't told me your name."

"You didn't ask . . ."

"I'm asking now . . ."

I raise my head. I do not know how to answer. Anything I say does not feel true. "Drina."

"And your family name?"

Zaporata is poised on my tongue, but I hesitate. No, I am not a Zaporata. "Muentes," I say. "Drina Honoria Muentes."

His drooping eyes lift.

"Your father's name?"

"My mother told me it was Diego."

"Mother?"

I sigh. "Nadja."

He leans forward in his seat. "How old are you, Drina?"

I shrug, impatient. "I think sixteen. Will you help me get my baby back?"

He stares at me. Reaches for the big black device on his desk. Lifts one piece between his ear and his mouth, turns the small wheel with his finger. Is this a telephone? I watch as he speaks into it, his voice reaching someone a distance away.

"Hello? Good evening, Carlita? It's Alvaro Vargas. I need to speak to Marisol. Would you please put her on the line? Yes, yes, I know it is dinner hour. But she will want to speak to me. Yes, I'll wait, of course."

His eyes meet mine as he covers the mouthpiece with one hand and whispers, "I am calling someone who, I'm sure, will want to hear your story."

He quickly shifts the device against his ear, sits up.

"Marisol, yes. Can Bernardo bring you down here? To the office? . . . Yes, right now, or when you finish your dinner. There is someone here for you. . . . No, not an emergency exactly, but it is a matter that will be of great interest. . . . Of course. . . . Yes, we will wait."

He replaces the speaking device in the cradle. Inhales deeply. Exhales. Leans back in his chair. "She is on her way."

CHAPTER 15

I have finished the thick slab of bread and chunk of sharp cheese provided by Señor Alvaro Vargas. When he is not looking, I press my fingertips against the surface of the desk, picking up the last of the crumbs and bringing them to my mouth. My eyes dart about as I eat. Señor Vargas sits, rearranging the objects on his desk. But he watches me closely.

"Have you had enough?" he asks.

I nod, although hunger still turns my stomach in knots. He eyes me thoughtfully, reaches behind him to a narrow table, takes three dried dates and some almonds from a ceramic bowl, and places them before me.

My mouth waters at the very thought of the sweet fruit. I hesitate. I will not stuff my mouth like a desperate stray dog. I pick up a date, look it over, roll it in my fingers.

Halfway to my lips I stop, interrupted by footsteps in the corridor. Alvaro Vargas stands, moves to the door, and I pop the date in my mouth. The insides of my cheeks fill with saliva at the shock of sweetness. I chew quickly and swallow. Then I perch at the edge of the chair and lean forward, straining to get a glimpse into the hall.

A small raven of a woman moves along the corridor with quick, short strides. She is wearing a black lace dress, stockings and shoes—but not the widow's garb of a peasant. The cut of her dress is elegant, the fabric rich, her leather shoes narrow and fine. Her silver hair is braided and wound in a tight knot at the back of her neck. A black lacy *mantilla* held up with a *peineta* perches atop her head.

I stare at this approaching force. Her eyes are small black stones deeply set in soft folds, her mouth pulled in a firm line. High cheekbones and an angular chin make the face, which must have been beautiful once, appear strong and sure.

As Alvaro Vargas takes her arm and guides her into the room, she peers at me. I realize my mouth hangs open and I snap it shut. Pulling my eyes away from hers, I slump back into my wooden chair, stare into my lap, my face burning.

Señor Vargas waves her into the seat beside mine. She arranges herself and looks between us. "Who is this feral child, Alvaro, and why have you called me here?"

"She has been accused of a terrible crime. Of stealing a baby."

"And how is this my concern?"

"She took the baby from Señora Castillo."

The old woman chuckles. "Well, good for her."

"Marisol!"

"I know. I try to be Christian, but with the Castillo clan, it is difficult. And, despite this one's feat—and nerve—I still don't see how it concerns me."

Alvaro smiles. "Well, I only know one other woman with that kind of pluckiness."

"Get on with it, Alvaro!" she says lightly. "You've taken me from my dinner."

"Have a glass of sherry, my dear." Señor Vargas pours her a goblet of golden liquid from a crystal bottle. I watch through the wave of hair falling in front of my face.

"Staring in that way is rude," Marisol says. "Do you think we cannot see you through that tangled nest?"

Startled, I look up.

"That's better," she says. And to Alvaro, "I hope you've arranged a bath for her."

"Marisol, I've questioned this young woman. I believe her story, which is quite an adventure and a tragedy. She had good reason to take the baby, who is her half sister. Her mother died of fever, leaving the infant to her care. Magdalena Castillo claims she adopted the child, whom she calls Paloma. But it is not possible; this I know. I have a friend serving on the National Council of Evacuated Children. This is where she claims she adopted the babe. But so far, the Council only places children of school age—not infants or toddlers."

The woman squints at Alvaro.

"Then what's the issue? Give the baby back and send her on her way."

I nod vigorously. "Yes, please!"

Señor Vargas raises a hand. "It's not that easy. How do you suppose the word of a vagabond Gypsy girl would hold up against the word of a Castillo? Found wearing the jacket of a slain Nationalist officer, and in possession of his personal articles, including a grenade." The woman looks at me with a renewed spark of interest.

"And this unfortunate waif has no means to support or raise the child. Banished from her group, separated from her lone supporter."

I cannot breathe.

"Get to it, Alvaro, please."

He turns to me. "Tell Señora your name, little one."

"What does it matter," I blurt, "if I'm not getting my baby back?"

"Tell her, please."

I swallow. "Drina."

"Your full name."

I sigh. Repeat what I'd told the man earlier. "Drina Honoria Muentes."

The woman suddenly sits up, her back ramrod straight.

"And your mother's name?"

"Nadja."

She stands abruptly, bends toward me, lifts my chin in her hand. She has the look of a *Gitano* inspecting an Andalusian horse, her intent gaze moving from my mouth to my nose, my eyes and forehead, cheeks and profile. She raises an eyebrow. Glances back at Señor Vargas.

"So, there's a resemblance. Anyone can adopt a name, especially when it might serve their purpose." But her words do not match her expression. She seems suddenly older, or perhaps her confidence has waned. She turns my face toward her. "How old are you?" she demands.

"Sixteen."

She sighs deeply. "Alvaro, I want to speak to you in private, outside, please!" Still eyeing me, she tips her head toward the door.

Alvaro nods. "Excuse us . . ." He pushes the door open and holds it as this Marisol sweeps through. It closes behind them, leaving me alone again. My head spins. A resemblance, she said. To whom? She thinks I am masquerading? Of all the people I might pretend to be, why would I choose myself? In my exhaustion, this thought strikes me as funny. I begin to laugh, but the laugh breaks down into a sob that I stifle with a fisted hand. I will not parade my weakness before them this way. I take a deep, trembling breath and strain to hear their hushed words in the corridor. Do I dare move closer to the door?

Sniffling, I stand, pad silently toward the heavy portal. Lean my head to the side, cup my ear against the wood. I hear Alvaro's muffled voice. " . . . would make sense . . . sixteen. It was—what—seventeen years ago Diego brought her home? And there were rumors, after all . . ."

" . . . a little too convenient, wouldn't you say? . . . no way to know for sure . . ." Marisol sounds uncertain. And there is something else. Is it fear?

Alvaro continues, calm, persistent. "... resemblance is striking ... same dark eyes, that barely contained fire ..."

"Many *Gitano* women share that trait, Alvaro. It's what distinguishes them as dancers ..."

"But, you've always felt great regret over Nadja. If it's true, this could be a way to make reparation ..."

"I will not be duped, Alvaro! I ..." Her voice trembles and cracks.

"There's no shame, Dearest, in extending the benefit of the doubt."

"What do you suggest I do?"

"What do you *want* to do?"

Silence. I can barely breathe.

"I want to know the truth."

"The girl could be ..." He does not finish the phrase.

"But, Diego ..."

"Perhaps he didn't know ... or didn't tell ..."

"And Camilla," she says, "O, *Madre de Dios!*"

"One step at a time, Marisol."

I try to piece together the meaning of their exchange. My heart is racing. I do not know what to feel. My *daj*, what am I to think? Diego? And who is Camilla? Their words have become a blur in the whirlwind of my thoughts. I force myself to focus.

"Bring her into your home. After all, is it not the Christian thing to do? Explore the past. See what Diego has to say."

"I need some time ... to think ..."

"Whatever you want, Marisol, of course, but if she's still

here, I'm certain they'll arrest her in the morning. There is a small window . . ."

I wait, breathless. Without warning, the door opens, knocking against the side of my head. I step back, skull pounding, ashamed to be caught eavesdropping.

"Well," Marisol snaps. "So much for speaking in private!" She casts me a withering glance, her mouth puckered. Then her face relaxes. "Ahhhhh . . ." she sighs, shaking her head. She raises her hand, index finger first, in a kind of resigned salute. "I would do the same if I were you, whoever you are. . . . So, it's decided. You're coming home with me tonight—"

Alvaro looks at me. "This is acceptable, I take it?"

I stare, open-mouthed. Paralyzed. Things are happening much too quickly. "What about my Little Red Squirrel? My baby?"

"Little Red Squirrel?" Marisol barks. "That is no name for a child! And say what you will for the Castillos, but the babe will want for nothing. You've done more than anyone could or would have done. And, to your good fortune, you wound up in the merciful hands of Alvaro Vargas. You will come home with me."

"But I do not belong here!"

"Where do you belong, then?"

I am crying now, torn as I am between my desires. Little Red Squirrel. Boldo. Yet, the chance to meet these people who could be family. My *father*. But, no matter what I choose, I am forced to turn my back on the rest.

"Drina?"

"I have nothing. I *am* nothing. I do not belong anywhere!"

Marisol shakes her head slightly. Softens her voice. "First, as I see it, you have nowhere else to go. More importantly, you've claimed that my son, Diego Honoria Muentes, is your father. If this is true, I am your grandmother. If it is not true . . ." Her face hardens. She purses her lips. I stare at her, try to recognize something that would connect this *grandmother* to me. I see nothing.

Alvaro places one hand on my arm, the other on Marisol's wrist. "Why don't we simply let this unfold? I trust that all things will turn out for the good. If, at any point, you want to leave, well then, that is your choice. Marisol, don't you agree?"

"I suppose."

Where do I want to go? I do not know what to wish for. It is feeling less and less that there is a choice to make. "But if I leave here, how will Boldo find me?"

Marisol looks at me sharply. "Is he your husband, this Boldo?"

I hesitate a moment too long.

"Good. You are very young yet. And where has he gone?"

Señor Vargas purses his lips. "Sevilla. They've taken the prisoners to Sevilla."

"But when he comes back for me . . ."

Alvaro Vargas looks at me with sad eyes. "Drina, dear, we must be realistic. Most likely he will not have the chance."

CHAPTER 16

Señor Alvaro Vargas stands by the curb as we leave. I shift my eyes sideways and watch the old woman sitting beside me in the back of the carriage. Neither of us speaks, and the sound of the horse's hooves on the cobbled street seems unreasonably loud. The old man driving the carriage whistles a tuneless melody, perhaps to fill the place where conversation should be. I could jump from the seat and run—what is stopping me? But I know I will not, and the old woman who might be my grandmother somehow knows it as well.

My gaze roams from Marisol's angular profile to the edges and corners of the many columned buildings and shops lining the avenue, the stone and concrete walkways laid out in repeated designs of overlapping squares and diamonds. Some of the windows are lit with the glare of electrical lights.

Storefronts and cafes are plastered with posters of war scenes—planes, bombs, and frightened, angry people.

I am lulled into a kind of numb, mindless watching. We round a corner. A thread of music breaks the trance. Clapping, the thrashing of a guitar. I sit up and turn toward the sound.

She nods in the direction of the music. "A *peña* where Lola Vega comes to perform. Bernardo, stop here for a moment!"

The old man pulls on the reins and the carriage rolls to a stop. I stare inside at the flash of color and sound. I feel Marisol's eyes on me, but it is hard to tear my gaze away.

"Lola was born here in Jerez—claims to have Gypsy blood. The most famous *flamenco* dancer in the world."

My pulse quickens. The rhythm of the music tugs at my feet, the beat draws my shoulders forward and back, my chin side to side. How long has it been since I've danced?

"Bernardo, pull up to the next corner. There!"

She points toward a wooden pole outside the club covered in large poster pictures, most of militiamen with red caps and bandanas and soldiers in blue coveralls, others showing children. All with print messages about the war—meaningless to me. Bernardo guides the carriage closer.

"There!" she repeats, pointing a black-lace, gloved finger toward a poster peeking out beside these war placards. A drawing of a man dancing with a beautiful woman. I stare at the fine clothing, marvel at the way the picture depicts energy and movement, the way their faces communicate passion. "My son," she says, "and Lola Vega, dancing here together."

I feel her gaze as I stare at his features, the shape of his face, the line of his nose, try to see something of him in me—strain to feel some kind of recognition, but no, there is nothing familiar in the likeness. But it is only a drawing, after all.

"See his name there, Diego Honoria Muentes."

I peer at the bold, black characters superimposed over the dancers' feet. My father's name. I think of my *daj* and me, alone, far from here, while he was dancing with this Lola Vega. But fascination trumps whatever resentment I might feel. Marisol waits, expectant. I do not know what to say, so I offer nothing. Drop my eyes to my lap.

"All right, Bernardo, thank you." With an abrupt flip of her hand, she motions for us to move. Have I angered her in some way? I fight the urge to turn back for one more glimpse of Diego, remembering my *daj* calling his name. We travel on, the music fading, and its absence conjures the spirits of other losses. I push these away, close my heart to them. How else can I ride on in this carriage? How else can I continue to breathe?

We travel in silence. Marisol pulls her shawl closer around her. Bernardo adjusts his cap. "We're almost there," she says, eyes fixed on the road ahead. "Diego is not here—he is in Cadiz. This is, likely, a blessing. He will be . . . surprised when he arrives home."

I can only imagine how surprised he will be. So many questions rise inside of me, but I cannot voice them.

We turn up a dirt road that winds up a hill and around a grove of palm trees. A sprawling, whitewashed house with a red tiled roof appears, orange trees growing around the terrace.

Curly, wrought iron grates surround the windows, and vines of small blossoms creep around the corners.

Bernardo makes a small grunting sound and the horse slows to a halt. He jumps from his carriage seat, tethers the fine beast to a post, and comes around to Marisol. Holding her elbow, he helps her down; then, without averting his eyes, he extends his arm to me. I feel his eyes judging me as they sweep over my torn clothes, my filthy hands and face. Avoiding his arm, I take hold of the side of the carriage and step out myself. I look up at the wide staircase with potted palms on either side. It is clear I do not belong here.

"Come," Marisol says rather briskly. We start up the steps and Bernardo plods ahead to open the door.

"Tend to the horse please, Bernardo," Marisol says. "We are surely capable of handling doorways on our own." He removes his cap, runs his fingers through a shock of gray hair, shrugs, and turns, reluctantly. Her black eyes glint as she shoots me a glance. "Congratulations," she whispers through barely parted lips. "You've caused a bit of a stir already."

A plump woman in an apron appears at the door, pulling it open as we top the stairs. Her eyes widen and her lips part at the sight of me, but unlike Bernardo, she is quick enough to rearrange her features before Marisol notices.

"Carlita, draw a warm bath for the girl. For Drina."

Carlita nods uncertainly. Now she feels free to ogle me up and down. I mumble a greeting, look away.

"And prepare a room for her—the south bedroom, for now."

"Si, Señora," Carlita says, already heading up a winding staircase. Her open-backed slippers slap each step.

"You're hungry," Marisol says. It is a statement, not a question. This is a woman who is used to being sure about things. She leads me into the next room, a kitchen.

I nod. Then shake my head. I do not know that I can eat. And now, I hear the running of water above me. A bath? *Marime,* I think. I have never washed except in fresh, running water. It is unclean to soak in one's own filth. And yet I am tired, and hungry, and dirty, and I have already crossed many lines of appropriateness— defying my Auntie, lying next to Boldo, wearing the dead soldier's clothing, exposing my ankles. With every transgression, the next is easier. I sigh deeply. Who have I become?

Marisol is not troubled by my hesitation. She turns to a large stove, twists a knob, and lights a match beneath a wide, cast-iron pot. Removes the lid, gathers a wooden spoon and a glass of water from the sink. Pours in the water, stirs. A savory smell fills the air.

"*Gazpachuelo,*" she says. "Have you ever tried it?"

"No . . ."

"A good way to stretch a little food—since this damned war there's never enough. Fish, potatoes, vinegar." She stirs. Sniffs. "Go wash your hands and get a bowl from the cupboard. Over there, beside the window."

I turn the curious knobs as I saw her do, and water runs. I wash, shut off the tap, and open the cupboard. What an array of plates and bowls and cups!

"What keeps you? A bowl, Drina. Your bath will be ready

and you won't have eaten." Her tone is impatient, snappish.

I get the bowl even as my stomach turns over. I am starving, yet I am sick with worry. Still, I sit at the table where she points, I lift the spoon, I eat the delicious soup until the bowl is clean. I burp quietly and swallow the sour repeat of fish and vinegar in the back of my throat.

"Now, upstairs, let's go."

Somehow I follow her up the stairs and through a dark hallway toward a lit room where, through the crack in the door, I see what must be the tub—a white stone vessel, steam rising from the top. Carlita steps out, gestures with her hand.

"Carlita will see to your needs," she says. "I'll gather some clean clothes." She stalks off down the hallway, leaving me with the servant woman whose neutral expression quickly changes to one of scorn.

"Your bath is drawn." Her tone is chilly. We avoid each other's eyes. I do not move.

"Problem?"

I shrug. "I can't . . . we don't . . . I mean . . ."

"Bathe? I can see that. But you'll not dirty our fresh linens by slipping into bed the way you are." Her upper lip curls in disgust.

"My people, we don't bathe in still water . . . we . . ."

"Well, you're here now. This is what we do."

Marisol sweeps back along the corridor, a pile of neatly folded clothing in her hands. "What's wrong, Carlita?"

"She's refusing the bath," Carlita says, distaste pulling at her features.

Marisol sighs. "Why don't you go tidy the kitchen, Carlita?"

Carlita hesitates.

"Go on!" Marisol says. "So much nonsense over a bath!" Carlita stomps off, shaking her head, muttering. I hear the words *these people*. That is who I am to her. One of *these people*.

Marisol studies me. "Surely you'd prefer to be clean, wouldn't you? Then what's the problem? Truly, it will be a gift to those around you!"

"My people wash only in running water . . ."

"You mean your mother's people. If you are who you claim to be, then you need to know that your father's people bathe. If that's half of who you are, go and enjoy half a bath."

Still, I stand in the doorway.

Marisol sighs. "You're trying an old woman's patience." She nudges me into the bathing room. "Look—take off these filthy clothes, over there, the toilet—you know how to use that, don't you?"

I nod, although I've never actually used one.

"Then here, if you need running water, how about this?" She reaches for a hose with a silver sprinkler at the end. She turns a knob, adjusts a switch, and water sprays from the sprinkler. "See how it works? " She turns it on and off." Get yourself in there and run this water. Will that do? Half and half. Half bath, half running water. Perfect for you, *si?*"

I am too tired to argue, and perhaps she is right. She places the clean, folded garments on the tiled floor. "Go on. I'll step outside. Just drop the soiled clothes by the door."

She is gone.

I stand alone in the bathing room. Stare into a looking glass above the sink. I do not know the person staring back at me. I cannot see her clearly, but it is not just the steam from the bath that clouds my view. The gold pendant around my neck still glints. The only thing left, it seems, from the life I knew before.

Stepping back, I remove my torn shoes, slowly unbutton my clothes caked with dirt, blood, and worse. As I peel the fabric away, my fingers fumble and shake. My heart races as I drop each tattered piece by the door. I lift one foot over the edge of the tub and gasp as the hot water touches my skin. Pull it back. Breathe deeply. Immerse the foot, grab hold of the rim, then step in with the other. I stand naked above the water, reach for the hose, turn the knob, then the switch. It sprays across the room and I drop it, nearly lose my balance. I recover, grab the dancing hose and aim it over my body, feel the warmth across my breasts and down my torso. I shiver, take a deep breath, and plunge myself into the bath. Hold the hose high, dowsing my head, my chest, my entire self, my hair running with it in streams over my face, my shoulders, my back. I gasp for air, hold the wand close enough to cause painful pelting, more, more, until my tears mix with the droplets and fall into the bath.

I turn the sprinkler off and sink back into the water. It is filthy now. I pull the plug, watch the dirt swirl down the drain. I lather myself with a sliver of aromatic soap, turn the sprayer on once more, and wash myself clean.

CHAPTER 17

I rub my body with a large white towel until my skin is red and dry. There, just inside the door, she's left a garment, folded neatly, of white eyelet cloth. I run my fingers through my hair, shake out the water, wrap the towel around it, and squeeze. I shiver convulsively—the water had been so hot, and now I feel cold in so many ways.

With chattering teeth and trembling fingers I reach for the garment, let it unfold in my hands. I almost do not recognize these hands—now shriveled and pink, the nails and knuckles scrubbed clean and smelling faintly of roses. The scent reminds me of something . . . I close my eyes and inhale. My heart races. Of course. It was the smell of my Little Red Squirrel clothed in the pink dress and blanket. I have an urge to throw the sleeping gown, with its fine, white, delicate fabric, to the floor, stomp on it, tear it in two, but the impulse leaves me. I hold it up, take the hem, and pull it over my head. I am a ghost in this garment, a ghost or an angel. It falls softly against my skin, and my body begins to relax.

I look at the toilet and feel a sudden urge. I push the door shut, hoist up the gown, and step closer. Sit my bare behind on the oval white stone rim and gasp. Jump up. Cold!

"Are you all right in there?"

"Yes." I stand, prepare myself for the shock of it, and sit myself back down. Not so bad the second time. I try to relieve myself, but somehow I cannot, despite the pressure. I wait. Close my eyes. There—the tinkling sound surprises me, and feeling rude, I stop the flow, then try and continue, quietly. But no, the water music echoes in the tiled bathing room, and, I'm sure, into the hallway.

"Good," Marisol calls. "Use the newspaper strips to wipe, then wash your hands in the sink." She heard me. My face heats up in shame, but I do as she says.

"Now, flush—pull the chain on the ceiling!" She must be right outside the door. I reach up and pull the chain, startle at the large sucking, swooshing sound of the swirling water carrying my pee away. Kizzy would laugh, I think, and again sadness sneaks up on me.

Marisol leads me down the corridor—"To your room," she says.

My room . . .

I stop in the doorway. Two narrow beds dressed in soft, white fabric stand high off the floor on solid wooden frames.

The shuttered windows are large. A shaft of moonlight shines in, slicing the room in two. Underfoot is a thick, fringed carpet in shades of wine, lapis, and gold, covering much of the polished pine floor. A massive chest of drawers, the edges carved in rounded swirls, is placed against the far wall with a mirror hanging above it. Another smaller cabinet sits between the beds, topped by an electrical lamp with a wide red shade.

"Come in," Marisol says. "I'll turn down your bed. You must be exhausted. Which one would you like?"

Still, I stand at the portal. She folds back the blankets of the bed nearest the window, fluffs the pillow, stands on her toes to adjust the shutters. I watch as from some far-off place.

The moonlight softens her features, and perhaps her heart. She reaches for my hand, leads me to the bed. I sit. She guides my feet beneath the blanket, I lie back stiffly. She draws the bedding up, covering me to my chin. Sits on the edge of the bed. Places a thin hand on my shoulder.

"You know, no one will stop you from leaving here in the night. If that is what you must do, I've left some clothing for you there by the closet." She pauses, a deep line forming between her brows. "But I'm asking you to stay. We both have many questions, I am sure, and stories to tell. For me, however awkward this may be, I prefer to face the questions and get to the truth. Though difficult, can we not give each other the benefit of the doubt? Ultimately, we both must decide if we can make that leap of faith."

I avoid her eyes. I want to say yes, I want to see my father,

I want to hear the story of him and my mother. But the words stick in my throat. I nod. It is the best I can do.

She stands. As she leaves I glance her way, see her in silhouette, framed by the light in the hallway.

"Good night." She closes the door, gently. I turn on my side, knees drawn to my chest, facing the window. The night sky spreads out like a bolt of black velvet cloth, the moon a silver coin flung in the middle. It is as though I could reach out and pluck it between my fingers, tuck it away in my pocket, or better still, stitch it into the hem of my garment for safekeeping.

So many things within my grasp and lost—a mother, a child, a friend, a lover, a place to belong. . . . And now, perhaps at stake—a grandmother. A father.

I am afraid to stay. Afraid to go.

The words come into my head of their own volition:

My daj, *what am I to do?*

Where am I to go?

I need you to tell me.

I lie there in the fine bed, the moonlight streaming in the window, and a night bird begins to sing. Its song is haunting.

And a single word comes back to me:

Sleep.

Chapter 18

I open my eyes to a room bathed in sunlight. I sit up, heart pounding. For a moment I don't know where I am, don't know *who* I am.

Yet here I am in this bed, in this room facing south. A room of strangely familiar things. Here, the red-topped lamp, there, the curvy chest of drawers. The clothes in a neat, folded pile on the other bed, towel on the rack near the window. These things recall the evening past.

And today, Marisol said, there would be questions, and stories to tell.

Perhaps today I will meet my father, the dancer. Perhaps he will embrace my desire to dance as well. I tamp down the soaring of my spirit at that thought, afraid to wish for too much.

I go to the pile of clothing, take the dress in my hands, press it against my body before the mirror. It is the loveliest dress I have ever touched—a soft cotton, the color of wine, with a floral print barely a shade lighter.

I am aware, suddenly, of the smell of coffee—coffee and something freshly baked. My stomach groans and churns. I place the dress on the bed, cross my arms, and peel the white sleeping gown up over my shoulders and head. A slender naked woman with a long graceful neck appears in the smoky mirror, a few tendrils of black curls escaping around her shoulders. Surprised, we look at one another, she and I.

"I am here?" I whisper. "I am me?"

I look away first, sigh, sit on the edge of the bed and begin putting on the white undergarments, then the claret-colored dress. It slips on easily, the waist cinched, the top slightly billowed, a row of small ebony buttons up the front, a narrow turned collar trimmed in ivory lace. But it falls halfway between my knees and ankles. This is *marime,* to show the leg. What am I to do? I will wear the stockings. Perhaps the sheer dark fabric covering my legs will suffice?

And shoes—the shoes, a bit too big, but the dark brown leather, soft.

I step to the mirror, wrap a rogue curl around my finger, draw it up, and pin it back in place. My fingers move to my mother's pendant lying in the hollow of my throat. This I slip beneath the high neckline of the dress. It is all I have of my old life. Feeling it hidden there, warm against my skin, gives me some sense of the familiar, of my *daj.*

There is a soft knock on the door.

"Come in."

I expect Marisol, but it is Carlita.

"So, you slept," she says, without meeting my eyes, "And you are still here. Señora Marisol wants you for breakfast." In an instant she is gone. I hear her plodding down the stairs. "Yes, Señora, she is still here. She's coming down."

I get up, fold the white sleeping gown. Tuck the bedding back, imitating the way the bed cover is laid on its twin. As I'm pulling the sheet taut I notice a pair of photographs on the nightstand. A young man staring from each. Both about my age, I'd guess. One, very handsome, with wavy dark hair, long-lashed, hooded eyes, a squarish jaw. The other, a narrower face, fuller lips, a straight nose, and high cheekbones. He seems to see me, this one—there is something about his eyes, close set and piercing. I take the photograph in my hands and meet his gaze. Glance up into my reflection in the mirror. The realization enters slowly, but there it is—the man in the photograph has my eyes, or rather, I have his. My heart quickens. Surely I am looking into the face of my father. Who else could it be?

"Drina . . ."

It is Marisol. I put the photograph down and move to the door. She stares up at me from the bottom of the staircase.

"It is time to eat."

I come down, sit in the chair Marisol offers. Sun pours in through small rectangular windows set high in the stucco walls. A wedge of light falls across my place at table. Carlita places a steaming cup of coffee before me and cuts into a loaf of warm braided bread topped with raisins. A little milk, a little sugar, butter for my bread. Her movements are quick, impatient.

"Thank you, Carlita," my grandmother says in a way that lets Carlita know she is to leave us.

Then Marisol turns her attention to me. "Eat. Would you like an egg?"

"No . . ."

But she is already taking an egg from a bowl, already lining a pan with butter, cracking the egg on the sizzling surface. She stands at the stove, her back to me. Quietly, she speaks, "I know this is not easy for either of us. But I'm pleased you decided to stay."

I say nothing. I don't know that I decided anything at all. Except to sleep. And dress. And now to eat.

She turns. "The dress—it suits you!" She chuckles. "It's Camilla's, but you wear it better!"

"Camilla?"

She turns the egg onto a plate, places it before me. "Well . . ." Takes a deep breath. "After your mother and my son . . . well, after Nadja left, many years went by, and then he met Camilla. Diego taught her son to dance. He is Diego's protégé. . . ."

"My father is married to this Camilla?"

"Yes."

My face tightens. My mother, calling for Diego at the end . . . And he is with this woman whose dress I am wearing.

But Marisol does not like her. There is something in the twist of her mouth when she says her name. I decide I don't like her either.

"They're in Cadiz—until tomorrow. Today we will shop for some clothes of your own. In town. We will talk. You have many questions, and so do I. And Drina . . ."

Something in her voice changes.

"I was saddened to hear of your mother's death. Alvaro called me earlier and told me the whole of it. You've shouldered much tragedy."

Tears press behind my eyes. I squeeze them back. Stand. Clear the plate and cup from the table.

Marisol turns to the stove, busies herself with the pan, moves to the sink. "But today the sun is shining. I will show you the compound?"

I nod. Follow her to the door, then out to the steps.

"Bernardo, bring the wagon around, please!"

We wait in silence until he pulls up, then climb into the wagon. Bernardo makes a clicking sound and we jolt forward. We pass the house, a barn, some smaller outbuildings, another large wooden structure. Then the land opens into rolling hills. Marisol points toward the fields. "Our people have been vintners for as long as anyone remembers. The land is perfect—the soil chalky from all the limestone. Diego's paternal great-great grandfather, or maybe it was his great grandfather—who can recall—planted these grapes—Palomino grapes—perfect for making Oloroso and Amontillado—the very best sherries."

I look across the fields covered in woven chains of vines, supported on wooden trellises. All so very neat and orderly.

"Who cares for all of this?" I ask stiffly. As if by speaking I am giving something up that I need to hold tightly.

Marisol sighs. "Ours is a small vineyard. It was my husband and my son, Felipe. Plus, a team of workers. Diego did not have the passion for anything but dance. They are twins, Felipe and Diego. Fraternal twins—they are not alike." She pauses, her mouth pinched. "Not alike in any way. But my husband—their father—has passed. And now, with the war . . ."

Her voice drops off.

"Felipe . . . is he a soldier?"

"No, but he supports the Republic in other ways. Quietly. It is very complicated."

"And my . . . father?"

She bristles slightly, draws a slow, deep breath. "Diego is a Nationalist—like most of the moneyed class."

Twins who oppose one another. Who share neither appearance nor ideas. Was it not the Nationalists who captured me? Who took Boldo away? Was not the yellow-haired man who violated my *daj* a Nationalist? My father is one of these? I cringe. My tongue feels thick, my lips dry. I roll the words in my mouth before I speak.

"What about you?" I ask. " Which side do you support—in the war?"

She laughs, but there is no humor in it. "I am for life, that's all. Not this side or that. Neither serves anybody well. It is always about greater interests. And I have two sons who disagree. What am I to do?"

I ponder this. For a time, we ride without speaking. Looking straight ahead, she finally voices the silent words that pulsate between us. "So, how to sort through the past to discover the truth about the present? I will tell you what I know. Then, perhaps, you can explain to me how you believe you came to share the Muentes name." She glances at me, and away. Her face is suddenly as twisted and gnarled as the thick, old vines creeping between the buildings. "Where to start. . . ."

"My husband was a harsh man. Dead now, for many years. He had strict ideas about the way things should be. Proper—everything had to be proper!"

She shakes her head, stares off toward the fields. "His sons were supposed to work at his side in the vineyard; that's how he saw it. But all Diego wanted was to dance. Ernesto saw this as frivolous—not respectable, manly work. And Felipe, he loved his books, went off to university and came back with high ideals and the heart of a servant. Championed the rights of our workers. Defied his father, who was a taskmaster."

She pauses for a moment, staring into the past. "Go on," I whisper. "Please." My voice seems to bring her back.

She takes a deep breath. "Diego met Nadja in Sevilla. Saw her dancing at a *peña* there, recognized something in her that was different. Fell for her, hard. She had what we call *duende*—a passion and darkness that bring the dance to life. They began to dance together. There was something wildly complementary about the partnering—anyone could see it. Diego was technically brilliant, Nadja full of . . . I don't know, a sort of primal power. There was tension and attraction between them that thrilled anyone lucky enough to watch."

Glancing at Marisol, I see her eyes fixed on the horizon as if looking into the past. I too think back—to Kak Hanzi speaking of my mother as a dancer, and now Marisol. It is hard for me to imagine, and yet, at the same time, I suddenly know it is true.

"There," she points to the large white stucco structure. "That is the *bodega*, where the casks are kept and the wine is aged. Bernardo, let us off here, please."

We climb down and begin to walk toward the building.

"So . . . Nadja and Diego became inseparable. She was a colorful, wild bird. Beautiful. Spirited. The way she lived in the moment. It was easy to see how she became the center of his world. He was different with her. Freer. Diego wanted to get married, to form a dance troupe, but both sides, our family and her clan, vehemently disapproved."

Her words render me numb, haunted by this person my mother once was. The person who died when my father left her. I am angry with her suddenly—with all of them. "You didn't want Diego to be with my mother?"

Marisol sighs. "At that time, I'm ashamed to say that it didn't matter what I wanted, or how I felt. Ernesto ruled the roost. He had the final word. And, to put it bluntly, he wouldn't have his son marry a *Gitano*. It was ugly. In the end, Nadja left. I believe Diego sent her away. He just couldn't stand up to his father. And neither could I."

"But what did you think?"

Marisol begins walking again. "I honestly didn't know her well enough to have strong feelings for her. But I respected her as a dancer. I could see why Diego was taken with her. Mostly, I was angry—at Ernesto for being a tyrant, at Diego for caving in to him, at myself for feeling powerless." We arrive at the *bodega*, she pushes open the heavy pine door, and we step inside.

I am grateful for the darkness, as it hides the parade of expressions I feel pulling at my face. It takes a moment for my eyes to adjust to the dim, filtered light. I look up . . . and up. It is the largest building I have ever seen, the rough hewn ceiling timbers high above us supported by tall white columns reaching from the yellow sandy floor. A nutty, yeasty smell permeates the air, which is cooler than outdoors. Rows of wooden barrels are stacked four high creating walls of casks with wide aisles between them. The only light shines from wrought-iron lanterns hanging from the ceiling on long chains and from several windows set high in the walls, covered with thick woven shades.

"Like a church, isn't it?" my grandmother asks quietly. I shrug, having never been in a church, but what she says seems right to me. "The height allows the hot air to rise, so as not to affect the wine. Come, sit here."

We sit side by side on some barrels standing on end. "Now, it is your turn," she says.

I take a deep, trembling breath. "I'd heard rumors—in the clan—that my father was a dancer—and a Spaniard—he wasn't *Gitano*. My mother never told me his name—until the end, when she was . . ." I swallowed hard. "She was sick with fever, delirious. Talking crazy talk about Diego coming back for her. When I asked her who this Diego was, she said he was her husband. It was the first time I'd heard his name."

"So, your mother said they were married . . ."

I hesitate. "No—well yes, but she was very sick then. When I was little, she married a *Gitano* who took us in, although he always let us know we should be grateful to him for doing her this favor—because of me." I thought of Raul, his smug manner and demanding ways.

"So, she married someone else. How do you know this Raul was not your father?"

"Everyone knew I was born of a Spaniard. That I was half of this, and half that. That Raul resented me. Everyone knew."

Her dark eyes bore into me. "Go on."

"Well, Raul was away when my mother . . . when she was . . ." I cannot roll the word *rape* from my tongue. Such a sharp, cutting word. "She was attacked by this soldier, and when she gave birth to his child—my Little Red Squirrel—she lost a lot of blood, slipped out of her mind, started living in the past. Thought the baby was me. Talked of returning to Jerez. To Diego."

A man in a cap and knit vest approaches. In one hand a piece of chalk, in the other a long metal implement with a narrow cup at the end. "Ah, Señora Muentes! To what do I owe this honor? And who is this lovely one?"

"Good afternoon, Javier," Marisol says. "Drina is my guest here. We're just enjoying a stroll, getting to know one another. Drina, this is Señor Robeles, the *Capataz* of the *Muentes Bodega*. It is his job to oversee the production, to taste, adjust, tinker . . ."

"Come," he says, "Shall we sample something?" Not waiting for a response, he removes a finial-shaped plug from the top of a cask, inserts the dipper, pours the amber liquid into a small glass that he pulls from his apron. "Amontillado," he sighs, rolling the liquid in the slender vessel. "Very fine indeed." He hands the glass to Marisol. She sniffs, swirls, closes her eyes.

"Ahh . . ." She lifts the glass upward, pointing it toward a high, round window I hadn't noticed before. I cannot draw my eyes from the stained glass fashioned into the familiar pattern—there the vines, there the clusters of grapes. My hand flies to my necklace. I draw it from the neckline of my borrowed dress, finger the raised gold design. Feel, for the first time, a connection to this place.

"To truth and light," Marisol says, then sips, moves to hand the glass to me. I let go of my pendant, take the glass, raise it to my lips. First the nutty aroma, then the heat of it on my lips, my tongue, the warmth spreading into my veins, slowing the moment. She watches me drink, and her eyes drop to the bodice of my dress. I dab at my chin, wondering if I've dripped on Camilla's frock. But it is not a spill she stares at. She steps forward, reaches toward me. I move to take a step back, but her fingers touch the pendant, turning it, her squinted gaze intense.

"Thank you, Javier," she says distractedly. "We will share a glass of our best Oloroso this evening and toast you then."

"*Gracias,* Señora." He tips his hat and is gone.

"This pendant?"

"My mother's," I respond, pointing toward the window. "I see the same design . . ."

"Yes," Marisol says. "The Muentes family crest. I suppose

130

Diego must have given it to her long ago. A lot has happened since then." She sighs. Turns toward the wall of barrels. "You know, sherry has to be aged," she says, pointing to the casks. "To make Oloroso, the newest wine mixture is added to casks of older sherries. The combination makes the richest, most complex flavor. This sherry here has been aging for about sixteen years."

We're both quiet. I care little for all of this complicated talk of wine, except, I realize, this wine has been here since my mother . . .

Marisol stops, looks at me closely. "In a sense, making fine sherry is like belonging to a family. The youngest shares the essence of everything that came before." Her eyes penetrate, seem to ask many questions. "But," she adds, "the test is in the tasting."

We walk back toward the house, both of us silent. I am a mixture of many feelings.

As we round the bend, a long black automobile pulls up the drive and rolls to a stop in front of the house. Marisol stops short.

The passenger door springs open. A tall, slender woman with chestnut hair steps out, pulling a camel-colored wool shawl around her. Looks our way, draws herself up. "Diego?" she calls, gesturing back toward the car with one hand. She is very beautiful, but the subtle lines on her face show that she does not often smile. A deep, double furrow cuts between her brows. The edges of her mouth pull down.

The woman stares at me, an arched eyebrow raised. "Marisol," she asks, "Who is this?" Her expression changes, eyes widening, then narrowing. She points. "*That* is my dress, and *those* are my shoes!"

"Yes," Marisol says, "The girl is my guest."

We all turn as the driver's door creaks and groans, then swings open wide. I peer at the man in the car even as my heart warns me to back away. He is with Camilla, so I know who he must be.

My father.

Chapter 19

Marisol takes me by the elbow, propels me past Camilla, toward the porch. Feeling like a prisoner being led away, I crane my neck for another glimpse of the driver emerging from the car, and I stumble on the steps. Marisol hisses into my ear, "Let me speak to them. Wait in your room. I'll call for you afterward. Go!" Her hand presses the small of my back.

I move inside, close the door, leaving a crack through which I can peer. Marisol strides toward the car as he climbs out.

I'm expecting the boy in the photograph—the one with the narrow face and eyes like mine—grown into a man. But, no. This man, my father, is the one with the lazy hazel eyes lined with thick lashes, the square jaw. Even more handsome now. I close my gaping mouth and stare at his face covered with at least a day's stubble.

"What's the matter?" he asks. "Who was that?"

My heart pounds. He looks between the two women. Camilla is abuzz like a hornet, her tone clipped, her voice darting between them, lamenting about her dress, her shoes, about Marisol overstepping her bounds. Neither of them pay her much mind. They are, perhaps, so accustomed to her complaining that her voice drones like a cricket on a summer evening, a sound there and not there.

The back door of the car opens and a young man climbs out. He is taller than my father, thinner. With his auburn hair and dark eyes, high cheekbones and straight, aristocratic nose he is clearly Camilla's son. He too, ignores her rant, looking between his mother, my father, and Marisol.

"Come, let's go inside," my grandmother says, touching Diego on the forearm, but looking at Camilla. "I need to have a word with my son. Alone."

Camilla crosses her arms, purses her lips.

Marisol's jaw tightens. "Camilla, may we have a moment, *please?* I wouldn't insist if it wasn't important."

"You want me to *leave?* Am I a part of this family or not?"

"Don't be ridiculous! Of course you are, but—"

"I deserve to know what's going on!"

My father runs a hand along his chin. "Even I don't know what's going on! Mother, will you enlighten us? Please?"

"When we get inside!" Marisol says, marching toward the door. I turn to rush for the stairs, and come face to face with Carlita. She frowns in disapproval as I step around her and hurry up the staircase. On the top landing, I stop, straining to

134

hear. First, the swoosh of the tall oak door. Then, the shuffle of feet and a sharp staccato sound that can only be Camilla's high-heeled shoes. Agitated, quick steps on the stairs. I steal toward my room, slip inside, and close the door.

Somewhere down the hall a door slams. Camilla, too, must have retreated to her room. My heart races. I need to hear what Marisol is saying to my father. Do I dare?

I slip off the fine shoes and pad toward the door, place my hand on the knob, my ear to the wooden panel. I listen. Wait. The corridor is silent. Carefully I turn the knob, push open the door, pressing it toward the frame to prevent a squeak. Like a ghost, I trace the wall toward the stairway, down the steps to the landing set halfway between the floors. I crouch against the wall near the railing, just out of sight, drop my chin to my chest, close my eyes. I listen, but I am terrified at what I might hear. Snippets. . . . "Alvaro called . . . She claims Nadja is her mother . . ."

"Did you know she was pregnant?" Suddenly they are silent. I lift my head just as I detect the footfall on the stairs.

It is the young man, Camilla's son. His eyes meet mine. Index finger to lips, I silently beg him not to acknowledge me. I stand. Back up, a step at a time. Turn, run up the last few. Glance over my shoulder. He is right behind me, his eyes laughing. "What are you doing?" he whispers. "And who are you?"

A door down the hall opens. Camilla stalks out.

"Since neither of them will tell me what's going on, perhaps it's best I hear it straight from you!"

I look from her to her son to the staircase. I want to hear what Marisol is saying, how Diego is responding, but now I have this hornet in front of me. I do not know what to tell her so I clamp my mouth shut, turn away, and walk quickly toward my room. As I step inside I hear the young man's voice. "Wait . . ."

I close the door, lean back against it, and slide to the ground, head in my hands. For so many years I dreamed of my father, but this is not the meeting I imagined. It is as though Marisol has brought home a stray dog that nobody wants. Given it food and a place to sleep until everyone decides what to do with such a sorry creature. Has it occurred to them that perhaps this dog does not want to be here? Has this thought crossed their minds? I sigh. Think of Boldo. Kizzy. How I long for a familiar face! Perhaps I should just leave and avoid the rejection that is surely coming.

But where am I to go? Resigned, I go to the bed, lie down, and close my eyes.

Finally, a sound startles me. Did I doze off? I sit up, dizzy and confused. Someone is knocking quietly on my door. The door opens and Marisol slips inside.

"I'm sorry this had to unfold this way, but you understand what a shock this was."

I say nothing.

"I've told Diego your story. Now I think you should meet him."

My *story*. As though I have written a fairy tale. My mouth is suddenly dry, my tongue sour.

"He is outside on the terrace. Come." Marisol takes my hand, pulls me to my feet. I slip into Camilla's shoes and plod behind her. Through the hallways, down the stairs, through the main house, out the back. I squint into the bright sun. Sweat trickles down my back, yet I shiver in the heat.

He is standing along the wall, gazing out across the fields. Turns when he hears us approach. My father's eyes meet mine. His face drains of color.

"Yes," Marisol says softly, "the resemblance is unmistakable."

He stares, his mouth open a bit. An expression just like my own. Runs his fingers through his hair, once, twice. His greenish eyes dart from me to Marisol and back. He shifts his weight from one foot to the other. Slips a cigarette from his pocket, fumbles to light it. Leaves it, unlit, between his lips.

I shrink within the strange clothing I'm wearing. Silently beg him to say something that will make me feel less of an intrusion. The seconds stretch between us. I look down at my clumsy, borrowed shoes. Turn away so I do not have to watch him struggle. My own heart is a tangled knot. I hear Marisol walking away. *No,* I shout silently, *do not leave me with him.* I look up and she nods over her shoulder. *Please!*

"Drina . . ."

His voice is deep, but unsteady. I meet his eyes, feel my face tighten. My jaw aches from clenching my teeth.

"I don't know what to say. You are the very image of your mother. I'm sorry. I wish . . . I mean, I should have . . ."

I shake my head. I do not want him to make excuses.

"We were young. Foolish. I just didn't think . . ."

What am I to say? I stand before him like a dumb sheep, my mind blank.

"Staying here . . . Camilla . . . I just don't think . . ." His face reddens as he trips and stumbles over his dwindling words. He reaches into his pocket, removes a leather wallet, fingers a wad of bills. "I can help you. Whatever you need. I accept my responsibility. Here." He thrusts the money toward me.

It is as though I have been struck. I step back.

"Well," he stammers, "then what is it you want?"

My words come of their own accord, like bullets from the *machina*. "My mother was a dancer?"

He blinks. Shakes his head. "What a thing to ask! Of course. Surely you knew that." There is an edge of accusation in his tone.

"Never. My mother never danced again."

His face and shoulders sag. A bill slips from his fingers and blows across the terrace like a fallen leaf.

"She called for you at the end. Said you were coming back for us."

"I'm so sorry, I . . ."

I take a deep breath. "And you are a dancer. I knew that."

"Yes . . ."

I pause, the words poised on my lips. "I . . . dance . . ."

Something in his eyes and posture shifts. "You are your mother's daughter then."

"And my father's?"

He hesitates. Stuffs the money back in his pocket. Studies me in a new way.

It is easier, I suppose, to talk of dance than of betrayal. Abandonment. Yet, it is a hint of encouragement. Despite the ache I feel, I cannot deny the thrill of this small flicker of interest.

Of hope. Of dancing. My father and I remain, many feet apart, staring at one another.

"Diego!"

We both look up. Camilla is standing in the window above. My father nods slightly and heads inside.

I remain perfectly still until my heart slows. I close my eyes, see my father's face, his long-lashed, hazel eyes, his squared-off jaw. My hand flies to the pendant at my throat. I finger the raised vines and delicate clusters of grapes. *Oh,* I think, *oh, how I wish . . .*

Suddenly I hear my mother's voice: *Be careful what you wish for. Your desire can be your undoing.*

CHAPTER 20

It is a good long time before Marisol returns to the terrace where she left me. "So, you spoke. And?"

I stare off across the fields before looking her in the eye. "Nothing. He tried to give me money." My words fly like shrapnel. Marisol cringes and I feel a small wave of regret.

But she recovers quickly. "My son seems to have a knack for doing the wrong thing. For this, I am sorry. By all accounts, it appears to be true that Diego is your father. You are my granddaughter. So, now we will find a way to become family." She pauses, watching me closely. "I'm not fool enough to think it will be easy. That we can be thrown together and embrace and feel something toward each other that has not grown from experience and years. But, as family, we all have a responsibility. I'm willing to try. No—I *want* to try. Do you?"

The words spring from my lips. "Does *he?* Want to try?"

"It will take time. But I was asking about you."

I lift my chin, look away. Shrug. I refuse to want them more than they want me.

"I will take that as a qualified yes," she says. "The thing to do now is to just get on with it. We'll muddle through for a while. That's as it should be. In the meantime I am going to call Bernardo to bring the wagon. We can go into town to buy you some clothing. By the time we come back, things will have settled down a bit."

I sigh. My only interest in clothing is that it will allow me to peel Camilla's garments from my skin.

I follow Marisol inside, lagging a step behind, past Carlita's peevish eyes and the curious ears straining behind closed doors.

We ride silently into town, the streets familiar, yet different in the daylight. To my right is the large church we passed last night, up ahead, the cafes and shops. I close my eyes, blotting out the vision of riding these avenues in the back of the military truck, Boldo beside me, the taunting guards, my Little Red Squirrel squalling in the cab on the other side of the glass. Now they are both gone, to places I cannot reach.

"Look, over there." Marisol nudges me with her elbow. It takes a moment for me to tear myself from these memories. I look in the direction she points, shading my eyes from the assault of the sun. "Slow down, Bernardo," she calls, gesturing for him to pull toward the curb. The window of the shop is one large pane of glass revealing a garden of dresses. Flounces and ruffles, brightly colored polka-dotted fabric, each frock hung to best highlight its unique details: embroidered blossoms, lace overlays, pearl buttons. One is topped with a delicate lace shawl trimmed in long, fine fringe. Another, accompanied by a brilliantly hued fan. These are the dresses of *flamenco* dancers I've watched at the *ferias*.

"I had a dress like that . . . in a deep shade of turquoise. I was no older than you."

I snap my head in her direction.

"Yes, I used to dance. Which is how I recognized it in you when we rode past the *peña*. I saw how the music drew you out, how your body responded in time. Only natural, given who you are." I watch her reflection gazing back at us in the glass, her face, in shadow, hovering between the finery. "And me? Once I married, that was that. Ernesto wouldn't stand for it. It was a long, long time ago." With a wave of her hand, she instructs Bernardo. "Thank you. Please take us to *Ropa de Mujer*, around the corner. You know the shop."

I continue to watch her out of the corner of my eye. I should have guessed she had been a dancer—the way she holds her back straight, her head high, chin raised. How her steps are clipped and rhythmic, her movements decisive. Generations of dancers. *And I am the next.* The thought sends a tingle through me. Perhaps in this house, with these people, it could happen.

But then I think of my *daj*. It hadn't been possible for her. And yet . . .

Bernardo rounds the bend, pulls in front of another

storefront, and we climb down. Marisol strides ahead, pushes open the door. A bell jingles merrily, announcing our arrival.

"Beatriz," Marisol calls. A short, stout woman sits behind a black machine, a garment lying across it. The contraption has a wheel on one end and sits upon a small table with an iron treadle below that she pumps with her feet. A collection of pins sprout between her lips. The woman glances up, pulls a length of thread that she quickly snips with a small pair of scissors. She removes the pins, jabs them into a felt cushion, and pulls herself to her feet.

"*Buenos dias*, Marisol," Beatriz calls. "Who is this lovely one?"

"Drina," Marisol replies. "She will need a number of things. She has come to visit and her baggage has been lost." My grandmother nods at me, as though encouraging me to verify her explanation. I notice she does not tell this Beatriz that I am her granddaughter. And I wonder how long she intends to have me visit.

"Oh my," Beatriz says. "We can take care of this. Come here, Drina. Let me have a look." My face heats up under the woman's gaze. She circles me, considering my hips, breasts. Around my waist she runs a finger, then her thumb from shoulder to shoulder. "All right, step in there, clothes off." She pulls back a curtain revealing a small, closet-like room. I hesitate. I do not want to disrobe in there behind just this flimsy cloth. My face burns. "Go on! What are you blushing about? Silly girl!" Beatriz pushes me good-naturedly into the little closet, draws the curtain. "Hand me the dress you're wearing. I'll hang it for you."

I shiver as I remove Camilla's dress, embarrassed to be standing in my undergarments, but relieved to be free of her clothing. I wrap my arms around myself, huddle in the corner. I hear the two of them conversing about this item or that, this color, that print. I shut my eyes and beg them to hurry.

The curtain flies back and Beatriz thrusts in a number of garments, each on a metal hanger, and hooks them on a peg. "Start with these," she says, whipping the curtain closed again.

I exhale, realizing I'd been holding my breath. My arms that had been shielding my near-nakedness relax, then spring into motion. Remove the first article of clothing—a midnight blue dress—pull it over my head. The fabric feels smooth and cool, the shape of the dress so very different from the full skirts and flouncy blouses I am used to. The opening is in the back. A zipper like a long narrow train track runs up my back—I cannot grasp it on my own..

"Come out. Let's have a look!" Beatriz yanks back the curtain again, and I step out, holding the dress closed as best I can.

"Turn," she commands. I hesitate. She steps behind me and, in one fluid motion, zips up the dress. She tips her head critically. Turns me around. Pinches the waistline and produces several pins from her lips. I wonder if she holds a collection inside her ample cheeks.

"Here, we take it in," she says, gripping and pinning a fold of fabric on both sides.

"Yes?" she asks Marisol.

Marisol eyes me questioningly. "She has to like it." I begin to shrug and she raises her index finger. "No. Decide what you like, and say so. Do you like this dress or not?"

I do not know how I feel about the dress. I stare at my reflection, and someone I do not recognize stares back. But it is better than wearing Camilla's dress.

"I think so," I manage.

"Good. Finish pinning it, Beatriz, and then, on to the next. A skirt and a couple of blouses. A sweater. Another dress. While she's trying the rest I'll gather some undergarments and hose."

I slip on this and that, under the critical eye of Beatriz, who grunts her approval or expresses dissatisfaction with a simple "No!" Only the blue dress needs altering. The rest—the brown slim skirt and cream-colored blouse, the forest green dress, the gray sweater and skirt, and the flared navy blue skirt and pale blue blouse—all fit without the benefit of a pin. They are all soft and well-made, but despite the fact that they cover my arms and most of my legs, they feel as though they show too much of me, tailored as they are to hug the body. Beatriz collects them, tying the tops of the hangers with a red ribbon before carefully folding them into a large brown bag with a twine handle—all except the green dress that I leave on. Marisol adds Camilla's frock to the bag, and a collection of silky white undergarments, skin-toned silk stockings, and several pairs of short white and black socks. We walk to the door and leave to the accompaniment of the bell, the soft green cotton sashaying against my calves, the silky hose like a second skin stretching over my feet and legs.

From here we head into the small shoe-making shop next door where I slip on numerous pairs of shoes. I come away with two—black leather with a thick raised heel and a button strap; the other, brown canvas with ribbons that tie around the ankle, and a woven-grass sole. As we leave, I cannot help but glimpse my own image echoed in the glass windows. It is like observing someone I can only think of as a familiar stranger.

Marisol sets the bags in the front of the carriage, beside Bernardo, and we climb into the back. As we ride, my eyes roam the streets, and I realize I am constantly searching for those I have lost—as though Señora Castillo and my Little Red Squirrel or Boldo, might step from the curb or round a corner. I press my eyes closed for a moment to try to wipe the slate of my memory clean.

"We will meet Alvaro at the café. He will, no doubt, be astounded at your transformation."

I say nothing. I see him before she does, at an outdoor table, the dome of his head inclined toward a newspaper spread on the surface before him. He stirs a small cup of coffee with a miniature spoon. We climb from the carriage and he looks up, as though sensing our presence. His eyes sweep over me, his face widens in a smile. He stands, pulls one, then another chair out for us.

"My, my," he says. "I see you've been shopping! Lovely, Señorita Drina! Lovely! Marisol?" As we seat ourselves he looks at her questioningly.

"Well," Marisol begins. "We've talked—Drina, me, and, of course, Diego."

146

"I thought Diego and Camilla were in—"

"Came home a day early."

Alvaro's eyes widen. "Oh." He sits up, leans forward. "And . . ."

"You were right, as usual." Her expression belies the edge of her words. Her features are soft, her eyes affectionate. "Diego confirmed it, in as many words. And then there was this. She's wearing our family crest. Drina, show Alvaro the necklace."

I do not like that she somehow claims as hers that which belonged to my *daj* and then to me. Grudgingly, I slip the pendant from my beneath my dress, stare at the table as I hold it between thumb and index finger.

"And so, now . . ."

"Drina will stay with us, and we will learn about one another." She looks at me to agree. Thinking of my father's reluctance, I hold back a shrug, nod slightly, and smooth my dress across my lap.

Alvaro waves a waiter to the table, orders for both of us. Small plates of this and that, two glasses of *vino fino*. Sliced *jamón*, *manchego* cheese, sardines. I eat in silence. And as the two of them converse, I lose myself in the abundance of food, the variety of tastes.

"Slow down," Marisol chides. "Take your time. The plates aren't going anywhere."

I put down my fork, stop chewing. Feel my face color.

"Oh, it's all right," she says. "Try not to be so sensitive! I'm old. I say what I think. Isn't that right, Alvaro?"

He chuckles. "It certainly is, my dear. That's what makes

you such a delight. Keeps me on my toes!" His smile fades and he turns his attention to me. His gaze is penetrating, and once again I sense that he sees more than what is before him. He places a hand over mine. "It may not seem so now, but Drina, you are blest to become a part of this woman's life. Try not to judge the situation just yet. Give it some time. Each of you has much to offer the other. This I know."

Marisol and I glance at one another. Our eyes meet and mine quickly dart away. She clears her throat. Addresses me. "Shall we choose to believe him about this?"

I want to respond, but the words get stuck, and then it is too late. She stands. "Thank you for lunch, Alvaro. We should get back. Drina . . ."

"Thank you," I mumble and follow her to the carriage.

Chapter 21

As we round the bend to the house I see that the long black automobile is gone. Marisol notices too. She glances down the drive toward the main road but says nothing. Bernardo reins in the horse, the carriage slows in front of the entrance, and my grandmother reaches forward to hand me the bag. We climb down and I follow her into the house. I feel my father's absence even before Carlita speaks.

"Diego and Camilla have gone back to Cadiz."

"What for?" Marisol asks. Her words match her gaze. Flat and hard.

Carlita shakes her head, lips pursed. "Camilla . . ."

The son, Renato, appears, cutting her short. "You're back." He eyes the shopping bags and then me, his gaze sweeping from my head to toes and back. "New dress," he says, nodding his approval, a smile playing at his lips. "Very nice."

Marisol glances between us. Drina, Camilla's son, Renato. She gestures toward the stairs. "Go hang your things." I feel his eyes on me as I climb the steps, feel the tension as I escape to my room. I close the door and exhale, relieved to be alone. It seems my father has run from me. I feel equal parts relief and disappointment. I drop the bag, flop on the bed, stare at the ceiling. A small spider with legs as fine as Beatriz's thread works nimbly in the corner where the wall and ceiling meet. I watch the jointed legs lift and drop, the deliberate rhythmic dipping movements the creature makes, completing some mysterious chore. Its determination spurs me. I will take the garments from the bag, hang the clothing. I set about it, slowly. When I finish this task, then what?

I carefully unfold and examine each item. Mine, I think, running my hand over this fabric and that, but still, they feel foreign. I hang the clothing in the large armoire, place the undergarments in a drawer built inside. Then I sit on the bed. What to do now? I am restless, without a purpose, with no place to go and nothing to do. I do not know how to live here, do not know how to be. My throat swells and I feel the pressure of tears behind my lids.

A knock at the door interrupts. I rub my eyes, inhale, brace my voice so it will not wobble. "Yes?"

"Come on out."

It is the young man. I don't know what to say, so I go to the door, open it.

"Drina, yes?" He watches me through the small space, peering around the corner.

I nod.

"Renato. What are you doing? Are you busy?"

"Nothing . . . no . . . I mean . . ."

"Then come out. I want to talk to you. We can walk the vineyards."

I step into the corridor beside this Renato, anxious, but relieved to have something—anything—to do.

He smiles widely, turns, and I follow him down the stairs, my hand on the railing. I am unsteady in my slippery new black shoes, or perhaps it is my nerves.

I trail him to the kitchen. Marisol looks up from the table, lays aside a book, removes a pair of silver spectacles.

"Drina and I are taking a walk," Renato announces. This he says confidently, but I notice that he stops, waiting, I am sure, for Marisol's approval.

She glances between us, considering. It is her turn to shrug. "It is a glorious day for a walk," she says. "But don't overdo it."

I'm not sure what she means exactly, but it seems she gives me permission to return whenever I like. I am grateful for this and decide to pay attention to the path we walk, so I can come back as it suits me.

We walk in silence, away from the house. His hands are thrust into his pockets and he steals sidelong glances my way that I pretend not to notice. His eyes flicker with curiosity.

"So, where did you come from? Is it true? You are Diego's daughter?"

As soon as he utters the words, he must see that he has asked too much, too soon. Still, he presses. "I mean, did he know about you, or not? How did Marisol find you?"

I stop, look down. Hesitate only a moment before I turn to leave him. He reaches for my arm. "Wait!"

Even as I tell myself to go, my feet remain planted.

"I'm sorry," he says. "I'm just trying to figure out what's going on. My mother—she's hysterical anyway—well, she's in a state. Diego couldn't get a word in. I heard them fighting, and I thought my mother said you were his daughter. I just want to know, that's all. Do you blame me?"

"No . . ."

"Then? . . ."

We stand there staring at one another.

"Come," he says, "Let's find a nice place to sit."

Silently, we walk side by side toward the rolling hills of the vineyard. A warm breeze ruffles the skirt of my dress, lifts and skims a tendril of hair across my cheek. For the first time, I try to imagine what it must have been like for them to have me arrive, seemingly out of nowhere. But hadn't my father ever anticipated this? That one day his child might appear? Or had he forgotten, completely? A piece of history pushed aside for so long that it no longer seemed real?

"There." Renato points to a tall cork oak, a layer of thick bark cut away along the trunk, its green pointy leaves forming a canopy overhead. Renato moves toward the shade, clears the ground of the long-capped acorns that litter the grass. I bend, gather what I can, slip them into my pocket. They can be roasted and eaten like chestnuts. My mouth waters as I think of the grainy, sweet taste. The late afternoon sun hangs low in the sky, like liquid gold between the leaves and branches.

We sit beneath the tree, Renato's legs thrust out in front of him, mine folded beneath the wide skirt of my dress. His questions hang in the air between us.

"You're really pretty," he says. "Those dark eyes . . ." He looks at me and then away.

I blush deeply, and to divert his attention, rush to answer his questions. I speak quickly, staring into my lap. "Diego and my mother were supposed to be married. She danced with him. But his father didn't approve. So my mother went away. Then I was born. That's the story as I know it." A jolting thought suddenly occurs to me. "Is Diego your father too?"

"No," Renato says. "Good thing. If he was, you'd be my half-sister." He smiles, raises an eyebrow suggestively. "That would never work!" It takes me a moment to understand what he implies. "He's my stepfather. He married my mother a few years ago. My father had left us. I guess we have that in common."

These last words have a different tone. Meant to sound like a joke, but I know better. I say nothing.

"So, how did Marisol find you?"

What am I to say? That I was captured trying to steal back my baby? No. This I cannot tell. "I met Señor Vargas. He called Marisol."

"What did Diego say when he found out?"

"You ask a lot of questions."

"There's a lot I want to know."

153

I sigh and look up through the fluttering leaves. The image of my father pushing his money at me comes to mind. The bill blowing across the terrace. For a fleeting moment I wonder if I should have just taken it and left. Use it to buy what I'd need for Little Red Squirrel, and then, somehow, get her back. The intensity of Renato's dark eyes pulls me from that thought. He is staring at me, waiting.

"He was surprised." It is all I will say, and after all, that much is true.

"So was my mother—surprised." I cannot determine the emotion behind his words. Renato plucks another acorn from the grass, absently peels pieces from the rough textured cap. "He's a great dancer, you know. He's taught me for the last few years. You'll have to see him perform."

At the suggestion of dance, something in me stirs and comes alive. This small spark doesn't escape Renato's attention. "We'll both dance for you—when my mother isn't looking." He grins. "How long are you staying here?"

His prying makes me weary. "For as long as I like," I answer, with much more confidence than I feel. At least, I reason, if my father forces me to go, I can save face—pretend that leaving is my choice. I hope my snappish tone will discourage him, but he doesn't seem to notice. Or perhaps he notices, but doesn't care.

"I should warn you, my mother usually gets what she wants, mostly because she wears us all out." His words are spoken in a joking way, but to me, it does not feel like jest.

"We'll see." I say this in the same tone that my *daj* used to use when humoring me, or putting me off. I realize I've made it sound like a challenge.

Renato whistles softly through his teeth, shakes his head, looks at me with laughing eyes. "I can hardly wait until they get back!" he says.

"When will that be?"

"Whenever my mother decides."

"My father cannot decide for himself?"

Renato shrugs. "You just don't know my mother. But you will . . ."

I do not want to hear of my father's weakness, or how Camilla manages to get her way. I stand and begin to walk back along the path.

"Where are you going?" I hear him scrambling to his feet. "Wait! I didn't mean to upset you."

"I'm not upset."

"Then why are you leaving?"

"I'm tired." As I say it, I realize how true it is. The last two days have felt like a hundred.

"I'll see you later?" Renato calls. I do not answer. I do not much care if I see him later or not.

Marisol looks up as I slip through the door. "Did you have a nice walk?"

"I'm tired. I think I'll go lie down." I avoid her eyes, climb the stairs, go to my room. I drop on the bed, try to think of all that has happened. How many days since my *daj* breathed her last? Since Luludja stole my Little Red Squirrel? Since Boldo woke me and we went after her? Since we got captured? The events blur together like shattered images in a nightmare. How, I wonder, did I end up here, in this fancy room, with these people who are supposed to be my family? How is it that everything I knew is gone? Tears come and I turn my head into the pillow.

I only barely hear the footsteps on the stairs as I sob and gulp air. I turn on my side to muffle the sound. The door creaks and in a moment I feel her sitting on the edge of the bed, her soft hand smoothing back the strands of damp hair clinging to my cheeks.

"Yes, cry all you want, for all you've lost. . . . Yes, go on and get it out, as much as you can. . . ."

My grandmother strokes my back, continues murmuring words of comfort. At first I stiffen under her touch, but the effort it takes is just too much. The tension begins to melt away, and I feel myself cave in to her care.

CHAPTER 22

The days flow, one into the other, in much the same way. A meal, a walk in the vineyard, some chore or other, a ride into town. Even as Marisol and I become less awkward in the presence of the other, we never really relax. There is a constant underlying sense of waiting—listening partly to the words we exchange, all the while straining to hear the sound of the black automobile. We look at one another as we speak, then shift our gaze toward the long drive leading to the house. Renato, too, is restless, spending most of his time at the place he calls the studio. I hear music pouring from this small building set beside the vineyard road. Sometimes I walk nearby, feeling the pull of a *rodeña*, the rhythm of a *Sevillana,* or the haunting melody of a *petenera.* I do not venture near the door, though the music invites me. We all agree, without saying so, that life must wait until Diego comes back and things can be sorted through.

On the sixth day I am sitting with Marisol on the terrace, sipping a glass of sherry, looking at an album of sepia-toned photographs mounted on black pages. She points to this person and that, each stern face some relative or other. At the same moment, we raise our heads to the hum of the motor, to the sound of the tires spitting gravel on the drive to the house.

At first neither of us moves. But then she flips the thick cover of the book closed, sets it in my lap, and rises. I feel as though I have become one with the chair, the picture album a heavy weight in my lap. I hear Marisol's footsteps tapping across the stone floor, the squeak of the door, the exchange of voices. I cannot make out the words, but the rhythm and tone are quick and sharp. I catch a snippet of Camilla's voice, a question that isn't a question. *"She's still here . . ."*

I put the album aside, push myself to my feet, step toward the terrace door, peer inside. I can glimpse them standing in the entranceway, Marisol's back to me. Camilla's voice rises. *"Unacceptable,"* she says. Marisol glances back over her shoulder and spies me in the doorway. I draw back to where I believe I can see and not be seen, but Marisol ushers them onto the front porch, closing the heavy door behind her. This, I am sure, to shield me from harsh words.

I walk silently across the space between us, hesitate before the door. They are arguing on the other side. I do not want to hear the words I can imagine being spoken, but still I strain to listen. Like having a toothache that I probe with my tongue to gauge the pain. Renato suddenly appears at the top of the stairs and starts down. "They're back finally? What are they doing out there?"

I push past him, up the stairs, and escape to my room. I hear him open the front door, their words pouring in for a moment before the door shuts them off again.

I sit on the edge of the bed.

My father doesn't want me.

My hands shake at the realization. I clasp them together, let go. Shove them beneath my thighs to keep them still. He didn't want my mother, and now he doesn't want me. Something in me clenches, resists the thought. Perhaps it is Camilla; maybe she is standing in the way.

I am torn between wanting him and not wanting to want him.

The downstairs door opens and I hear the sound of luggage being dragged across the floor. They climb the stairs, pass my room, continue down the corridor. I hold my breath as they pass, stare out the window. The sky is a wall of bright, solid turquoise that assaults my eyes. I look away. The photographs on the nightstand stare back at me—my father, and the brother with my eyes—Felipe.

A muffled blur of voices rises and falls. I stand and go to the window, push the pane open. I step closer, place my cheek against the glass. Leaning out, I turn my ear to the sound, which must be coming from a nearby room.

At first I detect only the back and forth of two hushed voices, one high, one low. There is little give and take. Camilla's speech, though quiet, is more pointed and sharp. She batters him with words. The lower-pitched mumble in between belongs to my father.

I move the chair to the window, step up, and crank the casing open as far as I can.

"Well, she's still here! Now what?"

". . . don't know. I didn't think . . ."

"Your mother had something to do with it! . . . trying to drive me out!"

"That's not true . . ."

"It *is* true. . . . brings her here . . . gives her my clothes? What will it be next?"

"Camilla, we've been through this a hundred times."

Their voices drop for a moment. Perhaps they are aware I am listening, but no, Camilla speaks again, something I can't make out. Then my father . . .

". . . everything is always my fault?"

"Well, this is your fault, yours and Marisol's . . . treating her as if she's a part of this family . . ."

"She's not one of us, Camilla, you know that."

"Then send her back to wherever she came from."

"Her mother is dead. She has nowhere else to go. Have a little pity!"

I climb down from the chair. Move to the door. I am suddenly sure of what I must do. I will walk to the edge of this town, to a place where *Gitanos* gather. Find a new clan. Perhaps Boldo's people. Or Jascha's.

Something sinks in my heart as I move soundlessly down

the stairs. Even as I silently open the front door, I am filled with the certainty that I will not find a new clan to accept me, that I do not know Boldo's people, that I cannot go back to Jascha. All this I know as I slip out undetected, round the house and cross the yard.

As I go, I see and do not see. My mind is unfocused. The teal sky, golden fields, the graceful palms, and the house, there and not there, just visible behind the veil of my thoughts. All of this fades as I walk steadily along the edge of the vineyard, taking me back to other times and places. I see my mother's face, recall slices of long-ago days—singing together *Gitano* songs, my little-girl voice high and thin, my mother's rich and soft as a length of satin cloth.

As the kilometers pass beneath my feet, I feel her hands guiding mine around the half woven strands of a rush basket, remember the touch of her fingers arranging my hair. Other images I push away—what I saw through the slit in her tent on the day our lives changed, of the way her spirit escaped into death. My Little Red Squirrel wrapped like a butterfly. Boldo staring from the back of the truck as it pulled away. All these I have lost—my *daj*, Kizzy, Little Red Squirrel, Boldo. And then, for a fleeting instant, Marisol's face appears to me as well.

The sun has become a white blinding light on the horizon, telling me it's late afternoon and I'm moving to the west. My fine shoes have rubbed my heels raw. The stockings have begun to unravel in long straight paths. I walk to a grove of trees and rocks. There, a small mound of moss, spongy and soft. I peel it from the base of the stone, gently tear it in two, one half to cushion the back of each heel. I remove my shoes and line them, soil to leather, so that the lovely green pillows will sit against my feet.

I sigh, look around. The sun shoots through the trees in thin sharp rays, throwing stripes across a small clearing. The bars of light and dark, side by side, make me think of prison, of Boldo in Sevilla. A melody weaves through this in my mind, one of the old songs, a sad, haunting tune. There is no place big enough to hold the feeling, except . . .

I stand, the light crisscrossing my face. I begin to hum the tune aloud, startling in this out-of-the-way place. But each bar moves me, my body aligning itself with the soul of the song. I close my eyes and lean my head back, the hum of the notes buzzing on my lips, then on to my feet, my legs, my arms, hands, fingers.

Oh, even when there is nothing else, it is good to dance, to breathe, to move like a free bird. I feel the air on my skin, turn into, then away from the sun, warm and cool, light and dark. It is as if I am tasting life again—if only a small sip. I raise my arms above my head and spin, spotting my gaze at a distant point with every turn until I am spent.

I stop. Close my eyes. Then I slide my feet into my moss-lined shoes and walk. Marisol will have missed me by now. When I first arrived she did tell me I could leave, that I could take what I needed. This does not lessen the pang of guilt I feel.

I follow a narrow path, veering around a steep hillside. Perhaps it will lead to Cadiz, or another town. It snakes around, up into higher ground, and down again. And there, up ahead, is a small wooden building, the grass around it wild and high. Abandoned? My heart jumps. Here, a place to spend the night! Shelter from the evening chill.

I pick my way through the waist-high grass. There is a window on one side. With some caution I sidle up to the broken glass pane. A torn shade blocks my view. I move to the right, my face against the wall, to peer behind the canvas.

A shadow falls. I turn.

"Move a muscle and you're dead!"

CHAPTER 23

He wields a pickax in his short, thick arms. Stares at me through narrowed eyes. His mouth curls. "Who are you? What are you doing here?"

I back against the wall. Shake my head.

He grabs me, wrenches my arm behind my back. His stale breath warms my ear. "Nationalist spy? A Fascist informer? You think because you're a woman you're safe?"

"No. I'm nobody. I . . ."

He whistles loudly through his teeth. The door creaks, many footsteps pad the ground, urgent voices hum. A group of about twenty comes around the corner. Some with the stocky stature and carriage of peasants, all with bright, angry eyes. Some with tools, one with a rifle. Some in aprons. One holds a paintbrush.

A woman is among them. She has long golden hair, a smudge of blue paint on her cheek.

What have I stumbled into?

The man yanks me by the arm, shoves me around the corner. I trip, fall to my knees. He drags me up, shoves me forward. The crowd presses in behind, the woman with her hand over her mouth, eyes wide.

My daj, *please . . .*

We come to a door. Gripping my arm with iron fingers, the man leans back, kicks it open, flings me against the far wall. I hit, slide, slump as another drags a metal chair across the floor. Its legs scream against the concrete. Many hands push me onto the chair. I land off-center, its steel arm connecting with my tailbone. I drop onto the seat. Pain hammers my spine.

They face me, arms crossed, brows furrowed. The stout man with eyes of slits nods and gestures with one gruff wave of his hand. Several rough-looking men duck out the door, fanning in both directions. Are they lookouts? Guards? Watching for what?

"Where did you come from?"

What can I say? I look down. He kicks the chair. "Answer me!"

"I came from my grandmother's house."

"Really? Just taking a stroll? Like Little Red Riding Hood?" The men laugh, but with a glance, he silences them.

"No, yes, I . . ."

"Who is your grandmother?"

"Marisol. Marisol Muentes." This sends a twitch through the group. They exchange glances, shuffle their feet.

The thick, short man with piggy eyes squats before me. Puts his beefy face directly in front of mine. He smells of ham and sweat. "Really? And since when does Señora Muentes have a granddaughter?" The crowd mumbles, nods.

"Diego Honorio Muentes is my father."

"You're lying . . ."

One of the men steps forward, lays a hand on my interrogator's arm. They incline their heads, whisper. Piggy eyes me again. "A bastard *Gitano*?" He chuckles. "If what she says is true, she's a long way from grandmother's house." He kicks the chair again. "How do you explain that?"

"I was . . . leaving . . ."

"There's one way to find out if you're lying. We'll check out your story. But in the meantime, you're going nowhere." He raises his chin, juts it toward his men. "Agustin! Juan Carlos! You stay here with her. She's not to leave that chair. Felipe is due back before evening. He'll know if her story is true. I'll go ahead to meet him."

Felipe!

Piggy leaves. Hands the pickax to the tall, lanky one, Agustin. The other men follow him out. My eyes dart about. Parcels wrapped in brown paper are piled everywhere. A peculiar machine with cranks and levers and two flat surfaces stands in the corner. Tacked to the walls are the type of bold, colorful posters plastered throughout the city—war planes, soldiers, cowering children, thick black letters. It is a workroom of some kind. Tables hold stacks of rectangular metal sheets and cans of something like salt. Through all this I look for a way out, but there is none.

Juan Carlos closes the door, props himself against the concrete frame. Agustin sighs. Rubs his face with both hands. "I didn't come here for this—guarding a girl—with an ax."

"So, an artist is too good for menial work? Don't want to get your hands dirty?" Juan Carlos sneers.

"We all have our roles," Agustin says. "That's all I meant."

"You schoolboys are all soft. You talk, but when you have to act, it's another story."

"Shut up. I'm so tired of you." Agustin dismisses him with a wave of his hand.

Juan Carlos's face reddens. "Defending the Republic takes more than painting poster pictures! What are you going to do when the real fighting begins? Run to the studio? Paint the German Fascists away? You have no *cajones*. No balls."

"And to you, having balls means being a tough guy, right? Tough in front of the girl, here? So—what? You want me to swing the ax at her? That shows my loyalty? Makes me a man?" He picks up the ax, steps toward me.

I scoot the chair back. It topples over and I sprawl on the floor. Agustin puts down the ax. He grabs me by the hand. Rights the chair. "Sit down. Please."

"*Sit down, please,*" Juan Carlos spits. "No balls."

I feel for the chair behind me and sit. Artists? Soldiers? They are crazy, these two.

Suddenly there are footsteps outside the door. Voices. Agustin and Juan Carlos forget their argument.

Juan Carlos pulls me up, steps behind me, rams his thick palm across my mouth. I taste salt and metal. His other arm

clamps my waist. His body presses against mine. I squirm. "Not
a sound," he hisses.

Agustin goes to the window, pushes the shade aside with
two fingers, tips his head. Juan Carlos inches me ahead of him
along the wall beside the door.

Agustin steps back.

The door opens.

It is him. Felipe.

His eyes are my eyes. His cheeks, my cheeks. I look at myself
in my uncle while he stares. Piggy comes in behind him. Points.
"There she is. Claims to be your *niece*."

"Easy, Juan Carlos. She's not going anywhere."

I wipe my mouth on my forearm. My uncle walks toward
me, his mouth open slightly. He shakes his head.

"Where did you come from?"

"The house, the vineyard. Marisol brought me there."

"Brought you from where?"

My words spill. "I was captured by a militia. Brought to
Señor Vargas. He called Marisol and she came for me, a week
ago now."

Still he stares. "Your mother's name?"

I swallow. "Nadja." I take my mother's pendant in my fingers, hold it out toward him. "This was hers."

He glances at it. Studies my face. "Well I'll be damned," he
whispers. "But what are you doing all the way out here?"

I tell him about Diego and Camilla, about the welcome I
received.

He nods. "And your mother? Is your mother here with you?"

I press my lips together. "My mother is . . . no more."

"I'm sorry . . ." He pauses. "I don't even know your name."

"Drina."

"Drina," he says. "I'm very, very sorry, Drina."

Piggy steps forward. "You better make sure she's telling the truth."

Felipe nods. "Drina, what were you doing outside here?"

"I thought this place was abandoned. That I might spend the night." I point at Piggy. "Then he grabbed me."

"Where were you planning to go?"

"I don't know . . . away . . ."

My uncle rubs his chin. "I need to take you back to the house. To be certain you're telling the truth. I do believe you, but I need to be sure."

Piggy nods. I nod as well. What else can I do?

"It's a long way to the house and it's getting late. We'll need to ride. Bring my horse around, Pedro, please. And bring two more horses, for Agustin and Juan Carlos." My uncle looks at me. "There are militias, both Republican and Nationalist, scattered in the hills between here and Valencia. No one is safe. Agustin and Juan Carlos will ride ahead of us."

Piggy gathers his things and we prepare to leave. Outside, three tethered horses nicker and stomp. The largest, finest steed, a pearly white Andalusian, belongs to Felipe.

So I am returning to all I left behind.

I watch Agustin and Juan Carlos mount and come around to

where we are. The woman with the golden hair lingers in the shadow. My uncle walks toward her. They incline their heads together for a moment. Then he is back.

"Safest route is west around the Arroyo land," Juan Carlos says. "Ride close to the main house and then onto the back road." And with that they are gone.

Felipe lifts me onto his horse, sidesaddle, in front of him. A thin slice of relief cuts through my anxiety. Like tendrils of vines creeping over trellises in the vineyard, my mind wraps around thoughts of a grandmother, a room, a bed. How quickly these illusions reach and grab.

As he steadies me, takes the reins, ankles the beast forward, I wonder—can any of it really ever feel like mine when my father doesn't want me?

I rock gently with the gait of the horse, close my eyes. The hoof-beats fall in common time. Every other beat our bodies sway slightly forward, then back.

My daj, *how can I win my father's heart?*

The halter jingles on the upbeat. The horse's mane streams back in rhythmic waves, brushing my face.

My mother's word rises in my chest. It is sweet and bitter, all at once.

Dance . . .

CHAPTER 24

Dusk falls. Our shadows stretch long and thin. The horizon is painted orange pink, lined with violet, above that, blue slate. The moon floats like a ghost behind the veil of sky. Soon it will be night.

We ride quietly in and out of wooded places, from path to forest to field. The light sinks and the first star rises.

I watch Felipe through sidelong glances. His voice is soft and steady, his expression changes little, except for his eyes. They hold clouds, then reflect light; they are deep, then bright. He has many questions. *Was it hard to love this Little Red Squirrel? Where is the grave of your dear mother? How did you meet Alvaro?*

I explain, piece by piece. Something in his manner, in his listening, makes me hunger for the next question.

"What do you think of Marisol?"

"She is strong. Used to getting her way. She wants me to stay, though I'm not sure why. I . . . do not want to disappoint her."

I am surprised by my own words. The wall I feel between myself and others somehow does not exist with him. It is as though he is mining truths that have been hiding inside me.

"This Boldo—do you love him?"

"Yes, of course I love him. I . . ."

"What is it you love about him?"

I think of Boldo's eyes on me, of the way he wanted me from the first glance. How he risked everything to save me and my Little Red Squirrel. Of the price he has paid.

"I love that he loved me." I suppose I can say many things, but this is what crosses my lips. "The way he *saw* me." That he did see me at all, is what I am thinking, the miracle of it. My face warms at the memory.

Felipe lifts his index finger to silence me and reins in the horse. He stares into the darkness. I sense the stiffening of his posture, the intensity of his listening.

I sweat fear before I feel it.

Hoof-beats.

Felipe draws our horse to the right. The beast sidesteps, lifts its hooves high, silently moves into the cover of trees and shadows.

"Sh! We need to dismount. Careful . . ."

He jumps down first, takes my hand, and I slide to my feet. Quickly, he leads the horse deeper into the darkness. Pulls me along behind.

They come closer. Many horses and many men. Hoof-beats

and a frenzy of voices. Felipe ties our horse to a sapling. We hide behind a large boulder.

"Stay down. Don't move."

I duck my head to my knees, peer out beneath my arm. The commotion is near— in the spot where we were just riding.

The brigade gallops through. As the thunder fades and the voices diminish, my chest expands. I breathe again.

We wait.

Wait until the only sounds left are those of the evening.

"They're gone. Rebels—Nationalists," Felipe whispers. "Terrorizing people—anyone they believe might be sympathetic to the Republic." He wipes his brow. "We can't take any chances."

As we mount again and move forward, I struggle to block out the memory of the sounds of warring men. Of being trapped, cowering in the cave. Will this fighting never end?

We ride in silence until lights appear.

"The Arroyo estate," Felipe says. "Their vineyard borders ours. We'll ride by the house and cut back, as Juan Carlos suggested."

Felipe slows our horse.

Something moves below the terrace. I squint.

Felipe gasps. "Don't look, Drina. . . . No, don't . . ."

But of course I look.

Bodies hang from thick ropes—five, six. Two women—ragdolls—skirts rippling in the breeze, arms limp, heads drooped like wilted rosebuds. Four men—scarecrows—shirts billowing, shoulders slack. Fingers curled. One shoe on, another off. Dead fish on a line, pigs in a slaughterhouse. Gently they sway.

He reins the horse around, but what you see, you cannot un-see.

"Our house could be next!"

Felipe hauls me back, shoves my leg over the saddle. One arm holds me, the other slaps the reins against the horse's neck. Once, twice. He kicks with his heels—kicks, kicks, kicks. The beast charges. Its powerful neck bobs. I grab the mane with both hands, bury my face in it, hunker down, press with my legs. My skirt flies. Hold on. Hold on. . . . Behind my eyes bodies swing below a balustrade. . . . *Our house could be next . . .*

The roll of hoof-beats slows. We are still in motion as Felipe jumps from the saddle. I look up at the familiar house. My hands tremble as he helps me down.

Marisol looks out from the terrace—a starling perched on a ledge. She does not yet notice us. A man comes from behind, encircles her. Places his chin on her shoulder. I know, somehow, it is Señor Vargas, and I understand something new about them.

"Mother!" Felipe shouts. "Alvaro!"

They turn. We run to meet them.

"Felipe? Drina? How did you—where? . . ." Marisol grasps me against her small frame, presses me tightly.

"I found her at the studio. They were holding her there."

Behind me she grabs Felipe's arm, pulls him into the embrace. Holds us both for a long time before she lets us go.

Agustin and Juan Carlos appear suddenly around the side of the house.

"Did you pass by the Arroy—"

"We saw."

"It was too late. There was nothing Agustin and I could do."

I glance at Marisol, her jaw tight, fists clenched.

Felipe blows air through his lips, rubs his chin. "How much longer can we hold out, Juan Carlos? We've gotten by on borrowed time. They already suspect . . ." He turns toward Marisol. "It would be wise, Mother, to find safe haven elsewhere. I have friends. I could arrange safe passage. To France, perhaps."

"No. No! I will not leave my home. Our workers depend on us."

Felipe pinches the bridge of his nose, closes his eyes for a moment. "We've done all we can here . . ."

"So, you too, Felipe?" Juan Carlos says. "Turning your back on the Republic!" Along his jawline his cheek pulses.

Felipe inhales deeply. "We've placed everyone involved in danger. Our posters can no longer help the cause. Not here in the south. I say we finish this last run and close it down. The benefits no longer outweigh the risks."

"Felipe is right," Alvaro says.

Marisol's eyes burn. "I will *not* go!"

Felipe takes her hand and closes the space between them. "Mother . . . our friends, the Arroyos . . ." He hesitates, but something in his face betrays his silence. My grandmother seems to shrink, instinctively, and then brace as Felipe continues. "They are now hanging by their necks from ropes under the balustrade of their home. Dead. All of them."

Marisol gasps, turns away.

"I'm sorry," Felipe says. His face is the color of ash. "But it could have been *you*, Alvaro, Carlita, Bernardo. Don't you see?"

We stand silently, waiting, I realize, for my grandmother to speak, to act. I see that everything depends on her. Her shoulders move as she breathes deeply, once, twice. Her face is pinched. Brows furrowed.

"Shut the factory down if you need to. But either way, I—will—not—leave." She looks at us, one to the other. "We are not weak people! We are not dumb goats! We must make a plan. A plan of defense, and, if necessary, a plan of escape. There is always a way to survive! But for now, Felipe, you must find your brother. He went after Drina."

I stare at her, mouth open.

"Yes," she says. "Your father set out to bring you home."

CHAPTER 25

We sit around the table—Marisol, Alvaro Vargas, and me. No sign of Camilla or her son, Renato. There are two empty chairs—my father's and Felipe's. One brother going to bring back the other. I wonder—did my father leave in anger? Out of obligation? Guilt? Have I foolishly put both brothers in harm's way?

Carlita and Bernardo set out the meal. Thinly sliced *jamón*, a slab of cheese, a hunk of bread, olives.

No one asks why I left. Surely, without a word, it is clear.

Renato comes down the stairs, his handsome face flat, unreadable. Until he notices me.

"You're back."

I nod, though I cannot read the tone of his voice.

"You caused quite a commotion. Shouting. Finger pointing..."

"Renato, enough!" Marisol says.

"Some things are better left unsaid," Señor Vargas adds.

Renato shrugs slightly, a glint in his eye. I am not sure if he is amused or annoyed. I stare at him a moment too long. He raises an eyebrow and I look away.

"Sit down, Renato," Marisol says, gesturing with her hand. "Sit. Eat."

I shrink into my chair. Señor Vargas fills a plate for me, pours a glass of sherry. I am grateful for the eating. It fills the awkward space Renato carved with his words.

We lift our glasses and sip. The sherry warms my mouth with a nutty, sweet flavor, like drinking liquid gold. "Mmm . . ."

Marisol smiles slightly. "Yes—is it not everything I promised?"

"It is."

She is suddenly earnest. "Whatever I promise you will find to be true."

"She is a woman of her word," Señor Vargas says, laying his hand over hers.

Renato tears a hunk of bread, lines it with ham. He chews thoughtfully and stares across the table. "Do you dance?"

All eyes turn to me. Renato takes a sip of sherry. "I mean, if you take after Diego . . ."

I stare at my plate. "I dance, yes . . ."

"And, I understand, your mother was a dancer as well," Alvaro says. "With that combination—"

We are interrupted by the sound of horses. We jump to our feet. Alvaro Vargas steps in front, waves all of us back, but Marisol pushes his hand away, angles in front of him, her face against the glass.

"Step back Marisol, until I'm sure."

"One horse," she says. "I only see one horse."

"Come away from the window!" Alvaro takes her by the shoulders. "Please, dear."

But she is already running to the entranceway.

"Marisol!" He is a few steps behind her as the door swings open. Alvaro, then Carlita, Bernardo, Renato—they all follow.

I step back and wait.

And wait.

A blur of voices. I strain to sort them out.

Footsteps at the door.

It is him—my father. He sees me, closes his eyes, drops his head. Looks up again. They come in behind him, all but Felipe.

He moves toward me. Tightens his mouth in a straight line.

"Drina. I'd given up. Thought you were gone for good."

Hearing my name on his lips causes something inside me to buckle, and to yearn.

"I'm . . . sorry about . . . before. I was . . . well . . . I understand why you left. I don't blame you. I didn't make it easy. I . . . I'm relieved that you're safe."

Even this scrap of care I will accept. I can find no words, so I nod. Tears press behind my lids. I blink and they spill from the corners. With the back of my hand I wipe them away. We stand in a stiff embrace that begins to soften as he tilts his head against mine—when I feel his breath in my hair. The hard place inside me begins to slip, but something sharp catches and holds. And I am tired of this wall even as my fingers cling to it.

As he steps away I see Camilla frozen on the landing, her

face a bitter mask cut in stone. She turns slowly, the sound of her ascending, measured steps like a pendulum marking time.

For a moment we stand in awkward silence. Then Marisol leads us back to the table. "Now we just need to pray Felipe returns safely."

Chapter 26

No word from Felipe. Four days and four nights come and go. He has not been seen at the poster studio, nor in town, now firmly under Nationalist control. Alvaro Vargas is staying here with us at the house. Many officials in the city center have been beaten and tortured, lined up and killed, simply for not taking a strong enough stand against the Republic. Others, in the working classes, shot, accused of being communists. All over Spain the Catholic priests have been murdered by Republicans, their churches burned. Why, I do not know. Alvaro says the Republicans believe these priests teach people to be stupid sheep. If peasants accept their hardships, their poverty, how will they ever be angry enough to fight?

I cannot get my head around it, nor my heart. There are moments when feelings ambush me. They sneak up and strike hard—and then I miss my *daj*, my Kizzy, Little Red Squirrel. Am I to accept this suffering as the peasants do theirs? And if I do, does this make me an enemy of the Republic? It seems that we *Gitanos* are made out to be the enemies of everyone.

We wait for word of Filipe. The rhythms of the household resume, although at a slower, heavier pace. I go through the motions of being helpful, performing this chore or that. It is a pointless busyness, as my help is not really needed. But what else am I to do?

Camilla is a dark, silent presence. Worse than glaring at me, as she did in the beginning, she now stares through me, as though I am a specter. The ghost of my mother, perhaps.

But this I am not. I am me, and still I am here.

I stay by Marisol as much as I can. With her and Alvaro Vargas I feel safe. My father watches, and his eyes are no longer so shielded. He sees me, and as he sees, Camilla draws deeper into herself. Renato takes in all of this with little expression, but he notices much. His eyes betray his interest. Alvaro Vargas sees it too. I watch Alvaro watching Renato watching Camilla watching Diego watching me. And when they are not watching me their eyes creep to the windows. I feel their constant listening for sounds of Felipe. In this I join them, since I am, in a way, responsible.

On the fifth day Camilla brings an envelope to the table at dinner. She hands it to Diego.

"This letter was hand-delivered from Vicente," she says. She pauses, glances from me to my father. "There is an opportunity for you and Renato to dance in Sevilla." She pauses and her eyes glint in a way that says there is more to tell.

"Lola Vega has been asked as well. The Nationalists have set up headquarters there. A dinner is being planned for those in charge. They want you to dance for General Franco himself!"

"General Franco?" Alvaro's brows rise. "Going to Sevilla will be dangerous. Franco will be a target, for sure."

"Don't be foolish! This is the opportunity of a lifetime," Camilla says. "A chance to establish oneself with the powers to be, in the new Spain."

"With the future dictator, you mean?" Marisol levels a look at Camilla, then at Diego.

"Franco is a visionary," Diego says. "And if Felipe has fallen into Nationalist hands it wouldn't hurt to know people in high places."

Marisol looks down, lips taut.

"But what about Lola Vega?" Renato gestures with his fork. "You said they invited her as well? Will we be dancing together?"

"He doesn't say. But he wants you both. If you care to bring a partner that's fine. Or not. But the point is, with or without Lola, you will dance for Franco!"

"Enough!" Marisol snaps. She throws her napkin on the table, gets up, strides out of the room.

"Diego?" Camilla challenges him with her eyes. Turns to Renato.

"I say we go!" Renato stands, leans forward, hands on the table.

I sit watching, invisible.

My father leans back in his chair. Turns the letter over in his hands. His eyes wander until they settle on me. It is as though he sees me and something else.

"All right," he says softly. "We will dance in Sevilla for the great General Franco."

"Yes!" Renato shouts, and jumps to his feet.

Camilla smiles broadly. "I'll get word to Vicente. You'll have about a month to prepare. Vicente will provide the exact date and location when the time comes. Everything must remain discrete, for obvious reasons." She turns, triumph in her step, and marches up the staircase without a backward glance.

Renato's eyes glow with excitement. "A month. There'll be details to work out! Music, costumes . . ."

Diego is still eyeing me. "Yes," he says. He stands, looks between Renato and me. "We will go to the practice studio."

Renato is already out the door. Alone at the table, I stare again at my dinner plate. Listen to my father's footsteps behind Renato. Hear the door open.

"Drina."

I look up.

He pauses in the doorway. Gestures with his hand. "Come along."

Before thoughts form, my heart races. My hand flies to my mouth.

"Yes," he says. "Now we will finally see how the blood of your parents flows through your veins."

ℭHAPTER 27

It is one of the outbuildings I'd seen behind the *bodega*—the one where I'd heard Renato's music playing. A small wooden structure with a large window in the back.

Renato goes in first, next my father, who holds the door for me.

The room is plain except for the largest mirrors I've ever seen, stretching floor to ceiling, nearly covering the far wall. A platform of oak runs along the opposite side. Abutting one corner is a massive armoire with tall double doors. Beside the platform, which must double as a dancing floor, is a table holding a large, squarish mahogany box with a metal crank on one side. Two wooden chairs face the dancing platform.

"This is where we practice," Diego says. I watch Renato move to the armoire, open it, remove a pair of black leather shoes with thick heels. He steps out of his boots and into the black shoes, tightens the laces.

"Come, Drina, sit." My father drags one of the chairs off to the side beside the mahogany box. "You and I will let Renato dance for a bit."

I eye Renato with an edge of envy, so comfortable and familiar in this place.

"Have you seen one of these?" Diego asks, lifting the top of the deep, reddish box. The lid flips back, and with it, a large, golden, cone-shaped shell emerges.

I gasp. I'd heard of the machine called a gramophone—the invention that, through a small needle, somehow funnels music from a disk.

"A gramophone?"

"Yes. See, here are the records." I notice, for the first time, a stack of colorful cardboard sleeves on the table beneath the device. He flips through the disks. Words and letters, photographs and drawings of singers and guitarists, of *flamenco* dancers.

He slips one out, places it on the round, raised part meant to hold the disk, winds the crank until it will turn no more. Fascinated, I fix my eyes on the black whir on the turntable. "Seventy-eight rpms," he says. "It revolves seventy-eight times a minute!" I try to count, and he laughs in an easy way. I blush but continue staring, so hypnotizing is the sight. He lifts the graceful-looking arm that holds the needle and gently lowers it onto the edge of the disk.

A scratchy sound then . . . a miracle! Out of the blossom-shaped shell comes the sound of a guitar! My eyes and mouth gape. I cannot contain myself. My father smiles.

"It is a marvel!" I whisper. I wonder, as the words escape my mouth, whether I am referring only to the gramophone, or to the handsome face of this man who is my father. Smiling at me. *Oh, my* daj, I think.

A rhythmic roll of metal on wood. I look up to see that Renato has taken his place on the platform and has begun to dance. The music tugs at my spirit. He moves, and something inside of me goes with him. I know these steps, but his movements, his gestures, are clean and exacting. Precise. I am impressed and secretly ashamed. I, who think myself a dancer—I do not have this polish, this practiced flair. Compared to him—and, no doubt, to my own father—I am a peasant, a *Gitano* amateur.

The music ends and my father selects another record. A lovely woman—a *Gitano* —stares from the sleeve. Wide-set dark eyes, thick brows, a heart-shaped face. Her head tipped to one side, her cheek resting thoughtfully on her hand. Her face stirs something in me. Kizzy—she resembles my Kizzy.

"Pastora Pavón Cruz," my father says. "You might know her as *La Niña de los Peines.*"

I shake my head. "No, I do not know her."

"But your soul will recognize her song." He replaces the first disk with this one, turns the crank, drops the needle.

A flourish of guitar, then the clapping of hands. *"Olé! Olé!"*

The voice rolls from the shell. It is a *petenera,* a mournful, soulful song. The words draw me in . . .

I wish I could deny this entire world, to once again inhabit
the sea of my heart . . .

Something in La Niña's voice pierces me like a rusty blade. The tone, inflection—it is not this and not that. It is strident, then smooth, sweet but bitter, stretched and plied, each tone wavering between the shadowy colors of evening.

As though in a dream, my father takes my hand. His touch and the plaintive song carry me up, up from my chair, onto my feet, up the stairs to the platform. He backs away, slowly, more like a fading from me. I move with La Niña. Darkness in my veins pumps life into the dance. Her pulse drives the rhythm of my feet, her yearning, the stretch of my arms, her longing, the grasp of my fingers.

But I do not dance alone. No.

The spirits of my own losses rise as invisible partners.

How long I dance, I do not know. But when all that is left of the *petenera* is the scratch of the needle and the sound of my own ragged breath, I know I am done. Soaked in sweat, my skin turns to gooseflesh. I wrap myself in my own arms, trying to cover what I've exposed.

Renato leans against the mirror, back to back with his reflection, his face unguarded. He blinks, shakes his head.

My father sinks onto the chair, drops his face into his hands.

Hot shame crawls up my neck to my face. My cheeks burn. *What have I done? My* daj, *could you not have stopped me?*

I push myself to the stairs—down, down. Stare at my feet, will them on toward the door. My heart chokes.

Somehow he is there before me, his body in my path, his hands on my arms. My hands fly to my face. I cannot bear to see my father look at me. I am crying now, but I will not let them see. No.

"Drina!"

"No . . ."

"Drina! Look at me!" Something in his voice catches. I squint at him through splayed fingers. His expression is raw with an emotion I cannot name. He takes my hands, pries them from my face. His mouth twists. He swallows. Whispers, "You have embodied the spirit of your mother . . ."

A small, pinched sound escapes my throat. His arms are around me and I wet his shirt with many tears.

It is Renato who drags us from this deep place. "Why can't she come with us to Sevilla? We have a month. She could be my partner! Or she could dance alone. Diego, you can teach her well . . ."

My father draws back, still grasping my arms with his hands.

"Yes," he answers, his eyes never leaving me. "Drina will come with us to Sevilla. And she will reveal to the great General Franco the beautiful and wounded soul of Spain itself."

CHAPTER 28

It is only the dancing that makes waiting for word of Felipe tolerable.

The news from the streets is bad. Very bad. Alvaro and Marisol speak in hushed tones of thousands all across Spain—innocents whose only crime was being on the wrong side of this line or that—snatched from their homes, farms, and shops, marched into town squares, lined up and shot, hung, or beaten to bloody pulp. Some with family feuds use these violent *paseos* to settle long-standing grudges. Mean-spirited farmers eager to avenge some slight or another accuse their neighbors of aiding the Republic. A day later they have been spirited off to prison and heard from no more. Have they forgotten what this war is about? Or, like me, perhaps they never understood in the first place.

Renato, too, speaks of the war. Renato, now my constant

companion, whom I understand best and least of all. I know his touch, the breadth of his arms, the tilt of his head. I know the angles of his face and the deep cleft in his chin. But I do not know what is inside his head or his heart. He speaks, not of himself or his feelings, but of the latest skirmish or war crime.

"Even the penitentiaries have been opened," he says. "Inmates, thinking they are being set free, are shoved into a *paseo*, marched off to execution."

Our music begins. He sweeps his arms around me. I turn to wood, my heart hollow. My legs dead stumps, arms brittle branches.

"What is it?"

My knees threaten to buckle. I grab his arms. "What prisons? Where? Which prisoners?"

"I think we would have heard if Felipe was in prison. What is wrong with you?"

"Sevilla? What about Sevilla?"

"Felipe wouldn't be in Sevilla."

Renato doesn't know. How could he? He doesn't realize what he is telling me. Tears begin before I can hold them back. I face away so he will not see.

"I'm sorry Drina. I've upset you. I didn't think . . ."

I try to erase the image of Boldo marching in a line of ragged men . . . of clubs, guns, blood . . .

Renato turns me toward him, his face inches from mine. "You feel things very deeply. To me you are a mystery."

I close my eyes. Behind my lids I see Boldo. And then he

is kissing me. His mouth caresses mine gently, and something inside gives way. I part my lips, remember the way he stared at me when Luludja refused him my hand, the way he said, *Nothing is done—until it is done.* Remember lying against him in the night. I slip, spin, further and further into the past.

Then gasp. Step back. What am I doing?

Renato breathes heavily. "I'm sorry, I just . . . You were crying . . . I . . ."

My hands fly to my cheeks. They burn, scarlet. I see myself in the tall mirrors, facing him, the reflection of his back inclining toward me, the awkward slant of his head. My heart pounds.

"Drina. Drina, please . . . I didn't mean . . . I'm sorry."

What just happened? I am afraid of this nameless feeling.

Footsteps at the door. I wipe my face, take a deep breath. Renato pulls away.

"I brought Camilla to see for herself . . ."

Diego's voice is unnaturally cheerful.

"Mother . . ." Renato says, too quickly. "Yes, you must see. We've practiced very hard. You'll be pleased."

Did she see? She stares from me to Renato. Her eyes narrow and her nostrils flare as though smelling something foul.

My father fumbles with the record, winds the gramophone. Renato and I stand more than an arm's length apart. I force myself to breathe slowly.

It is an eternity before the needle scratches the surface of the disk, before the clapping pours from the golden shell, before, *"Olé! Olé!"*

The opening chord locks our bodies into position. Between

us, the distance prickles like the sky after thunder, before lightning. We dance a *siguiriya,* chins raised, circling, mirror images of one another. I turn, he pursues. He retreats, I follow. We move together—there, the release, the melting away into the hiding place where I feel without thoughts, remember without words. Where time stands still.

The music is over. It had taken us to another place, and now, suddenly, we have returned.

I cringe before Camilla's eyes, knowing, and yet not knowing, that we somehow showed her too much. Without a word, her crossed arms and tight lips tell me this.

My father claps, slowly at first, then louder, faster.

"Yes!" he shouts. "Yes! I don't know what happened between yesterday and today, but there is something . . . an ache in that dance I haven't seen before!"

Yes, I think, there is something. Does Renato blush?

"Camilla, did you see your son, my daughter—"

"Yes, I see," she says dryly, her lips scarcely moving. Renato and I glance away, avoiding one another's eyes.

"Still need to work on form—tailbones tucked, shoulders directly over the hips, chests lifted, elbows higher than wrists, wrists higher than fingers . . ." Diego motions with his hands in an expansive way. "But the undercurrent was powerful. Yes, they've discovered something new here today!"

I feel the color rise to my cheeks. He doesn't know what he is saying, but what he says is true.

"It is the *duende* that we see! The depth of her soul fuels the dance! Darkness bringing light, sadness calling forth joy."

And then, a commotion outside. Footsteps scrambling. Alvaro Vargas bursts through the door, grabs the edge to steady himself. His face is pale.

"Quickly," he says, panting. "Come quickly! Felipe . . ."

He leans against the frame of the door to catch his breath and waves us past.

CHAPTER 29

My chest aches. Heart rattles. Alvaro's words hammering in my head—*Come quickly—Felipe!*

An entire week he has been missing. It cannot be good.

Renato charges ahead, Diego right behind him. I struggle to keep up, over the hill to the house. Up the steps. Through the door.

My eyes adjust to the darkness inside.

There, around the sofa, Marisol bends, leaning in. Diego kneels. I shrink back. I want to see and do not want to see. I will my legs to move, and they do, thickly, as through water, closer to the murmuring voices.

Oh my daj, no. No more death. Please . . .

I taste the question on my lips, but my tongue feels swollen, my mouth swimming in spit. I swallow back the acid rising in my throat. A groan. Felipe or Diego? It is just as it was in the tent of my *daj*. The air suffocating, pressing on me, constricting my chest. The climate of death, dark, slow, and sickeningly smooth. They minister to the muddled form that is Felipe, laid on the couch like a corpse. A chilling sweat teeters down my back in a crooked path. My hands tremble. I clench my fists as the room closes in. Then nothing.

A sharp, biting smell stabs my nose. I try to turn away.

A slap on my cheek. A voice protests.

I realize it is my voice, distant, strained. I force my eyes open. Marisol's face, upside down, inches from mine. The bottle of acrid-smelling salts in her hand. I moan, close my eyes.

"Drina! Drina!" Cool, dry hands against my cheeks.

"What?"

"Breathe, my sweet! Yes, that's it!"

I struggle to sit up, but slump back. My head throbs.

"Felipe?" I whisper.

Three faces crowd above mine—Marisol's, Diego's, Renato's. So close I cannot focus. I strain to pull them into view. My stomach turns.

"Yes, he's badly beaten, but he'll surely live!" Marisol's voice is a balm to me.

Dark shoes make their way across the floor. "Good God, what in the devil? . . ."

The three faces draw back and Alvaro's looms over me.

"She fainted dead away!" Renato says.

My father holds my hand, awkwardly. "Renato—some water!"

They prop me up and the room spins. I glimpse Felipe on the sofa, his head wrapped in a bloody cloth, a gash along his arm.

But Marisol said he would live. He would *surely* live.

My fingers feel for the pendant around my neck. *Oh my daj, thank you.* I slide it along the chain. *Thank you.*

Renato brings a cup, tips it against my lips. I stare at him over the rim, feel the cool water tickle my tongue. A drop escapes from my mouth and trickles down my neck. From my throat, up along the curve of my chin, to my lips, Renato chases it with his finger. I pull away, wipe the trace of his touch, erasing the wet, the warmth, and the light in his eyes in one swipe of my hand.

"Renato, see to your uncle!" Camilla speaks to her son sharply but stares at me. He goes to Felipe. I cannot tear my eyes away from his back, his step, his hands. "Here, to the chair—yes, that's it." Diego and Marisol help me up, guide me to the armchair. Alvaro appears with a wet, folded towel. "Apparently misery loves company," he says, placing it on my forehead. "You didn't want to see your uncle suffer alone, is that it?"

I nod, trying not to displace the refreshing cloth. Here, from the chair, I get a better glimpse of Felipe. Carlita and Bernardo fuss over him, peel off the bloodied shirt, set down a deep pan of water, prepare steaming compresses and press them to his bruised arms and chest, gently dabbing and wiping, dabbing and wiping. Marisol brings a bottle of witch hazel and a sponge, whispers something about the sting, and delicately probes his wounds. Finally, a sound—breath drawn through clenched teeth. Yes, he is alive!

Eventually he rasps, a few words at a time. Alvaro, Diego, and Marisol kneel on the floor beside the sofa, stroking his forehead, his wrist, alternately encouraging him to speak, then quieting him.

"Almeida brothers . . . suspect . . . the studio . . ."

"Yes, well, what of it?" Marisol says, "The Almeida boys are like family. What would be their concern?"

"Nationalists." Felipe pauses. A weak wave of his hand. "Interrogation . . . worried . . ." He grimaces.

"Easy, Felipe," Alvaro says. "We don't need to discuss this now, do we?"

But Marisol presses on. "Felipe, are you saying the Almeidas beat you? They are responsible for this?" Her voice is tight, thin, a higher pitch than usual.

"Not now, Mother," Diego says. He takes her by the arm, tries to move away. She yanks her elbow from him.

"Don't patronize me!" she barks. "The Almeidas? Nationalists all of a sudden? And Diego, you support their cause! Attacking their neighbors—over what? Accusing us of being communists? Of supporting the Republic? It's come to this?"

Diego's face sags. Camilla pulls herself to her full height. "Don't be naïve, Marisol," she snaps. "Anyone can see which side is winning this war. If you were smart, you'd throw your support to the Nationalists as well."

Marisol whirls around. "It's all about knowing where your

bread is buttered, is that it? Opportunists who turn in their neighbors and families to save their own asses?"

Someone gasps.

"No," Camilla says, her voice ice. "It's about having the courage to stop playing both sides against the middle. It's about taking a stand for what is right!"

Marisol steps up to Camilla. "What is *right*? This?" She jabs at the air, pointing toward Felipe, "This is *right*?"

Alvaro takes her arm. "Marisol. Camilla. Let's not oversimplify . . ."

"Oversimplify!" Marisol turns on him. "Look at my son. Beaten to a pulp! I'm oversimplifying?"

I am frightened by her rage. Camilla and Diego silenced. Carlita and Bernardo frozen. Renato stares at his feet. Only Alvaro Vargas remains himself. He shakes his head. "All I'm saying is perhaps now is not the time . . ."

"Really?" Marisol interrupts. "Then when *is* the time?"

Alvaro nods, gently. "When Felipe is out of the woods. When we can speak quietly and decide, carefully, what needs to be done. When we can separate ourselves from rhetoric about this side or that long enough to consider what is for the best, for the love of our family, our friends . . ."

His words pour like an elixir, coating, calming. Shoulders slump, jaws loosen, fingers uncurl. I pick up the wet towel that had fallen to my lap, wetting the skirt of my dress.

Marisol softens. Sighs. Everyone waits. She looks at the ceiling and down again. "Alvaro is right. Now is not the time. It is only Felipe we need to be concerned with."

Felipe snores softly, a ragged uneven rasp. Marisol steps forward. "Bernardo will sit with Felipe. The rest of us, let's give him some room to breathe. In the kitchen, come! Carlita has soup on the stove."

Alvaro nods and we follow him toward the savory smell of *gazpachuelo*.

I feel Renato's gaze as he holds the door open for me. Avoid his eyes as I step into the kitchen. Before I take my seat at the table I glance his way. But he is gone.

The door waves, back and forth, back and forth, across the place where he stood.

CHAPTER 30

The days of Felipe's recovery pass slowly. So much unspoken worry about this vicious war that I do not understand. Then there is Renato and me. We have not talked about what happened. When I think of him I feel confused. Uncertain.

But one thing I *am* certain about is my shoes. For the first time in my life I have a pair of real dancing shoes. Crafted of fine black leather with a hundred small silver nails piercing the bottoms of the raised heels and the tips of their graceful rounded toes. Delicate button straps across the tops. What an arresting sound they make as they strike the floor. This alone would be enough to make me love them, but there is more!

These shoes that my father pulled from the armoire, that he gently cleaned with a soft, oiled cloth, that he knelt and strapped onto my feet like *Cenicienta zapatas*—Cinderella slippers. These shoes once belonged to my *daj* when she partnered with my father. He'd kept them in the armoire all these years. That must mean something, no? And now I wear her shoes! Each day I sit with my back to Diego and Renato so they don't see me hold my mother's shoes to my face, inhaling the musty, leathery smell, searching for some essence of her. It is not a scent I remember, but it has become the fragrance of my *daj*. Deeply, I breathe her in, then bend, creep my toes along the soft innersole, plant my heels securely, and buckle them in place.

We practice through the morning hours and past noon, then again later in the day and into the evening. Learning names for steps I've known by instinct alone, sculpting my movements into prescribed forms, memorizing "positions" from which the dance is supposed to flow and return. The precise motions and rigid requirements tie me in knots. I wonder—have I lost whatever I had that impressed my father in the first place? My concern for this step or that stifles what, before, had just poured from me.

"*Plantas*—toe—heel!" Diego shouts, striding across the room. "Now, *golpe*—stomp your whole foot—*golpe!* Again!" He keeps time with his hands, doing *palmas*, first cupped, then sharp, striking claps in syncopated *compas* phrases. "Drina—listen to the *compas*, be ready to change with a *llamada!*" Renato dances close beside me, reminding, redirecting, like a sheep dog nipping at the legs of a dumb lamb, coaxing it to move in the desired direction.

This day Marisol watches. Her eyes on me increase my need to do well. Not to disappoint. And my need increases the timidity of my arms, the uncertainty in my legs. My right knee aches from the hammering of my feet against the floor. I try not to favor it, but with the heavy heelwork—the *taconeo*—the weakness is evident. I cannot strike the floor with the same power as my left.

"Alignment!" Diego barks. "Posture! Shoulders directly over hips, hips aligned over legs! Shoulders back! Down! Chest high! Chin up! Back straight! Tailbone tucked!"

All this I try to remember as I sweep my arms through my positions—first, second, third—while I count the *compas* with my feet—fourth, fifth, sixth—as I weave blossoming *floreo* with my hands, pinkies leading, the petals of my fingers following, wrists rotating around and in, then thumbs leading, wrists spiraling back and around.

"Yes, better," Diego says, with little conviction.

He stops clapping time. I exhale. Deflate. He sighs slightly. "Yes, better," he repeats softly. Pauses. "But now, I wonder, where has *Drina* gone? Where has the *duende* fled? Where is the soul, the fire, we saw first? So powerful it seared our eyes!"

I look down to hide the trembling of my lower lip.

Renato shifts his weight toward me, brushing my arm with his hand. I cannot raise my face. Shrug. Shake my head. Stare at the shoes I cannot fill.

"Too much for one day, perhaps," Marisol suggests. "Drina will find herself again after everything new becomes second nature." She takes me by the elbow, steers me away from my father, on toward the door. "We two will go back to the house for *tapas*," she says. "Out on the terrace with Felipe."

I remove my precious shoes, stand them neatly beside the dance floor, slip into my woven *espadrilles*.

The worry we all share is the one no one speaks. What if all of this —the steps, the choreography—what if it does *not* become second nature? What if I cannot recapture what I've lost?

As if reading my mind, Diego calls after us, "Not to worry. There's time. It will come."

But I do not believe it. Two weeks of practice so far. Only two weeks left. My stomach churns at the thought of letting them all down—my father, Renato, even Camilla—although I care about her only to save face, to prove I am something. Marisol.

But worst of all, my *daj*.

Outside, we walk wordlessly toward the house, feet crunching on the gravel path. The sound is unreasonably loud.

"Drina," Marisol says, "You need to trust that you have what it takes. I do. So does Diego, or he wouldn't risk Camilla's wrath!"

I bite my lower lip, glance at her sideways. A long wisp of silver hair has escaped her coiled bun in back. It flutters against her face.

"That said, you don't need to do this. Only if you want it. Don't do it for anybody but yourself."

Her hand goes to her hair, removes a loose pin. In a wave, the rest of it escapes, rippling like the white wings of a bird. She sweeps and coils it around her hand, throws it over her shoulder.

"But what about . . ."

"Your father? He'll dance in Sevilla no matter what. What about *you* is the question . . ."

The yearning inside nearly paralyzes me.

"Stop a moment," she says. Turns her back to me. "Would you re-braid this unruly mane for me? Pin it back?"

I take her silky fall of hair, deftly divide it in three sections. I turn the thick plait round and round my fingers.

"Do you want to dance, is what I'm asking?" Marisol says. "It's all right if . . ."

"Being a dancer is all I've ever wanted." *That, and having a family,* I think. *To belong.* I fasten the twist securely with the hairpin.

"Well then," Marisol says. She turns to face me. "You see how beautifully you wove that braid? How your fingers flew? Did you say to yourself, 'I must separate three strands, weave right across the center, left over right, right over center, pull it tightly?' No! Years ago at your mother's side you did that, probably a thousand times, until your fingers remembered on their own. Dance is no different! Repeat the steps, over and over. A thousand times. Then think about them no more. Your legs and arms will remember. Then your soul will return!" She pats the sides of her bun with both hands. "Very nicely done!" Takes me by the elbow. "I'm hungry. What about you?"

Out on the terrace I lift my chin to the sun, feel it warm my face. Felipe drowses on the settee, a blanket across his knees. Marisol and Carlita arrange the food before us. *Papas* in oil with tuna. A hunk of *manchego.* Thin slices of *jamón.* Small croquettes of codfish. A plate of steamed barnacles—*percebes.*

A bowl of olives. I lift my glass of *vino fino,* feel the slight tingle of this light, crisp sherry. Allow myself just to be.

Finally, Marisol sits and we begin. I do not know I am hungry until the food touches my tongue. Then I must remind myself to chew, to swallow, to pause between bites. I take a *percebe* from the bowl, snap the crusty tubular body from the blossom of shell, slowly tease out the sliver of meat with my tongue. Marisol smiles across the table. "Delicious!" she says. Felipe lifts fork to mouth. Pauses.

"What is it?" Marisol asks. He tips his head, listening. Footsteps. My heart starts to race. Coming along the walk, then up the steps out front. "Someone's coming to visit," Marisol says. It seems she is not thinking, as I am, that it is a death squad, a militia with rope nooses, peasants with clubs and axes.

Felipe gets up, still favoring the side where his ribs were broken. Grimacing, he pushes in front of her. "You need to be more cautious!" he says quietly, his eyes narrowed. We three move inside, through the parlor, toward the door. Carlita is already on her way. Felipe waves us back, steps to the side where he can peer out the window without being seen. Marisol waits with her hands on her hips.

His shoulders tense. Then he relaxes.

I swallow. Breathe.

"Isabel!" he says, throwing the door open.

The woman from the studio with the golden hair stands on the stairs. She rushes forward. "I came back from Barcelona as soon as I heard!" She flings her arms around him.

He flinches.

"Oh, Felipe, I'm sorry! Your ribs . . . They told me . . ." She lets her arms drop, her cheeks coloring.

"It's all right." For a moment his fingers crawl through her hair, his forehead tipped against hers. Then he steps back. "Isabel, this is my mother, Marisol. Mother, Isabel is an artist. A really fine artist." His face has changed, softened. I can see that, to him, she is so much more than an artist. He turns. "My niece, Drina. I think you may remember Drina . . ."

"Yes, yes I do. Señora Muentes, a pleasure to meet you. Drina . . ."

I nod. Try not to stare. Marisol takes her hand. "Come in, Isabel. Come in."

We follow Marisol back to the terrace. Carlita prepares a plate, then pours the sherry. There is much talk of many things, good and bad. The Arroyos. Our dance in Sevilla. At the name of General Franco, Isabel and Felipe exchange a dark glance. Marisol asks about art, about painting, about Isabel's commitment to the Republic. We talk as the sun travels to the west and the light on the terrace shifts. Felipe and Isabel exchange many words, but even when silent their eyes speak. I watch them share this other language, the language of the heart, then embarrassed, I look away. Marisol sees it as well. This I know when she stands and raises an eyebrow my way.

"Well, Felipe and Isabel, you two enjoy one another. My granddaughter and I have things to attend to." We rise to leave.

"And you'll stay for dinner, of course," Marisol says. "8:30?" Isabel smiles. "*Gracias,* Señora Muentes. *Si.*"

I study her—them—as we head back to the studio. So

different, but somehow the same. She with her wide-set, green speckled eyes and golden hair, her soft-edged features, he with his dark intensity, high cheekbones, straight nose. There is an energy between them that reminds me of something. My mind stretches toward this unnameable thing. Renato and me? I blush at the half-thought, push it away, follow Marisol out toward the studio. The murmur of their voices fades into soft velvet.

"Well, he loves her, and she him." She smiles slightly.

"Isabel is very beautiful," I say.

"Yes, but that isn't it, is it? There's something else there, a kind of communion between them. Didn't you feel it?"

"Yes. Yes, I did feel it. I saw her at the studio, you know, the day they captured me."

Marisol nods. "If only it wasn't war time. If only they could be carefree. But then, when is love ever carefree, really?"

I know nothing of being carefree and little of love.

We arrive at the door of the studio, greeted by strains of guitar, the clatter of *taconeo* on wood, *palmas* driving the rhythm.

"Go," she says. "Remember! A thousand times—a thousand times is all it will take!" She pats my arm. "Start counting—and be back for dinner at 8:30."

CHAPTER 31

I repeat, repeat, repeat each step, calling out the moves in my head.

Again!

Again!

I do not use my brain. Only my muscles.

Five, six, seven, eight—right—*left left*—right! Right—*left left*—right!

Llamada!

This is how the afternoon passes, minutes divided into rote bars of eight, then twelve.

It is dusk when we stop. My hair hangs limp across my forehead. Dark rings of perspiration dampen my dress.

Paco, the *tocaor*, puts his guitar back in the case. *"Bueno! Bueno!"* he says, thumb raised. My father nods. "Yes! Great practice!"

Renato steps close to me, bends, gently dabs my sweaty forehead with his small white towel.

"Lovely," he whispers.

I smile as I bend over to unbuckle my shoes. Blush.

Together we walk to the house, calculating weeks, days, and hours to Sevilla. The lit windows of the house blink in the distance.

"There is a *feria* in Cadiz next week," Diego says. "I've arranged for us to go and perform. A dry run."

I think of the *feria* in Cadiz the last time. Of the dancers I'd watched while my mother, alone in her tent . . .

"Are you all right?" Renato asks, touching my elbow.

"A *feria* in Cadiz," I say, my mouth dry as leaves.

"You'll dazzle them!"

I cannot think of Cadiz. Grasp for another thought. "Felipe has a friend to dinner," I say.

"A friend? Who?" Diego asks.

"A beautiful woman—Isabel." I am about to say she is an artist, but something stops me.

"Hmph," Diego says. He frowns slightly and I wonder if I've said something wrong.

At the house I bathe, still uncomfortable soaking in still water. But the moist heat soothes my calves, eases the tightness in my shoulders, loosens my knees. I dress, hurry to the table that has been set with candles, fine white plates and napkins. Introductions have already been made. Felipe sits across from Isabel. Diego and Camilla side by side. Renato beside me. Marisol and Alvaro at the head of the table. I watch Felipe stare at Isabel. She smiles back at him with just the edges of her mouth, adjusts the lovely, teal-green, flowered scarf with long fringed edges that plays up the color of her eyes. I can't help but covet this elegant garden array with gathered silk rosebuds dotting it here and there. She meets my eyes and I blush, embarrassed to be caught staring.

She smiles, "I see you admiring this." She runs her fingers through the delicately raveled threads along the bottom. "It is lovely, isn't it? Felipe bought it for me in Paris."

This she does not say in a boastful way. I see, instead, how she enjoys my admiration, how she delights in my uncle's gift. She's turned my staring into a compliment and I am grateful.

Bernardo pours the sherry and disappears. Carlita carries in one, then another steaming pan of *paella*. Dishes are passed. The room fills with the comforting clink of spoons against plates, the aroma of savory rice, sausage, fish.

We are just beginning when Bernardo returns.

"It seems we have a guest," he says, his mouth twisted oddly.

Marisol tilts her head, puzzled. "Who?"

We all fall silent.

"Monsignor Muñoz has come to check on Felipe."

Felipe narrows his eyes, exchanges a look with Isabel. "Is that so," Marisol whispers, teeth clenched.

"Well, don't make him stand out there," Camilla hisses. "Invite him in! Carlita! Set another place!"

Alvaro places his hand over Marisol's. "Let's not assume the worst," he says quietly. "We need to be hospitable."

Camilla and Diego leap to their feet. I turn to Renato. Mouth the word, "Monsignor?"

"The priest," he whispers. "A Nationalist."

Diego and Camilla escort in a tall, long-limbed man with a beakish nose, dark bushy eyebrows, hair combed severely back. He is wearing a long black gown, tied at the waist with a red cord. A silver cross of Jesus hangs around his neck, shining against the black garment. A flat red cap covers the dome of his head.

Marisol stands. "Monsignor. We were just sitting down to dinner. You'll join us?" Her lips smile, but her eyes are flat as black stones.

"Please, sit down," Alvaro says, pulling out the chair Bernardo has produced.

The man smiles thinly, accepts the seat. "Thank you." He eyes Felipe.

"Rumor has it that you had . . . an unfortunate encounter." Pauses. "I wanted to see how your recovery is coming. Perhaps offer you a blessing." He smiles as if enjoying a private joke.

"I'm sure you know exactly what happened," Felipe answers. "Don't you?"

The air in the room changes. The Monsignor chuckles. "The Almeidas mentioned something to me." With a snap of his wrist he unfolds his napkin and tucks it into his black and white, stand-up collar. Digs his fork into the mound of *paella* on his plate.

Marisol stiffens. Alvaro squeezes her hand.

"It was a warning," he says, between bites. "There are rumors, you know . . . posters . . . a factory . . ."

Isabel straightens up, eyes wide.

"Nonsense," Camilla says, too quickly. "Just nonsense. You know we support the church one hundred percent . . ."

Felipe stares at his plate. Grips the fork in his hand. I expect to see the shaft bend from the pressure. The Monsignor clears his throat.

"Say what you came to say," Marisol snaps.

The Monsignor chews for a moment. He is the only one eating. Looks at Felipe over his glass of sherry.

"It's just a shame that after years of a Catholic education you turn your back on the church. That you forget all you learned."

Felipe leans forward. "*I* forgot what I learned? No! The Jesuits taught me too well. *You're* the one who chooses to forget what your gospel teaches! Didn't Jesus say, 'blessed are the poor?' But his gospel had teeth—bite! His message was like a wolf snapping at the heels of the rich! Isn't that why, in the end, they crucified him? So, what do you people do? Domesticate the gospel! Bastardize the wolf into a fat, lazy house dog, gobbling scraps from the tables of the poor!"

"Shut up, Felipe!" Diego is on his feet. The Monsignor's mouth hangs open, beads of rice sticking to his tongue.

"No, Diego, *you* shut up!" Felipe erupts, pointing his fork at his brother. "You know I'm right! Across a good part of Spain, the biggest patrons of the church have been shooting starving peasants as they gather rotten acorns from the grounds of their farms! While the church and its benefactors get richer, more powerful!"

Camilla stands, leans toward the Monsignor. "He doesn't mean that," she says. "He's ill, is all." Her face is pasty white.

"Ill—yes, I'm ill!" Felipe yells. "Sick over the hypocrisy of the church! Lining up with Franco and Mussolini! Hitler! Marching behind the Sacred Heart of Jesus, killing the workers, the poor! Kissing up to the rich!"

Monsignor Muñoz stands so abruptly his chair topples behind him.

"I don't have to listen to this! Don't say you weren't warned."

Felipe steps in front of him, blocking his path. "Just so you know Monsignor—my family supports your cause." Felipe shoots a look at Marisol, whose mouth is open. Alvaro is squeezing her arm. "It is only that I love them so well that I tolerate their blindness."

"So well you compromise their safety?" the Monsignor says as he moves toward the door.

"Stop!" Felipe reaches for the wide sleeve of the Monsignor's robe. "If you harm my family . . ."

The Monsignor yanks his arm away. "You already have." He strides out, his fork still in his hand, his white napkin flapping at his neck.

We sit around the table, food untouched. Silent.

Felipe drops to his chair, his head in his hands.

"You've put us all in danger," Diego warns. "Have you forgotten the Arroyos? Are you *that* selfish that you'd sacrifice all of us for your precious cause?"

"We need to leave here," Camilla cries, her voice high-pitched, hysterical.

"Let's calm down," Alvaro says, but strain crosses his face in pinched bands.

Isabel reaches for Felipe's hand. Renato takes mine beneath the table. "I'm sorry," Felipe says softly, almost to himself. "If you'd seen what I've seen . . ."

Everyone looks to Marisol.

She grips the edge of the table. "Felipe, what you said is true. But you should not have said it. It doesn't change anything. The Monsignor and his Nationalist comrades will make us pay. We all know what happens to Communist sympathizers."

Felipe looks around the room wildly. "We'll close the factory tomorrow. Send them all away. Then Isabel and I will head to Madrid."

Isabel nods. "Yes," she says, "we have connections. Once we leave, you will be safe."

My father's jaw pulses. "No, we won't be safe here. We'll go to Cadiz. All of us. We would be going in a week anyway, for the *feria*, and then on to Sevilla."

"My sister has a villa in Cadiz," Alvaro says. "We can stay there. It is a good plan. A necessary plan."

Marisol walks to the door and turns. "I said I would not leave my home." She looks around the room, everything flickering in the candlelight. Her eyes glisten with tears she will not shed. "But we must sometimes do what we do not wish to do. Carlita. Bernardo," she says. "Begin closing up the house. Everyone, pack only what you need. We leave for Cadiz in the morning."

215

CHAPTER 32

Before dawn, Renato and I meet, slip from the house, leave for the studio to collect our things. Bernardo nods as we pass, sitting in the shadows with a rifle across his lap. His thick finger loops through the trigger. All night he sat watch, although it did little to ease our worry.

"Eyes open," Bernardo grunts. "Keep your wits."

We hurry on. Halfway down the path Renato takes my hand, our steps fall together, we move as one.

Neither of us speaks, and yet a conversation takes place. A silent exchange about fear, regret, uncertainty. We are finally comfortable together here. And now we are leaving.

We veer off the path into the darkness, stay out of sight. No place feels safe.

"This way," he whispers. He leads me beside a *pino piñata* tree, the thick layer of pine needles spongy beneath my feet.

He stops abruptly. My heart races. I squint into the darkness. "What is it? What?" I spin about.

His lips suddenly cover mine. His hands cup my face, run through my hair, tingle along my neck, sweep my back. I gasp, for an instant tense up, then sigh into him.

Careful.

It is the voice of my *daj,* but I pretend to be deaf.

To our knees, to the ground, the sharp prickle of pine, his tongue, my lips. We fall back, my arms surround him, touching hair, skimming shoulders, my head thrown back. He kisses my throat, my tongue follows the hollow of his neck, his chest presses against my breasts. I arch my back and feel him against me. I lift my hips to meet him, and this is how we dance . . .

We almost do not hear the footsteps. Muffled. Quick.

Renato rolls over next to me, we lie side by side, breathing heavily. Hands clasped. Two possums playing dead, waiting for whomever it is to pass. The silent questions between us—*Who? Diego? Felipe? Rebels? What if . . .* Even as I worry, I still taste him on my lips, smell the sharp green pine that has become his scent. Secretly bless and curse the interruption, because without it, I wonder, what next? We lie silent long after the footsteps pass, until all we can hear is our uneven breathing.

He pulls me to my feet. "Hurry . . ." We run, hand in hand, brushing away the sharp needles stuck in our hair, our clothes. I fear too much time has passed, that we were missed. That they will look at us and know.

The morning creeps across the sky, gray and misty. A line of molten orange burns the horizon.

We unlatch the studio door, step inside, everything different in the early dawn. Collecting our things, we gather up the trunk in the corner. I check—yes, there are my shoes. There, the train of polka-dotted ruffles on the *cola* of the dress Carlita stitched for me. My large *manton* of fringed silk, the shawl embroidered with flowers. My *peineta* and combs for my hair carved from shell. Renato's shoes, bolero jacket, and pants, his flat-topped hat.

Without a word we each take one handle and carry our trunk toward the house. I am grateful for the quiet. What do we say now? What does this mean? As if in response, Renato whispers, "Look!" He gestures upward with his chin.

A hawk, huge, its wings spread wide, swoops overhead. I feel the color drain from my face. It is an omen, surely. The bird calls out, a high-pitched, piercing cry that raises gooseflesh on my arms.

"What is it?" Renato asks softly.

I close my eyes. Shake my head. When I open my eyes the bird is gone. Renato looks at me strangely. Before he speaks, Diego appears. "Finally! Bernardo should not have let you go. We were worried."

"We needed to get our things, is all," Renato explains. My father takes my end of the trunk, and as they move faster, I lag behind.

"Boldo?" I whisper. I wait for something. Perhaps my *daj*

will speak again. Some word or feeling. A message. I linger, holding my breath. Nothing. I exhale, glance up, but there is only sky.

I follow them to the front of the house, the drive now lined with trunks. Bernardo has the horses harnessed to the largest carriage, the rifle propped against it. Beside the carriage, the big black car. Marisol points to this and that. Camilla sits in the automobile, impatient. Alvaro has gone ahead by train to Cadiz to prepare the villa. Carlita secures the straps on the trunks. When Marisol sees me, her face relaxes. "Come, get in."

I walk toward the motorcar, meet Renato's eyes fixed on mine. I should look away, but I cannot. He smiles, a smile that asks a question. *Do you still feel it?*

I am about to push thoughts of omens aside, allow my smile to touch him, when a thunderous explosion rocks the earth.

We freeze, turn in the direction of the blast.

"What was that?" Camilla shrieks, shoving open the car door.

Marisol takes a step, her lips parted, face white. "Felipe," she murmurs. "Isabel." She runs toward the path. "They went to the factory!"

"No, mother! No! You aren't going anywhere, you—" Diego grabs her arm. His face is a mirror of hers. Ghostly. Twisted.

"Let go." She wrenches her arm from him.

Bernardo blocks the path. "Señora, you mustn't. We will go, Diego and me."

"No! Bring the carriage," she says. "It can carry us to the end of the back *bodega* road. Then on foot! Hurry!"

In the east, a funnel of black smoke rises. Diego climbs into the carriage, pulling my grandmother in beside him. Before she is even seated she shouts, "What are you waiting for, Diego? Go! Go!"

"And leave us here?" Camilla's voice is stretched thin.

"Renato—stay with your mother," Diego orders. "Carlita! Bernardo! You, too." My mouth fills with spit. I look between them—my grandmother, my father, Renato. Diego slaps the reins against the backs of the horses.

"Wait!" I bolt for the carriage, reach for the handle alongside.

"Drina!" Renato pleads. I hear his footsteps behind me. "No! *Drina!*"

I grab hold, pull up, cling. Marisol catches my hand and hauls me in.

I turn in time to see him standing helpless as the carriage rumbles away, a cloud of dust roiling up between us.

CHAPTER 33

At the end of the trail, we rush from the carriage toward the spiral of smoke. My lungs burn. I sweat ice. Shiver.

We slow at the clearing. Could it be an ambush? But then Marisol charges ahead. My father tries to hold her back. It is useless. I do what I can to keep up.

The edge of the factory is finally visible through the trees, a hole blown through one side. Flames explode from the window.

The heat presses in. Flames lap the wall, ripple across the roof. They snap. Flash. Glass pops. A crackling roar rolls beneath it.

We watch, as though it is something misunderstood. Something that cannot be. There are no survivors, this is clear.

Then another sound. High pitched. A hollow cry that could not belong to human lips, and yet I know that it does, and I know that it is Felipe. Oh my *daj*, it is the moan of a broken spirit.

Marisol leads us to him, and even as we step closer, everything inside me shouts *No! No!*

Felipe kneels before the body, her skirt smoldering. I see her scarf, strangely whole, the flowers floating on the sea of blue, fringe shimmering, the silk blossoms blooming through the haze of smoke. But, oh my *daj*, her hair, what happened to her lovely golden hair? Gone—her head a ghostly white dome he cradles in his lap. Oh, how he strokes her face, how he traces her lips with his fingers. Touches his cheek to hers. Places his arms beneath her. Lifts.

Her shorn head falls back, neck arched, arms hanging straight and limp. My *daj* . . . Boldo . . . and now Isabel.

Diego steps forward. Marisol stops him. The agony of wanting to go to Felipe and needing to hold back pulls my grandmother's face into a gnarled gray mask.

How long we stand this way, I do not know. But now he carries her toward us, splayed across his arms. Soot blackens his cheeks. A gash on his forehead leaks scarlet into his eyes. His eyes like windows in a vacant house.

My father steps forward, extends his arms, takes Isabel gently from him. I inch back, helplessly. I do not realize that my fingers rake my own hair, until Marisol gently lifts my hand, smoothes the wavy mass, and touches my cheek.

Felipe crumples to his knees, covers his face, and weeps.

My father, Renato, and Bernardo dig a shallow grave in the woods, beneath a stand of pines.

"I've heard rumors about this," Renato whispers, wiping his forehead. "The Nationalists—they shave their heads before they . . ."

"Enough!" My father silences Renato with a cold glance.

Before they . . . I begin to sweat again. At least my *daj* was allowed the dignity to keep her hair.

Marisol begins to wrap Isabel's head with her lovely scarf, covering the knicks and scratches on her scalp.

"No!" Felipe cries. He takes the scarf, buries his face in it, tucks it inside his shirt, against his chest. "Wait, please . . ."

He stops. Blinks. Stares into the hole in the ground. "Leave us for a moment."

"Of course," Marisol murmurs. Together we walk a short distance into the woods, sit together, our backs to the grave. Renato reaches for my hand, but it is not a time for touching. I slide my hand away.

After a time, Marisol rises. Retraces her steps. We stay where we are. Wait for her word. The minutes stretch, weigh us down.

"Come," she says, finally. "It is time to lay her to rest."

I take a deep breath. Return with the others.

Isabel has been placed in the grave. Felipe has not pressed her lids shut. She stares up with sightless eyes, still green-gold, still lovely.

Felipe stands back from the rough hole, his sleeves rolled

to his elbows. His eyes fixed above our heads. Several times he swipes a hand across his forehead and down over his face, as though wiping something away. Though he is right beside us, he is distant. I do not know where to look, what to do.

Marisol has picked some yellow flowers—weeds really, but lovely all the same. Hands one to each of us. We drop them in. They land this way and that. Silently we stand. Perhaps they pray. I don't know how to pray, not really. But I hold Isabel in my heart, touch Felipe's pain with brittle glass fingers. These feelings scrape the scabs of my own losses. Again they bleed.

The men shovel earth over her.

It is done.

Marisol looks at the fresh grave, and then to us. "Bernardo," she says, quietly, "Go. Pull the cart as close as you can. We cannot leave for Cadiz quickly enough."

CHAPTER 34

Marisol, Diego and Camilla, Renato and I travel in the big black motorcar. Bernardo and Carlita take the carriage. Our belongings are piled in the cart Bernardo hauls behind the carriage and in the large trunk of the automobile.

In front of me, my father grips the wheel tightly, leaning forward, a deep crease between his brows. Camilla sits beside him, arms crossed, her mouth pinched shut, thank God. Occasionally she sighs, placing her fingertips above her eyes, thumbs along her cheekbones. She glances in the small rectangular mirror, I suppose to see if we, in the back, notice her angst. I sit between my grandmother, who seems as frail as a bird, and Renato. I try not to pay attention to his leg pressed against mine, how it pulses warmth through his trousers, my skirt, all the layers between us.

Had Felipe come, one of us would have had to ride in the cart with the baggage.

But he would not come. "Too dangerous," is all he said. That, and there was something he needed to do before he left. Marisol looked at him, through him, her lips pulled tightly together.

"Please don't press me, Mother," he said, his voice stretched and thin. She placed her hands on his shoulders, embraced him. Then let him go.

He took us in, each in turn.

"Godspeed," Diego said. They embraced, and I saw my father's shoulders hunch, shake. They clung to each other for a moment, then Diego thumped Felipe on the back, once, twice, as much, I think, to muster some strength for himself as for his brother.

I stepped forward. My uncle—the one with my eyes, my cheeks, my profile—nodded. "Drina . . ."

Tears spilled over my cheeks, into my mouth.

My uncle pulled me to him. I lowered my face into his shoulder.

"Go on and cry," he whispered. I felt his hands in my hair, at the nape of my neck. "Cry for all of us. For Isabelle. For Spain itself . . ."

I missed him before he was even gone.

I feel my connection to him as we glide along the southbound roadway. If only it hadn't been so rooted in sorrow and loss.

Now we ride in silence. What is there to say? The motor-car hums along the pavement. I am lulled by the soft, steady vibration. My eyes are heavy. My head bobs. Several times my chin dips and I jolt awake. Then finally I give way to it.

I awake as the auto slows and turns sharply. Open my eyes, lift my head that had dropped onto Renato's shoulder. Marisol's hand covers one of mine, resting on my thigh. Even as Camilla glares at me in the mirror, I am touched by the fact that, here in the cocoon of the automobile, I have been surrounded and supported by some who love me.

I squint into bright sun and blue sky. To my left, the ocean sparkles beside rows of buildings the colors of tropical fruit. I have been to Cadiz, in the open spaces where the *ferias* take place, but never along the edge of the city proper. A golden-brown brick wall lines the promenade along the sea, marked at intervals with fancy black street lanterns. The shiny gold and orange dome of an enormous church shouts against the turquoise sky. Two white concrete towers reach up alongside it. People hurry along the seawall, in and out of the block of gaily colored buildings—tangerine, peach, lemon, and some so white they hurt my eyes.

"This is Cadiz," Marisol whispers, squeezing my hand. She smiles quickly—a smile that flashes and fades. Even the brightness of the city cannot overcome the darkness of what happened in Jerez.

"Alvaro said to follow this road around to the opposite side of the city," Diego says, slowing at a place where the busy roads cross. We roll along, crank the windows open and breathe the brackish ocean air. I close my eyes, feel the breeze on my face.

It is hard to believe this is the same day Renato and I walked in the dark through the woods, when we nearly . . .

When Isabel . . .

It feels like a lifetime ago.

We weave through one street, then another, all looking the same and yet different. Travel along a wide avenue, the ocean now to our right, the seawall marked by concrete lookout stations with small domed roofs. All of this I see and don't see.

Finally we pull down a cobbled street lined with palms, double- and triple-storied buildings rising on both sides.

"On the right," Marisol says, pointing toward a wide entranceway adorned in blue and yellow floral-patterned tiles. "Yes, I think it's this one here."

Diego slows the car and pulls to the curb. "Come," Marisol says, her voice belying the strain on her face. The car doors creak open. Marisol is out in an instant. Renato takes my hand. I am stiff, sore, tired in a way that has nothing to do with bone or muscle.

We walk into the tiled foyer toward the massive, oak double doors. Diego lifts the large brass doorknocker in the shape of a sea siren, her long head of hair tumbling around her naked breasts, her abdomen scaled with fins, ending in a wide flipper. There is something strangely familiar about the tarnished brass face—her eyes, the hair . . . My lids close as the image of Isabel's final gaze comes to mind. Fixed. Unseeing.

The brass knocker sounds barely twice when Alvaro Vargas throws the door open, arms outstretched. He waves us in, but his eyes are on Marisol. One look at him—at the way he goes to her, how he inclines his head, wraps an arm around her small waist—and I realize he knows, in one glance, about Isabel, about Felipe, the factory attack. Exactly how and what he knows is a mystery, but I remember now how he told me he reads hearts. Did he read Marisol's?

Beyond the doors, a large room, the floor a checkerboard of black and white marble tiles, stone columns around the outer walls. I look up to blue sky—it is an inner courtyard with rooms, some open and some with arched oak doors, lining the perimeter. Palm trees grow in huge pots along the open air space in the center. A shaft of sunlight cuts across the private courtyard, giving the sense of being outdoors, and yet I have the feeling we are very safe within.

"Welcome, welcome," Alvaro says. "This is my sister's summer home. Right now she is in Malaga. It's large, plenty of room for all of us."

Camilla glances about, her narrowed eyes widening. Perhaps she expected something less grand. "Very nice, Alvaro," she says approvingly. "What is it your brother-in-law does?"

"Oh, he's passed, many years now. It's just my sister, Alma, and my nephew, Guillermo. He is a *militar*, in Sevilla, I think."

She waves her hand across the courtyard, the shining marble, carved columns, ornate wrought iron railings, potted palms. "Yes, but what did he *do*?"

"It has been a most difficult day," Marisol says, cutting her off, shooting her a black glance. "I, for one, would like to rest."

"Come, dear," Alvaro replies, "I will show you your room. I've prepared it especially for you."

My father and Renato are already carrying in our trunks and belongings. Alvaro escorts Marisol to her room, and Camilla's question drops like a dead bird. I wander to a staircase that curls around one side of the atrium, my hand sweeping the graceful black railing that swirls up to a second story. I pause here, peek through an archway. Another set of doors around the sides. Bed chambers? A sitting area at one end. I continue up the spiral of stone steps to a large wooden door, push it open, step through.

A warm breeze ripples my hair, dapples my face. The sun draws me out, but as I move onto the rooftop terrace my heart begins to race. My breathing becomes shallow. I must stop, grip the railing along the top of the balustrade, banish the image of that other terrace, of the diaper cloths hanging from a line, the cradle and the pink blanket. The delicate features of my Little Red Squirrel. Every time I think I am someone new, something jumps out to remind me of where I've been and who I am. I close my eyes, let the sun warm my face. Tell my Little Red Squirrel how sorry I am. Then shake my head. My eyes fly open. I cannot allow these thoughts much time or space. No, there is enough right here before me.

I clutch the warm iron railing, gaze out over the city. The bright blue sea to my right, the city sprawling to my left. Behind me, the countryside.

"Drina!"

Renato waves from the sidewalk below. I smile. Lean forward.

"Stay there. I'll be up in a minute. We're almost done."

I nod. "Yes, come be with me here." Suddenly it is all I want. I turn, and there she is on the terrace, watching me, arms crossed, forehead wrinkled. When did she slip through the door?

"It is *not* a good idea. Not something you should even consider."

"I don't know what . . ."

"Oh, but of course you do," Camilla says. "My son and you. You may be dance partners—for now—but that *will* be the extent of it. Do you understand me?"

Her feelings, spoken aloud finally, give rise to something inside me. I stare at her, unaffected. Tip my head to one side, feel my eyebrows lift.

"You are not . . . *appropriate* . . . for Renato. You may be Diego's daughter, but Renato's future is not yours."

I say nothing. Shrug. This, I see, infuriates her. And then I understand that what I feel is something like power. And she feels it too.

Renato comes through the door, walks to the railing, leans over. "What a view here!"

Camilla brushes past me. "Remember what I said." This whispered through clenched teeth. And with those few words, the power I felt just seconds ago drains away. All that is left is exhaustion.

CHAPTER 35

My grandmother's room faces the ocean. She lies on the bed, her back to the door. Alvaro has thrown the windows wide, a gentle sea breeze tickling the sheer white curtains.

I approach the doorway, and despite Alvaro's assurance that she would welcome my presence, I pause. She appears so very frail lying atop the bedcovers, her small frame curled into itself, long silver braid lying across the pillow. I notice, with a start, that there is nothing to her—a sharp angle of elbow, a pointed jutting shoulder.

I try to detect the rise and fall of her shoulders, the rhythmic in and out of breath in slumber, but I cannot. I step nearer, straining to hear the hush and sigh of her breathing. I come even closer, perching at the edge of the bed, lowering my face beside hers.

She suddenly turns toward me and I gasp.

"I'm not dead yet," she says quietly, with a crooked smile.

"I didn't think you were . . ."

She pats my hand. "It's all right. I'm old and it has been a hellish day. Help me up and you'll see, I'll look less like a corpse."

We both cringe. Nothing funny about a corpse, not today. I take her by the arm, she swivels upright, nods to the two chairs facing the window. "Come. Sit," she says, slowly rising, reaching for the arm of the chair, steadying herself, then dropping to the seat. I push back the curtains, opening the view to the ocean, sit beside her.

She sighs deeply. "There are days that determine who we are. For Felipe this is one of them."

She plays with the end of her braid, brushing it against the open palm of her other hand. "Felipe—I pray for him. That he won't indulge himself in bitterness, won't become hard, cruel, cynical. A gentle, sweet boy he was. Caring deeply, always serious. But this . . ."

Her voice trails off. She turns, looks at me. "Somehow you've not allowed yourself to be swallowed up by your losses. Why? What inner strength kept you whole, made you choose to keep on fighting?"

"I don't know," I mumble. Her words catch me unprepared. "I don't think I really chose anything. You came and I . . ."

"Oh, but of course you chose! We *always* choose. Even not deciding is a choice."

"My father . . ."

"Of course. You wanted to know Diego. You took that chance. It was a brave choice."

She sighs. "We remember those decisive moments for a lifetime, regardless of whether we chose rightly or wrongly."

I think of how I defied Luludja, went off with Boldo, stole back my Little Red Squirrel. She is right. I will never forget.

Marisol stares out across the sea, as though water was time, the ripples of waves, years past. "I remember, as though it was yesterday, being in Madrid, newly married. Do you know there are mountains outside of Madrid?"

I shake my head no.

"Yes. I was there with Ernesto—your grandfather. Even as a new bride I felt lonely. Lonely together with him."

"Did you love him?"

She inhales deeply. "He was handsome and moneyed, and my parents were impressed. He wanted me. He was used to getting his way." A flash in my mind of Boldo, the dead rabbits in his grasp, telling me, *My aim is true. I always get what I want.*

She pauses, considering. "I loved that he wanted me so much. A girl can be bowled over by a man's desire. But there in Madrid, I knew. I would sit on the small veranda outside our room and stare at those mountains. A large bird, a hawk perhaps, or a raven, flew past, swooping, gliding, riding the breeze." She closes her eyes, remembering. "It was beautiful—the freedom with which that bird soared, the mountain, planted behind it. But my heart ached."

My throat constricts. Everything in the room seems abruptly clearer, more focused. I lean toward her, force myself to unclench my hands.

"In that moment," she says, "looking at the mountain, I knew I'd made a terrible mistake. All I wanted was to fly free. To be a bird." She touches fingertips to her lips. "But no, I'd become the mountain—my life, my future with Ernesto—permanent. Fixed. I was a mountain—with the heart of a bird."

My own heart threatens to burst. My strong, sure grandmother a caged bird?

She turns from the window, dark eyes piercing. "You, Drina—what I want is for you to be a bird with the heart of a mountain. Grounded. Solid. Understanding you have a place that will always be there for you. Knowing that, you have the freedom to fly wherever your wings take you."

The questions, "How? With who?" stick in my throat.

A wry smile spreads across her face.

"With Alvaro, dear Alvaro, I can finally fly. Life is strange that way. How poor choices can lead you to make better ones. Good to remember, as I think the time is ripe for some difficult choices."

A strain of music interrupts us. It is a *Sevillana*.

"They've found the Victrola. Go on. There's no reason in the world not to dance. All the more important on a day like today. Go on. Feel the life pulse in you. Go."

The music draws me to my feet. My grandmother sits, staring out the window, silhouetted against the sunlight. I hesitate only for a second before I lean over and brush my lips across her soft, cool skin, let my face linger against hers.

Her hand comes up, open palm caressing the contour of my cheek.

I close my eyes and ease into the unfamiliar feeling of being loved.

Chapter 36

The day of the *feria* dawns hot and dry. With only two days of practice in a new place, and worry about Felipe enveloping the house, I feel skittish, unsettled. My father is edgy, barking orders at Renato and me. Camilla is at her worst, casting black looks in my direction when other heads are turned. Marisol and Alvaro stay behind, savoring, I'm sure, an empty, quiet house.

My dress—red cotton with large black dots—clings, sending a trickle of sweat down my back. I hold the huge, ruffled *cola* of my dress up around my shins as Renato helps me out of the car. My hair has been curled and piled high, held in place with shiny combs. Small curlicues are pomaded in front of my ears, and Carlita has placed scarlet flowers around the combs. Long, red, beaded earrings flick against my jaw as I move my head.

Bernardo has polished my mother's shoes. They gleam on my feet. My red, fringed *manton* sashays around my shoulders. I have been transformed. Again and again I finger the pendant hanging at my throat.

As we walk toward the stage area, crowds of people step back, allowing us a clear path. We are special guests. Children point, little girls look at my finery with gaping mouths and wide eyes. Uncomfortable, I look away.

And then, out of nowhere she appears, her raven hair pulled severely back to reveal high cheekbones, lightly rouged cheeks, polished lips. I stop mid-step, torn between my instinct to turn and run, and the urge to confront. For in her arms, plumped like a lovely, ripe, golden berry, I see my Little Red Squirrel. Catching sight of my earrings, she coos, reaches out a chubby arm, small fingers splayed. I cannot breathe, caught as I am in her sight.

My Little Red Squirrel smiles at me, squirms in the woman's arms. My heart stops. Señora Castillo will surely recognize me and scream, hurl accusations, call for help. The moment stretches between us. I wait, my arms, longing to reach for my baby, numb at my sides.

"Oh, Paloma, see the pretty lady," Señora Castillo croons. "Look at her shiny, shiny jewels!" She leans in toward me, turning so that my baby can touch my earrings. I wake from my stupor enough to step closer, tip my head so the jewels swing. I stare, open-mouthed, at my baby, everything inside me swooning as her soft fingers pat my cheek, open and close clumsily around my dangling earrings.

"Oh, don't pull. We don't want to hurt the pretty *señorita*. We want to see her dance!" She jiggles the baby on her hip.

Renato, who has walked ahead, turns, puzzled.

"Drina, come on," he says.

Señora Castillo smiles. "You'd better hurry. Your handsome partner awaits."

And she is gone. Blind to me. I am anonymous. Invisible. Or maybe I am someone entirely new. I feel suddenly empty, lost to myself.

"Drina," Renato says, reaching back for my hand, "What is it? Come! No need to be nervous. We'll be fine!"

I let him lead me on, torn between wanting to look for her, to spot her in the crowd, and wanting to run. Instead, I walk. Follow Renato. Move toward the music. The music, the place I am mostly myself.

We reach the stage where musicians ready their instruments. The tuning of guitars, the chatter of castanets. A crowd forms—fifty or sixty people at first, then a hundred or more, and still they come. My mouth is dry, my palms sweaty. What if . . . What if . . . The number of things that can go wrong bombard me. Forgotten steps, a missed beat. Oh, my *daj*, I can barely breathe! I am here, and not here.

Diego speaks to the musicians, talking through the *llamadas* and tempos. I see him gesturing with his hands, nodding his head. The *cantaor* stares at me admiringly, his eyes trailing from my face down to my neck, my bosoms, down, down the curve of my hips. Renato shoots him a black glance, and the singer turns away. This I see as though watching from the outside.

We climb the stairs to the back of the open-air stage and wait. Then my father is beside us, his hand at the small of my back pushing me forward, the strum of the guitar by the *tocaor*, and Renato is facing me.

"*Olé! Olé!*"

The hundreds of faces blur, their cheering dulls, and all I know is that the music transports me beyond myself.

The raspy, clenched voice of the *cantaor* grabs me by the throat. The castanets urgently roll and clatter, driving my metal-clad shoes. I dig my heels into the floor, straighten my spine. Raking the strings, the *tocaor's* fingers send a rough flourish of sound that launches my arms, arches my back. My chin snaps left, right, and up. The fan in hand blossoms, shielding my face, revealing only my eyes. I dance for my mother. For my Little Red Squirrel. For Isabel. For Boldo.

There is Renato, his face fixed on mine. Bloom of fan withers, closes. I slip it into the bodice of my dress in one fluid move. Arms, hands, fingers, feet speak. Tease. Invite. Demand. Electricity flows between us, eye to eye, and the power we share builds to a climax. Faster, more intense, the rhythm pushes us on, and on, and on . . . I have forgotten the routine, have left it behind in the wave of passion that overtakes me, but somehow Renato moves with me, perhaps by instinct alone.

"*Baila* Drina! *Olé! Olé!*"

The pulse bleeds from me. It is a voice I know. Renato searches my face, alarm pricking his eyebrows.

I will myself to move, and I do, without thinking, but my eyes scan the crowd. "*Baila* Drina!"

I spin, improvising my steps, looking, seeking, needing to find the voice.

There, off to the side, is my Kizzy. She is perched on a large boulder so she can see above the rest.

Somehow I continue to dance as my eyes take her in, bloated with child. Even at a distance, I know she is smiling. She raises a hand and I raise mine, lift my chin in acknowledgement. Others in the *campagna* mingle around the edges of the crowd. I turn, flash a glance over my shoulder. There, Luludja. Snap my head to the right. There, Jofranka. Kizzy stands apart, having taken a dangerous risk in shouting my name—after all, I am *marime*. To the rest, I do not exist, therefore they do not see.

One more bar, one more circle, and she is gone. The rock on which she stood, empty. The music ends, my body freezes in the final position. The crowd roars. Renato takes my hand, bows. I follow his cue. Turn, walk to the back of the stage. They cry for an encore, a collective chant. I keep walking, chin held high, my eyes above their heads so I do not see their faces. My father, before me now, motions for me to turn. Renato takes my hand. I walk on. The crowd seems to think I am playing a coy little game. They shout all the louder.

But I am done.

Renato and Diego are disappointed, confused, this I see.

As we leave, the throng steps back, murmuring, staring after me.

My father's expression slowly changes. He tips his head and looks at me anew.

"Yes," he whispers excitedly, "you're creating a myth!" He speaks quietly, his lips barely moving through his broad, public smile. He nods to the crowd, continues whispering in my ear. "A mystique. Left them begging for more. Brilliant. Absolutely brilliant."

I am taken aback. Does anyone really see me? Or do they just see what they need to see? Renato eyes me curiously. He, at least, senses something more.

Along the fringe we pass booths and vendors. A boy sells newspapers and Diego stops. Pulls a coin from his pocket, puts it in the boy's hand, and folds the paper under his arm.

Bernardo brings the car around. We climb in the back. Beside me, my father nods. "Great, all in all." He touches my arm. "Thought we lost you for a minute, there in the middle, before the *llamada*. But you turned it around. And then, the way you worked that crowd!" He chuckles. I bite my lip. Slump against the seat.

My father relaxes, flips open his paper, and pauses. "Perhaps in Sevilla I'll have the two of you dance separately. In some ways it makes a bigger statement—but we'll leave that to Vicente to decide." Renato and I exchange a glance. My father smoothes the front page with a sweep of his hand and settles in to read.

Suddenly he sits forward.

"Oh my God," he murmurs. "Oh God, no!"

CHAPTER 37

A large photograph of a church, burned and charred, dominates the front page of the newspaper. Billows of smoke pour from the broken windows. Nailed to the massive double doors in front, fluttering like a flag, is Isabel's scarf. Even in the colorless picture, it is impossible to mistake its flouncy silken blooms. Diego shushes our questions with a glance of his hand. As the automobile winds along the route back to the villa, he peers intently at the columns of print, again and again.

Camilla meets us at the door, waving another copy of the newspaper. She speaks in hushed tones, eyes darting this way and that, as though the Nationalists might be nearby, watching. My father pushes past her, her words pinging off him like bugs on a screen.

Marisol and Alvaro sit at the table, shadows darkening their faces. She turns an envelope over in her hands. A newspaper is splayed on the table before them.

"We heard," Marisol says. "Even before the paper, Felipe sent word. A messenger delivered this."

"Who could have been followed here!" Camilla's voice is thin and pinched. "I know he's your brother—your *son*." She shoots a look from Diego to Marisol accusingly, "but we need to distance ourselves from him!"

"What are you suggesting?" Marisol barks. "That we disown him? Banish him?"

"Call it what you will. He has placed us in grave danger! We need to look out for ourselves!"

Marisol snaps, "Well, it *is* what you do best."

Camilla narrows her eyes. "Really? May I remind you that now Felipe is not only a Communist sympathizer but a common criminal?"

"Enough!" My father slams his fist on the table. "This isn't all about you! *Yes*, it is dangerous, *yes*, he made some poor decisions. But he is my brother! My *brother!* Do you even care? At least he has the courage to act on his convictions! I may disagree with him, but I still respect him! Still love him!"

My throat throbs. This is a new Diego. I recognize my sentiment mirrored on Marisol's face. Camilla's mouth drops open. She is, for once, speechless.

Alvaro clears his throat. "It's natural for emotions to flare. But let's focus on the facts. Felipe has survived. We know this. He has safe passage to the south of France. Fortunately, no one was hurt in the blaze. We are here, miles and miles away from these events. Soon you are off to Sevilla. Yes, Camilla, we need to exercise caution. But we do not need to become hysterical."

Camilla points a long, thin finger from one to the other. "Don't say I didn't warn you! I have a good mind to take my son and leave here. Go to my sister in Barcelona."

"*I'm* not going to Barcelona!" Renato's face reddens. "I'm going with Drina and Diego to Sevilla. If you want to go to Barcelona, go ahead." He bolts through the door. I jump as it slams behind him.

"Well, Camilla," Marisol says, "it looks as if you've accomplished something here today, although clearly not what you intended."

Camilla glares. "What are you saying?"

My grandmother shrugs. But it is clear to me. Camilla has made men of them, in giving her husband and son the ammunition to stand up to her.

The moment stretches. "I will pack my things," Camilla says. Her voice is flat. She moves slowly toward the stairs.

"And miss our triumph in Sevilla?" Diego asks sarcastically. "Give up your chance to meet Franco?" She turns and he closes the space between them. "Do what you need to do Camilla. I'm not going to stop you."

"So you think you can toss me aside like you did your Gypsy whore?"

My father's hand flies up, palm open.

"Diego, no!" Marisol cautions.

He drops his arm. Anger contorts his face.

Camilla laughs a bitter laugh. "I certainly won't let my son end up like you," she says, "stuck with an illiterate, half-Gypsy, bastard child!"

Marisol gasps. Oh, my *daj*, I cannot breathe. My face burns. My father closes the space between them.

"You don't know what you're saying!" He speaks softly, but each word explodes. "I loved her mother, but I sent her away. All because I didn't have the balls to stand up to my father. I *swear*, on my father's soul, I won't buckle under again! I have a chance to try to make this up to her . . ."

"And what about *our* life? Her or me, Diego! Stop pretending you can have both!"

Marisol takes my arm, tries to usher me from the room, but I have turned to stone.

"Why do you *do* this Camilla?" My father spits words through clenched teeth. "Nobody's tossing you aside! You force us away! Punish me for a past I can't change. Make me pay for your *own* past as well! Demand that I love you, then put me off every time I try! If you loved me, even a *little*, you'd see that! But you can't see me—you can't see anybody but yourself! So, if you leave, it's *your* choice. *Your choice!*"

Camilla turns and stalks to the stairs. Her high-heeled shoes hammer the marble steps.

In an instant his arms are around me. I rest my face against his chest.

"I'm sorry, Drina . . ."

I melt into him, the rocky places in me crumbling to sand.

"I'll go to her," Alvaro says quietly.

My father sighs and buries his face in my hair. I nestle into the softness of him, unsure if what I feel is a surrender or a defeat. Nothing comes without its price.

"Why not go and get out of that dress," Marisol suggests gently. She's placed her hand gently on my arm, the other on Diego's shoulder. We step apart, and I am both resentful and grateful for the interruption. Without her words I do not know how I might ever step away. My father fixes me in his gaze. I nod, lift the weighty *cola* of my dress to climb the staircase.

In my room I sit on the edge of the bed, exhausted. The effort it will take to undo the row of hooks down the back of my frock is more than I can muster. I lie back, stare at the ceiling. What now?

Then a hollow duet of voices—one deep and slow, the other higher, faster, more intense. They echo along the marble hallways. Alvaro and Camilla, of course, just down the corridor.

I get up. Their words roll toward me as through a tunnel. Alvaro, who championed me from the start. My ally, my friend. Who better than he, in his careful, measured way, to put Camilla in her place once and for all?

Quietly, I move to the other bed, the one closer to the wall. Tilt my head just so to hear them better.

"I suppose you came to help me pack? And escort me out?" Her words drip sarcasm.

"No, Camilla. I thought you might need to talk." Alvaro's calm seems to trigger her wrath.

"Stop playing the righteous do-gooder. I don't need your help!"

"We all need each other, Camilla . . ."

I am impatient with his gentleness. So, apparently, is Camilla. Her voice stretches thin, cuts like a blade.

"You—so superior! The perpetual peacemaker. I know whose interest you have at heart—Marisol's—and that's it. You—so holier than thou—well, I know better! Everyone knows about you and Marisol carrying on, even before Ernesto died . . ."

Her venom strikes even though I'm a room away. Surely Alvaro will not tolerate it. I hold my breath, brace for an explosion. But Alvaro's voice softens.

"On the contrary, I don't see myself as superior to anybody at all. I appreciate others' difficulties. As you've so aptly pointed out, I've had many struggles myself, but I like to believe we all do the best we can. Come Camilla, sit a moment, please . . ."

Silence. I picture them facing one another.

Then, the creak of bedsprings. I can almost feel the rage oozing from her, leaving her spent. I resent both her bitterness and Alvaro's mercy. Why doesn't he chastise her? Put her in her place? Defend himself—Marisol—and me?

"Camilla—Diego loves you, you know . . ."

Loves her? Like loving a badger—a sleek creature with a vicious bite.

"From the beginning, there was always something he held back from me . . ."

"Well, we all have ghosts from our past. Can't you see why he kept quiet? Look what's happened now that his story has been revealed."

I grasp the *peineta* from my hair with trembling fingers,

loosen the pins, shake my tresses free. Fumble to remove the earring from one ear, then the other.

A new sound, a higher pitch, in an undulating rhythm. I tuck my hair behind my ear, incline my head toward the wall.

Camilla is weeping. I want to believe she is posturing for Alvaro, but this is not the sound of vacant tears. I stand, step against the wall, place my forehead against the cool surface.

"When I was a child, my father left, leaving my mother, my sister, and me. I grew up, married, and Renato's father abandoned us. I had to be tough to care for my son . . ."

"Of course, dear, yes, that's what a mother does . . ."

"Now the girl comes along and I'm losing Diego to her! Diego and my son! Her words unravel like tattered cloth. "Everyone I love, I lose."

Alvaro's voice, soft-edged, "You and Drina—have you noticed how your stories are so alike? No wonder your son loves her . . ."

I try to tell myself that I want nothing of her story, except perhaps, her son. But in spite of myself, my hands tremble at her pain. My *mala madrastra*, my wicked stepmother, seems to be melting into something else.

"People think I am so strong, but I'm not. I'm not!"

Alvaro pauses. "Camilla, no one is ever as they appear. Our wounds masquerade in every conceivable way. When I look at you, there are many layers that I see . . ."

How much easier it is, I suddenly realize, not to see.

CHAPTER 38

Two days later the much-anticipated letter from Vicente Herrera arrives. My father takes the envelope from the courier, a frown creasing his brow.

"What is it?" Renato asks.

"The postmark," Diego says. "It's postmarked almost two weeks ago." My heart flips. Could we have missed the date altogether?

Alvaro steps forward, peers at the envelope with a look of distaste. It was his friend at the post in Jerez who was supposed to have the mail forwarded promptly.

My father tears into it, sending a shiver through me. Marisol has appeared, as have Carlita and Bernardo. Camilla suddenly slips into the upstairs hallway, out of my father's view, and hovers along the railing like a ghost. He reads silently. Renato and

I exchange a glance. I have a fleeting urge to reach for his hand, but of course I do not. Finally my father looks up.

"Three days. Three days from now we will dance for Franco. Pack immediately and we'll leave for Sevilla today. Bernardo, go to the telegraph office and send confirmation to Vicente. I only hope he has assumed we would be coming and has not taken our silence as reneging."

Renato's face breaks into a smile. We are leaving for Sevilla. I feel a blush of pleasure at his excitement, followed by a cold shaft of fear. Dancing before the Nationalists . . . I push the thought away.

Bernardo nods, takes the note my father holds between two fingers, and lumbers to the door.

"Renato. Drina. Collect your things. Make sure you leave nothing important behind. Mother, would you and Alvaro like to . . ."

"No," Marisol says. "Alvaro and I will stay behind. There could be news from Felipe, and if we're gone . . ."

Camilla's face clouds over and she goes to the door of the room where she's hidden since their fight. His back still to her, my father cannot see her retreat. But it is as though he senses her presence.

"Camilla," he says, quietly.

She grasps the wrought iron railing.

My father looks down. Exhales softly.

"Pack your most beautiful dress. Please. You know the one—the pale pink, the one that is the color of rosebuds."

His waiting is painful.

"I've always thought it brings out the dark flash of your eyes."

It seems forever before any of us take a breath. She turns from the door, bottom lip trembling. Her knuckles shine white on the rail.

We all stare up at her, all but my father. Alvaro nods her way, ever so slightly.

"All right," she says, almost inaudibly. "The pink . . ."

My father's shoulders relax, and he lifts his head. "Thank you."

I am relieved and disappointed, all at once.

Then everyone is moving—my father down the corridor, Camilla to her room, Marisol and Alvaro out to the terrace, Carlita to the kitchen.

Leaving Renato and me.

He looks about, and when he's certain we're alone, wraps his arms around me. I hadn't realized how much I'd wanted to be touched by him. But I cannot relax. My eyes dart from one door, one corridor, to the next.

"What's wrong? Aren't you happy? We're finally going to Sevilla! Dancing for Franco!"

I recoil at the name—Franco—the syllables so like the harsh sound of the *machinas* of warring men. But can I blame Renato for not understanding? He knows so little of my past. He hadn't heard his mother's ugly words about me the other day, hadn't witnessed the rest of her fight with my father. I am too ashamed to repeat it.

"Nervous, is all . . ."

He smiles. "I know how to fix that." He takes my hand, leads me downstairs to the room where we dance. Where our costumes and shoes are neatly stored. Where we can be alone.

There, he backs me against the cool tiled wall, his hands on my face, in my hair. When he kisses me I forget what he doesn't know and hasn't heard. There are only his lips soft and demanding, his tongue curious, insistent, his eyes closed, body tense against mine. I yield to the whole of him, grasping for proof that I am more than his mother believes. That I am to him what my *daj* was to my father. Yes, yes, I can feel that it is true. That his mother is wrong.

We barely hear my father's step on the stairs, pull away at the last instant. My hand flies to my chin, rubbed raw from our hunger. Renato turns toward the cupboard.

My father walks in, eyes us for a moment. He is flustered, his intention forgotten, but he sees.

"Please," is all he says quietly, looking between us. I understand all that the single word holds. There is nothing I can promise in response. And I see that he understands this as well. It is only Renato who cannot see, who busies himself with the shoes and clothing, who tries to distract with the opening and closing of doors and drawers.

"I'll help you," is what my father finally says. And we pack, all three of us, grateful for something to busy ourselves with.

By the time we lug the trunks up to the sidewalk, Carlita has laid out a meal and Bernardo has returned from the telegraph office. The big black car hums at the curb. Marisol and Alvaro sit at the table and press us to eat, to wrap something for the ride, to drink. "You must keep up your strength."

Jamón and *manchego,* olives and pistachios, oranges, sherry. We grab, nibble, sip, anxious to be off. Alvaro and Marisol walk us to the door.

My grandmother takes my hands.

"I am proud of you," she whispers, squeezing my fingers in hers. "Remember—a bird with the heart of a mountain. There is *nothing* you cannot do, Drina Honoria Muentes. I will be with you—here—the whole time." She lets go and pats her palms over her heart, then reaches into her pocket and hands me a small wrapped parcel. I remove the red silk ribbon, let the bundle of white folded tissue hatch in my open palm.

It is a comb carved from abalone shell, crafted into the shape of a bird—wings spread, beak open, as if singing. I allow it to nest in my hand for a moment, then secure it firmly in my hair.

As my tears well, she grins wickedly. "And when you dance for Franco, dazzle him senseless! The Republic—and your uncle Felipe—will thank you!" I smile, throw my arms around her.

"One more thing," she says, suddenly serious. "Do not forget that this is wartime. There can be unexpected confusion, chaos." She presses a small cream-colored paper into my hand. Points to the print. "If you should get separated, this is the address here. You'll need to know the way back home." Again her hand flies to her chest. I stare at the mysterious marks on the page, and at her. Carefully tuck the paper into the slot in my luggage tag. "Now go," she says, nudging me toward the car.

Camilla appears, a valise in each hand, and climbs in front. I am relieved that I will not need to look at her. Renato and I get in back. My father slides behind the wheel.

We wave to Alvaro, Marisol, Bernardo, and Carlita. They remain on the cobbled walk until the car rounds the bend. I've placed my finely embroidered shawl, my *manton,* across the back seat. Renato slips his right hand beneath it, exploring the shrouded space between us. My left hand follows. We gaze out the side windows, my eyes to the right, Renato's to the left, noticing little of the blurred colors of Cadiz, focusing instead on the dancing of our fingers beneath the shawl. Our fingertips touch until intertwined under the covers of lacy fabric. Our secret teases a smile from the edges of my mouth. With my right hand I adjust the abalone bird perched in my hair. The smooth, polished shell reassures me of many things.

I ride, strengthened on one side by the partnering of our hands, bolstered on the other by my bird poised for flight. My father and Camilla stare straight out the windshield, their silence filling the car to overflowing.

Chapter 39

The evening is hot and steamy, and the air in the private *peña* where the party is taking place is thick and heavy with smoke. The stuccoed walls hold photographs of dancers and singers, famous *cantaors* and *tocaors* dressed in colorful finery, in dramatic poses. There are many tables all covered in white linens. Beautiful women and military men lean toward one another, speaking and laughing, smoking expensive cigarettes, tipping heads to the side and elegantly blowing smoke over their shoulders. The sight of so many men in uniform chills me, conjuring memories I would prefer to forget. A man they call Oro, the owner of the *peña*, seems to appear everywhere at once, fawning and flashing his toothy white smile over guests to his right, while snarling over his shoulder at employees. Waiters slip through the crowd with trays of *tapas* and pitchers of *sangria,* replenishing drinks, setting heaping platters before them. The guests lift glasses, gesture with their hands, throw back their heads and laugh.

My eyes scan the room until they settle on the stage—a deep, elevated wooden dance floor along one side of the wall. A wave of panic seizes me. They have decided—my father and Vicente—that I will dance alone. To better focus their attention on something new and exciting, as my father put it. But who am I to dance for these grand, powerful people? The hum of conversation, the clink of silverware, and the counterpoint of laughter dim as I force my attention to the music inside my head, to the beat and rhythm that own me. I must let the music sweep me away, let my body become one with it. This I tell myself, but can I accomplish it?

Renato and I are led to a pair of dressing areas behind the stage. Camilla is supposed to help me into my outfit, to lift and juggle the heavy rows of its ruffling *cola,* to fasten the parade of small buttons along the curve of my spine. But Vicente has stopped to introduce her and my father to this dignitary and that. I am impatient for her to come, yet dread her arrival.

There is no time to waste. I hang my dress on the hook, lay out my shoes and *manton,* my brush and combs, hairpins and jewelry. Sweat trickles down my back.

Alone, I close the door, remove my street clothes. They drop, then puddle around my ankles. I push them aside with my bare foot, fan myself with my hand, pat the perspiration from my brow. I gingerly take my dress from the hanger, step carefully between the blossoming petals of scarlet fabric. Pull it up over my breasts, slip my arms through the ruffled, capped sleeves. Hoist. Reach behind to try to fasten a button or two, but no. It is impossible. Instead, I pick up my brush, drag it through my hair. Again and again, maybe twenty times, maybe one hundred. Where is she?

There is a knock and the door abruptly opens. I brace for Camilla. A woman in a deep blue silken robe sweeps in.

"I had to see for myself this new young thing everyone is whispering about! I certainly hope that you live up to your advance billing!"

She is striking, her jet black hair streaked with a single slash of gray, as though someone had drawn a brush with silver gilt through that one lock. She raises her chin for a better look at me, tossing her thick mane over her shoulder. Neither young nor old, she is more handsome than beautiful, her strong face full of confidence. Her presence fills the room.

"Come dear, you do speak, don't you?"

I nod, blush. "Yes," I mumble. I feel the color darken my cheeks.

"Well," she says, smiling, "I do hope you have greater ease on the dance floor than you do with conversation!"

I cannot tell if she is teasing or trying to humiliate me. "I hope so, too," I say.

She lifts my hair from my shoulders, winds it back to study my face. "Well," she says, "at least you pass the first test."

"The first test?"

"At least you look good. These military types love that." She extends her hand. "Lola Vega, darling. I know your father."

"Oh, Señora Vega!"

"Let me help you with that dress. You can't do it alone! Where is that stepmother of yours?"

Stepmother? The word renders me dumb. If Lola Vega notices, she says nothing, her fingers already at the small of my back, coaxing buttons through loops, adjusting seams with a tug and a pat, lifting and shaking where fluffing is needed.

"Now your hair . . ."

I sit, mute, while she expertly sweeps and coils, tucks and curls, adjusting pins and clamping combs into place.

"Your *peineta*?"

"Yes, here." I hold out the fanlike tortoise shell crowning comb and the abalone bird.

"Lovely," she murmurs. I try not to wince as she pins my coif securely in place. I slip in my earrings, the ones that mesmerized my Little Red Squirrel.

"There!" she says finally, swiveling me toward the mirror.

My eyes widen.

"Indeed," she says. "You'd better dance as well as you look!"

"Lola," a voice calls.

"*Si, si,*" she shouts, rolling her eyes. "Coming." She studies her reflection for a moment. "Now I need to pretty up."

"Thank you!" I'm left with my image staring back at me in the large looking glass above the dressing table.

Voices in the hall—Lola's and another. "Too late. She doesn't need you now," I hear Lola saying. "By the time you got yourself here the poor thing would have fainted dead away."

In the mirror I see Camilla rushing in, flustered, her face red. "I'm sorry," she says. "I didn't mean to be—"

"It's all right. Señora Vega helped me. I'm all ready."

She looks away first, takes a deep breath, then meets my eyes. "You look . . . quite beautiful."

"Thank you," I manage. My eyes sweep over her pale pink satin gown that flows around her body in soft waves. I swallow. "So do you—look beautiful."

Camilla's face colors and her fingers flutter across her throat.

"That is kind of you to say . . . Drina."

It is the first time she has addressed me by name. "And you were kind to come." It seems I should call her by name as well, but "Camilla" seems forward, and what else can I call her?

"Well then . . ." She opens the door, steps around it.

"Good luck. You and Renato . . ."

"Yes. Thank you."

She leaves me. My heart is still pounding as I hear Renato's music begin, take in the sound of his footwork, gauge the progress of his routine by the applause of the crowd. It is over, it seems, in a heartbeat, and then he appears at my door, flushed and breathless, sweat trickling down his face. I do not need to ask how the performance went. As our eyes meet, I see a fire that I have never seen before. Beside him, Vicente gestures to me. "Five minutes," he beams. "Ah, but you look lovely! Truly arresting! Your father did not exaggerate!"

"I told you," Renato gasps. "She'll be wonderful." Vicente laughs and we follow him down a long, narrow hallway. The shoes of my *daj* carry me closer and closer to the buzz of voices, the distant strains of music, one small stride at a time. Each step echoes in my ears.

I touch the pendant at my throat, the precious metal cool against my fingers.

Gently caress Marisol's bird in my hair.

There, the stage door. There, my father. A few steps more. There, the faces of the crowd. Renato steers me forward, his hand on the small of my back. The curtain swishes aside. A blinding light.

I blink.

A wave of applause.

The music begins.

CHAPTER 40

"Olé! Olé!"

The music, raw and sharp. Rough, but smooth.

I throw myself into it. Surrender. My heels hammer the floor like the roll of a *machina*. My head, I throw back. Arms become wings of a bird. I fly.

Soar.

The *tocaor* rakes his guitar. Slashes the strings with furious fingers.

I am here, but not here.

There, the crack of castanets. I dance, sense my *daj* watching in the shadows, Little Red Squirrel in her arms. Inside my soul they dwell.

"Olé! Olé!" The *cantaor's* neck swells in ropes of tension. His hands jab the air as he sings, calling Kizzy to heart. *Baila* Drina!

Now the *cantaora* points right. In my mind I see Marisol, then my father. My fingers curl and blossom like lilies. Chin up—Felipe. Down—Isabel. My body dips and swings with the Arroyos dangling from their balustrade. The shoes of my *daj* pummel the floor where the memory of the yellow-haired man lies. Then Boldo—my body contorts, face twists. The many threads of my heart, woven through the dance.

The final chord. I freeze. A moment of silence. And then the crowd roars.

I open my eyes. They are on their feet. Their applause like the winging of a thousand birds.

CHAPTER 41

Oro, with his blinding smile, escorts me off the stage and into the audience where Renato waits. The musicians begin to play a set before my father and Señora Vega go on. Renato and I acknowledge the crowd, *"Gracias! Gracias!"* I try not to recoil as many men in olive *militar* uniforms bow, take my hand. Vicente, Oro, Diego, and Camilla join us, shaking hands, exchanging meaningless talk.

It is then I remember the great Francisco Franco. Where is he? Many times I have seen his likeness on the posters and pamphlets—the high forehead, drooping eyes, small, thick moustache. I scour the faces of our admirers, searching the room. Where is the head table, the place of honor? It is said that

Franco is felt but not seen. He is mysterious, reclusive. Perhaps, after all this fuss, the famous *Generalisimo* is not here?

But no, there he is, seated at a small table, a group of six military men surrounding him. One younger officer stands, motions for us to approach. "Ah, this is the lovely flower—even more beautiful up close!"

The *Generalisimo* smiles, just a little, as if saving the motion for something more important. "You have made your father and mother proud," he proclaims, lifting his chin toward Diego and Camilla. No one points out to the *Generalisimo* that Camilla is not my mother. I think of my *daj* and hope his words are possible—that I have made her proud. "In your dancing you have captured the spirit of the new Spain as well."

I stare at him as he speaks, trying to see whatever quality it is that makes men fear and follow him. But this I cannot detect. To me he seems a small, tightly wrapped knot of a man with rather ordinary features. If not for his erect carriage, the measured manner in which he speaks, and the way those around defer to him, I would guess him to be a common clerk, perhaps a butcher. For a moment, I see him in a white apron smeared with blood, behind the meat counter, wielding a cleaver. The waxy legs of *jamón* hanging from hooks surrounding him, waiting to be carved. I think suddenly of Isobel and Felipe. Hadn't they too envisioned the spirit of a new Spain? A Spain very different from the one this man is forcing on us. "I'm certain you have a stellar career ahead," he says, as one who is used to having whatever he says come to pass.

"*Gracias,*" I manage. I cast my eyes down as if out of respect. But in my mind I spit on the ground. Yet even as I imagine this, a small part of me, I am ashamed to admit, is pleased by his compliments. My father thanks the *Generalisimo* profusely, shakes his hand, then leaves to prepare for his dance with Lola Vega.

The tall, youngish officer who beckoned us looks from General Franco to me. "The general is very pleased," he whispers, leaning toward me. "*Very* pleased." He presents me with a rose—vivid gold with bold scarlet edges.

"*Muchas gracias.*" I accept the bloom, sniff the unfolding petals. Its perfume is heady, sweet. "Ahhh . . ."

The officer nods, his eyes creeping from my face to my throat, to my breasts. "It *is* lovely," he says, looking back into my eyes. "But it pales in comparison to you, my dear."

My skin crawls. I cross my arms, hug my torso, glance toward Renato to see if he's overheard.

Thankfully, Vicente sweeps over, ushers us away, speaking softly all the while. "I am told the *Generalisimo* is not one for chitchat or idle praise—from him, his words of admiration—effusive! Now, there are other key players here. I'll seat you where you can make an impression. Be charming. When in doubt, smile." This, I can tell, is directed toward me.

"Renato, go and get the ladies something to drink. Come Drina, Camilla, sit here." He places us on opposite sides of a long table. Camilla immediately extends her hand to a couple beside her. I remain frozen in my chair. What to say? Vicente said to smile. Will I not look like a fool, grinning stupidly at strangers? I force a smile that feels more like a grimace, and stare into my lap. Suddenly, a hand on my shoulder. Thank goodness! "Renato," I say, turning.

"Not your handsome young dancer, I'm afraid." It is the officer who brought us to Franco, who gave me the rose, now wilting on the table before me. I glance at Camilla for help, but she is deep in conversation.

"Capitán Guajardo," he announces. "Come, I can see the heat is getting to you. I will escort you toward the window where you can get some air."

"No, really, I'm just . . ."

"Don't worry dear, I don't bite. There are just some opportunities for all of you that I'd like to discuss."

Camilla sees us. Her eyes tell me to get up. Capitán Guajardo takes my hand. "Come."

I rise, knees weak. I will not walk outside with him, will not be alone with a *militar*, no matter how important he is.

Linking his arm through mine, he leads me to a table near the door. A beautiful woman approaches and stops. Glares at me, and then at him. With hardly a glance he dismisses her. She sighs loudly, stalks off. He seems not to notice. Snaps his fingers and a waiter appears.

"Get the señorita a libation, some refreshment. *Vino fino*? Oloroso?"

I hesitate. Scan the room for Renato. "*Vino fino*," I mumble, and as an afterthought, "thank you." Renato will come back and find me talking with this man, who pulls out a chair, gestures broadly. "Please, join me, Señorita Drina."

I take the seat, reluctantly, the dress binding me, making it hard to breathe. I fold my hands in my lap. He sits in the chair opposite me, leans back, crosses his legs, fingers clasped around his knee. "Tell me, Señorita Drina, are you shy?"

It is as though he is talking to a puppy. I shrug. Grit my teeth. Look away.

"Not bashful on the dance floor though. Not at all. I like that. The dance exposes a hidden side of you. Offstage, a demure little kitten. Onstage, a tigress."

A chill ripples my skin. I wrap my arms protectively around myself.

"Ah, but I'm making you uncomfortable. Forgive me, please." He smiles, showing his large, straight white teeth. "You know, Drina, you are gorgeous in a dark, mysterious way. It captures a man's imagination."

I shake my head. "Capitán Guajardo . . ."

"Salvador. Please call me Salvador."

"Capitán . . ."

"Salvador."

"Capitán Salvador . . ."

"I am a powerful man, Drina. I can make all kinds of things happen. Can make you a star. Introduce you to the right people. You have talent. Looks. Presence. Tell me, what is it your heart longs for?"

I hesitate. "Nothing, really. Nothing . . ."

"Oh, come now. Every woman holds a secret desire. And often, the man who can deliver the object of that desire becomes intriguing. Indispensible. That's what I'd like to be. Indispensable and intriguing to a stunning creature such as you."

In my gut a slow rage continues to churn. What do I want? Can this arrogant jackal undo what happened to my mother? To Isabel? Felipe? I stare at him and my mouth becomes a thin line, my teeth grind together.

"Is that a little feistiness I see?" His eyes narrow. A sly grin curves his mouth. "Oh, how I appreciate that in a woman! A sign of passion! All right then. I relish a challenge. Name your desire, Drina! I will see that it comes to pass. And when I do, you'll look at me differently. Of this I am certain."

Something beyond my control rises. Brings me to my feet. "You can give me anything?"

He licks his lips. "Yes. I daresay that I can."

"What will I owe you?"

"Well, Drina, I'm impressed. You are nobody's fool! It's very simple. Dance for me again. Lola Vega can arrange it. I'm confident the rest will follow."

My eyes dart about the room for Renato. He is carrying a pitcher of *sangria* to the table where we sat. Soon he will see that I am missing and come looking for me.

I take a deep breath. "There is a man—one of my people. He was captured by your army and imprisoned here in Sevilla. His only crime, that he helped me in my hour of greatest need. Find and release him. Then I will dance for you again."

"Is that all?" He chuckles, but at once becomes earnest. "He could be dead, you do realize that?"

"He isn't dead. I know it here." I tap my heart.

"Your hero's name?"

"Boldo."

"His family name?"

"I . . . don't know," I mumble, trying to hide my shame. I conjure up a bravado I do not feel. "A powerful man such as you should be able to find a *Gitano* named Boldo. He is a falconer. There cannot be two such men."

"And when I have released this prisoner, will you run off with him? I'm sure this would displease your father greatly, not to mention your young partner. And me."

Renato sees me, waves. Time is short. "Is this really a concern for one as confident and capable as you, Capitán? Salvador?"

He stands, a glint of amusement and something else in his black eyes. "I'm glad, Drina, you don't underestimate me. No one should underestimate me."

I glance across the room, smile over the crowd at Renato. The effort it takes strains my face. "One more thing," I say, turning back toward him. The Capitán raises an eyebrow. "How will I know you've done it—that you've released him?"

"Oh, you'll know."

He lifts my hand, brings it to his lips. Head tipped toward my fingers, he averts his eyes. "I will come back with proof. Then you will deliver your part of the bargain."

CHAPTER 42

Exhausted, the dancing done, party finished, we walk back down the long, narrow corridor toward our dressing rooms. My father and Lola laugh and talk, basking in our success. Renato watches me anxiously. The secret within presses on my spirit like a weight. Builds a wall between us. Confused by my reticence, Renato hovers too close. I want to reach out to him, but I cannot. The implications of my agreement with the Capitán paralyze me. *What if . . . what if . . . what if . . .* A million questions fly around my head like a swarm of anxious bees.

"What's wrong?" Renato asks, taking me aside. I feel his warm breath on my neck, close my eyes.

"The heat, the sangria . . . the excitement." My words fade, sounding false even to me.

"No, Drina, there's something else. Tell me." His dark eyes search mine.

"I . . . I wish my mother had been here." I am, at once, ashamed of this excuse and surprised by the truth of it.

"Yes, of course, but aren't you happy? Excited about our performances? The audience loved us! Didn't you hear the applause?"

"Yes. It was exciting." Even as I say this, I realize it is not the applause that excites. The dancing, for me, is like food, water, air. Sustenance. Another truth I cannot explain.

"It's my mother, isn't it? I know how Camilla can be. But she'll come around, I promise you."

It is an effort to speak. To focus. About his mother—at least about this I must be honest. "Renato, I know it hasn't been easy for her. To learn about my mother. And me. She's suffered many losses. I am going to try harder. I think it will be better. It already is."

He gathers me in his arms, speaks into my hair. "This is why I love you. I want us to be together forever, Drina. We can have a wonderful life. Things will improve. I know it."

My heart pounds. I feel myself dissolving into him. He takes hold of my shoulders, holds me at arms' length, his face suddenly animated. "Listen—Vicente spoke to Diego. We have the chance to dance in Barcelona. My mother has family just outside the city. We'll go there. Make a name for ourselves. A name we share."

"Drina!"

I turn toward Lola's voice, then back to Renato. He stares at me, lips parted, waiting. "Yes," I say, to whom, I'm not certain.

"Drina—a word with you! Come, come." Señora Vega motions for me to follow her into her dressing room.

"Lola wants me . . ."

Renato nods. "It seems everyone does." He pulls back. "Go. Talk to her." I cannot read the dark look in his eyes as he turns and disappears into his dressing room. I pause for a moment, staring at the place where he stood, then hurry down the hallway toward Señora Vega.

I follow her inside, my head cluttered with words . . .

Name your desire . . .

Your hero's name?

Boldo . . .

I realize she is watching me closely. "Where were you just then?" she asks. "Far away, that much I know."

I shrug. What is there I can say?

She sits down at the dressing table facing the mirror, unpinning her hair, dabbing cream on her face. "Well," she says, "you have a lot to think about."

I panic. Does she know about my conversation with the Capitán?

"Be a dear and unbutton this dress for me, would you? It's strangling me!"

I fumble with the buttons.

"I take it Diego didn't have the chance to tell you?"

"Tell me what?"

She steps out of her dress and into a stylish skirt and satin blouse. Reaches for a pair of pearl earrings. Dabs perfume behind her ears, between her breasts.

"I want to offer you a place in the troupe I'm putting together."

My mouth drops open. "You want me to dance with you? But . . . what about Renato? And my father?"

"Look, Drina—Renato is talented. Attractive." She purses her lips, turns her head, picks up a hand mirror and eyes her profile. "But, face it—he doesn't have the same presence you possess." She puts the mirror down, powders her nose.

"But, my father—"

"Wants the best for you. And that's what I can provide. He recognizes your potential and understands my influence. When I promote someone, people notice." She snaps the compact closed. "I'd love to see how much of the mother lives on in the daughter."

"What? What do you mean?"

"Your mother and I danced together when we were young. The two of us—we complemented one another. We were friends. Good friends. Confidentes. Listen. From Nadja I learned how to empty myself, to let the music consume me. She had *duende*—that mysterious undercurrent of darkness that wrenches the hearts of everyone who watches. You have it too. Let me teach you. Help you. In your mother's memory."

I finger the pendant at my throat, the familiar longing quickening my heart. The great Lola Vega offering me a part of my mother I never knew . . .

She looks absently in the mirror, applies a bit of rouge. "Diego never really recovered from losing her, you know—even though her leaving was of his own doing."

I swallow hard. "Señora Vega—does Renato know? About what you're suggesting?"

"He was there when I posed it to your father. Disappointed, to say the least. But he'll get over it. They always do."

Something inside me sinks. Had he spoken words of love, or something else?

I stare at this woman who possesses a part of my mother I have never experienced. It is all I can do to hold back the hundred questions burning in my throat.

Lola looks into the mirror, pulls the *peineta* and several pins from her hair. It tumbles around her shoulders in a rich dark wave. She runs a hand through it distractedly, shakes her head to loosen it further. She stops, turns from the mirror to face me.

"You'll need to decide quickly. I make an offer once, and once only. If all goes well, we'll leave on tour in a month or so. In the meantime, Oro has invited us to perform here at the *peña*. A way to practice, to gain experience together."

She pauses, studying me closely. "And make no mistake—you still have a lot to learn. Quite a lot. To be blunt, what you have going for you in style and passion you lack in technique and experience. Without that you will never realize the potential I believe you possess." She pauses, examines me closely. "I will tell you right now that I will not coddle you or afford you any special privileges because of my relationship with your mother and your father. That would do you an injustice." She turns back to the mirror, adjusts her collar, loosens one more button of her blouse, revealing her deep cleavage.

"Well, I . . . I'll have to think about it. Talk to my father . . ."

"Of course, you must."

There is a knock on the door. "Coming, darling!" She flips her hair over her shoulder, adjusts her skirt. Then she glides out of the dressing room.

I step into the corridor and watch her go. She is already on the arm of a *militar*, moving toward the stage door. She tips her head until it rests on his shoulder.

When they round the corner the man glances back. Smiles wickedly.

Our eyes meet.

It is Capitán Salvador Guajarda.

Chapter 43

Walking home from the *peña*, Renato is a silent presence beside me. Though we walk shoulder to shoulder, I feel a great glaring distance between us. Many strides in front of us, Diego and Camilla talk together with such animation that they seem not to notice us at all. It is as though they have become us, and we them. Looking straight ahead, I take a deep breath. "Lola told me things I would have thought to hear from you. Would you have professed love for me if she hadn't invited me to join her troupe?"

"That isn't fair, Drina. Don't you know how I feel about you after all this time?"

"I thought I did."

"And now you don't believe it? Because I want you to stay with me? Can you blame me? I don't want to lose you."

I can find nothing wrong with his explanation. I am flattered by his words of love, but there is something that hankers. Like a mosquito bite I continue to scratch until it bleeds. "I wish you'd told me first about what Lola was going to ask me."

"I wanted you to know what you'd be leaving behind." He stops. Closes the distance between us. Runs his finger along my forearm.

I step back. "And what if I decide to go with her? Will that change the way you feel?"

He pulls me to him, my cheek against his chest, wraps his arms around me. His breath warm against my ear. "If you love me, you'll come to Barcelona."

I stiffen. Lift my head.

"What if Lola invited all of us?"

"She didn't. And she won't."

"I never said I wanted to go with her."

"You haven't said you don't."

"She knows things about my mother."

"So does your father!"

As we approach the door to our hotel, an olive drab military sedan drives up and slows. The back window rolls down and Lola Vega's face appears. "Goodnight all! Diego, we'll talk. Breakfast in the morning to square things up?"

My father waves, looks at me, his eyes alight with excitement. The car pulls away from the curb. Diego takes my elbow, ushers me toward the stairs. Renato stomps up the steps ahead of us, flings open the door, and disappears inside. Camilla seems exuberant. "You've made quite an impression," she says. I wonder if she's referring to Lola, Renato, or the Capitán.

Inside, Camilla heads upstairs. My father lingers. "Drina . . . sit. Have a drink with me. Talk about tonight."

I follow him into the small bar with its shelves of books and soft leather chairs. He unstops a bottle of sherry and pours two small glasses. Puts them on a tray with a bowl of pistachio nuts and places it on the table before us. I sink into the cushions, exhausted.

"Before I say anything else, you have to know how spectacular you were tonight. I was so proud of you."

His eyes sparkle with admiration. I think of the moment months ago when I prayed to my *daj*, asking her how to win my father's heart. *Dance* . . . She was right. A rush of pleasure rises and then drops. I push away the feeling that there is something more I want from him.

"I know Lola spoke to you. Are you excited?"

I look down, unable to speak.

"Drina, you have to realize what an opportunity this is. You could spend a lifetime waiting for such a chance. To make a name for yourself."

Drina Honoria Muentes—I remember how it felt to hear my name for the first time—how it bridged past and present. "I have a name," I mumble, as much to myself as to him.

"I mean a name everyone knows. That inspires applause. Adulation."

I stare at him, thinking of tonight's applause—how it felt

like an intrusion, dragging me from the place inside where I go while I dance. And yet something thrills in me. To dance, dance, dance. How many years I longed to let my soul soar. How many years my *daj* denied me.

"Drina, do you hear me?"

"Yes."

"Vicente has a contract for Renato and me in Barcelona. Naturally, he'd love to have you as well. But he understands."

"Understands what?"

"That you'd never turn Lola down."

I close my eyes, think of Renato, the way he looks at me, how he holds me, how we . . .

"But . . ." I falter, the feeling of loss choking me. "Can't we all just go to Barcelona together?"

"Drina, listen." He takes my hands. "This is how we can fulfill your mother's dream. Her legacy. She would have been a star if not for me."

"You mean, if not for me." I swallow tears.

"No. I was the one who stood in her way. I won't make the same mistake twice."

"She never wanted me to dance."

"That was in the past. Now you can dance for both of you—set her spirit free."

Something in me clutches and holds. For my *daj* . . . my father . . .

"It's not forever. Only until your career is launched. In the meantime, Lola will take good care of you. But she'll push you hard. She is a taskmaster, but when you consider what you'd learn . . . After you've given it a fair chance, if you're unhappy, you can join us in Barcelona. I'll leave you the train fare. The choice will be yours."

I hear the words but do not feel as though I am choosing anything.

"It's late. Get some sleep. In the morning everything will seem clearer."

I nod, leave the library, my glass of sherry untouched. Scale the staircase to the dimly lit corridor leading to my room. The small, yellowish sconces throw imposing shadows. My silhouette stretches monstrously across the wall. I cannot catch up to it—it continues to loom before me, bigger than life. A dark ghost I cannot overtake. I hurriedly insert the key, unlock the door.

"Drina, wait."

I turn. "Renato."

"Shh! Let me come in, just for a minute."

I pull him by the hand, close the door behind us.

"Drina, I heard what Diego said. I know you don't want to do this. You want to be with me. Don't go with Lola. Or stay a day or two with her, for your father. Then tell him you didn't like it. That you missed us. Say whatever you have to, as long as you get on the train to Barcelona. Then we can be together like we are here. Please don't make me beg."

I open my mouth to tell him that no one has asked what I want, but I am silenced by his kisses. Kisses charged with a new urgency. Love? Pain? My body melts into his. The kisses

I return are deep and dark as *duende*. Longing tinged with something else. Gasping, he pulls away. "Was that yes, or was it goodbye?"

I do not answer. I reach toward his cheek but he takes a step back. "Remember this. I'll be waiting for you in Barcelona."

CHAPTER 44

What will tomorrow bring? I toss and turn, wrestling with the bedclothes. Sleeping fitfully, my anxious thoughts blur into dark dreams . . .

Boldo holding the string of dead hares. But no—they are wingless birds, plucked of feathers. He proudly holds one out to me. It has the face of my daj. I turn, run. Run! Unable to scream. Trip across train tracks. A locomotive thunders past. My father and Renato in the window of a passenger car. I wave. Cry out. But they do not see me. Cannot hear me. A brightly painted vardo follows the train, pulled by a sway-backed mule. The driver reins in the beast. Reaches for me. Capitán Guajarda, the yellow-haired man, sits beside him. "Don't make me beg," he says.

I awake with a start, my heart racing. The morning sun glares in my eyes. I get up, shower, dress carelessly, leave my hair wet and unplaited, walk down to the breakfast room. They are all there—Camilla, Diego, and Renato, plus Lola Vega. Renato sees me first. He leaves the table, creating a place for me. We exchange stiff, public smiles.

The rest look up, stirring their coffee, spreading pastry with jam. "Sit. Sit," my father calls. "I'll get you a plate."

"It is all arranged," Lola says brightly, as my father assembles my breakfast. "Of course you're feeling a bit unsettled. Who wouldn't? It's all very sudden. But not to worry. Your father has told me he's giving you fare to Barcelona in case I'm too hard on you." She and Camilla chuckle.

I pick at my food. My father hands me a small white envelope—train fare, I imagine. My insurance. And a slip of paper pressed in my palm with an address, a number that I am to tuck behind my luggage tag beside the slip Marisol gave me. Marisol!

A hollow feeling envelops me. I coax many thoughts to fill this empty space—notions of pleasing my father, fulfilling my mother. Returning to Renato. Of dancing. But still . . . the vacant place threatens to swallow me up.

Diego, Camilla, and Renato make preparations to leave as Lola waits for us to say our goodbyes. Somehow I remember how to place one foot in front of the other and walk with them to the curb. How quickly my fate unfolds. I force myself to smile as Vicente drives up. Hug them all, even Camilla. Renato, I embrace quickly, avoiding his eyes. Seeing what is before me is too difficult. His hand lingers on the back of my neck, then creeps up to the base of my skull. He gently lifts my damp hair, his fingers weaving through the limp strands, sending a shiver through me. He glances over his shoulder toward the car and back, pleading with me once more, with his eyes alone, to follow him. When I look away, he pauses for a long second, lets his hands drop, and leaves me.

My father remains beside me as Renato loads the automobile, Camilla settled in the front seat, watching through the window. "I am so proud of you, Drina." He looks at me in such a way that my throat thickens with emotion. His gaze holds mine. In his eyes I see the eyes of Marisol and Felipe mirrored. And yes, even mine. The Muentes eyes, deep and heavily lashed, full of a past we share. He pulls me to him, and I realize that I know the feel of his arms, his scent. My father, familiar to me after all the years of unknowing. This, I will hold close in his absence. He whispers into my hair, "I do love you, Drina. You'll see—this will all work out. And then we'll all dance together in Barcelona."

All of this I want to believe. I do not look back as the car pulls away. Finger the white envelope tucked carefully in my pocket.

Within the hour I have collected my bags and wait at the door with Señora Vega. The car of Capitán Guajardo pulls up. I see him sitting in the front beside the driver. He springs out, relieves me of my bags, and I slip in the back beside Lola. As we pull away, I glimpse his eyes in the rearview mirror, trying to engage mine. I stare, instead, out the side window, the sights of Sevilla flashing past. In scant minutes we are delivered to the hotel where the troupe will be staying.

"Be a dear and grab these bags, Salvador, would you?" Lola leads the way into the lobby. I follow a step or two behind. I feel the Capitán at my heels, see his shadow on the pavement, overtaking mine.

"It may take a week or so for me to free your man," he whispers, his lips barely moving, "but you've been patient this long, no?" I feel my face flush and I nod just enough for him to notice. He drops the bags beside Lola at the desk where she retrieves my key.

"Thank you, darling," Lola says, barely casting him a side-long glance.

"When will I have the pleasure of seeing you and your new charge dance again?"

Lola waves her hand. "Speak to Oro." She leans toward him, kisses the air beside his cheek dismissively, and turns toward the stairs. A young clerk gathers our bags and marches behind her. "Come along, Drina," Lola calls. "We've a busy day ahead."

"I'll be eagerly awaiting your next performance," the Capitán says, discretely brushing his finger across my arm. "Until then . . ." Without meeting his eyes, I follow Lola up the staircase. It is a relief to put space between us.

I barely have a moment to arrange my belongings before Lola calls for me. The morning is filled with fittings, being measured and wrapped and pinned into billows of brightly colored fabric, dotted and laced. A man comes with a crate of shoes, but no, this is where I put my foot down. There will be no shoes but those of my *daj*. We agree, instead, to have them repaired and reinforced, polished and shined right there where I can watch him.

After a brief lunch we walk to the peña where I will meet the troupe before rehearsals begin. In minutes we arrive, and inside, I meet a group of other young dancers. One named Luz, another Inez. And the young men, Jorge, Hernán, and Lope. They eye me curiously, sizing me up. The girl named Inez smiles. Her round face and dark eyes shine. An open, curious face, so like my Kizzy's. A shred of hope teases me. This one, perhaps, could be a friend.

Strains of a guitar or two, the chatter of castanets, the friendly banter of musicians—*tacaors* and *cantaors*—drifts in from the large open hall where the practice is to begin. "All right, dancers," Lola calls, clapping her hands, "Let's get started." I pull on my shoes, secure the straps, shake out my legs and arms, roll my neck, priming my body. My nerves are tense, muscles tight. I watch the others casually take their places, their bodies relaxed and loose. They converse together easily. Is no one else worried? Does no one else wonder where to stand, what to expect? I try to adjust my expression to match theirs, while pretending not to stare, find a spot not too close but not too far from anyone else, toward the back so that I can watch and imitate, no matter which direction I face. Beg my pulse to slow—how can I dance with a galloping heart?

Lola steps to the front, her feet in a T position, then right foot forward. We all follow, reach, stretch, hands undulating, waving, arms rolling like snakes. Loose, loose. I begin to relax.

I can follow her lead through this simple warm-up. She speaks firmly as she moves, "Arms up, inhale . . . stretch. Lean back, arch, tuck the navel, drop the hips."

Just as I begin to forget my fear she says, "*Plie* . . . straighten. *Demi plié* . . ." Her feet are turned out, knees bent. "Fifth," she calls. Without hesitation their arms fly up over their heads. "One, two, three, four-up-five, six, seven, eight . . . *Port de bras* . . . elbows lifted . . ."

I know the movements, not the names, so I cannot anticipate the motions as do the rest. A fraction of a second late, I feel as though I am playing a child's game of *Simón Dice*— Simon Says. I am always just behind the beat. Sweat dampens my face, my back. I see the stains on my dress as I raise my arms alongside my ears.

"Stretch . . . one vertebra at a time, shoulders roll back, five, six, seven, eight—lunge—one, two, three, four, five, six, seven, eight—reach . . ."

My face hurts from straining—watching, listening. And this is just the warm-up.

Lola turns to face us. "Let's jump right in with a *Soleá por bulerías*. For anyone who does not know (does she look my way?), this is a hybrid form borrowing the typical choreography of the *Soleares* and *Bulerías*, but following more of the rhythmic pattern of the *Alegrías*." I find myself nodding with the others, even though I am far from certain. "*Marcando*," she continues, ticking off one direction after another like a grocery list. "*Escobilla, llamada*, then the first *letra. Palmas, contra tiempo, subida*. Repeat, we'll transition into the *bulerías*. Two *letras*, one *falsetto*. *Finale*. *Si?"*

Something close to panic seizes my throat. I force myself to inhale. Double my concentration. The musicians begin clapping *palmas* in a twelve-beat pattern. Lola marks steps across the floor, then moves to a sequence of more complex footwork, ending in a rhythmic cue for the singer, the *cantaor*. Yes, this I can do, I think to myself, whether or not I know the names of the movements. I watch again, and the third time we join in. I move, distracted, trying to remember the terms she used, trying to connect language with form, so that the next time I will know what to do. Study them, try to fit in so that no sweep of arm or tap of foot stands alone. Over and over we move, pressing on into the dance, Lola calling directions. "Drina—right!" she snaps. I find myself facing the opposite way as everyone else. In anger, I throw my hands up, hammer the floor all the harder with my heels. Dance has always freed my soul. Now it constrains my every instinct. I have lost myself trying to imitate each move, and the concentration it takes is building a wall between me and the dance.

"Relax for a moment. Grab a drink of water." Lola waves us off and I follow the others to the table where the pitcher and glasses have been laid out. My thoughts wander to rehearsals with my father and Renato. Realize now how they made accommodations for me, why they had me dance alone, accentuating my strengths, camouflaging my weaknesses. I feel ashamed and foolish for not recognizing this before. And furious that, despite this, he chose to place me, unprepared, into Señora Vega's hands. Why? So I can be made into the star he wants? Or proven a fool? I gulp my drink, wipe my mouth with the back of my hand, and line up again with the others for more of the same.

Finally, the grueling rehearsal ends. The relief I feel weakens my knees and turns my muscles to mush. My lower back clenches and aches. The balls of my feet burn and knives of pain shoot into my calves. I desperately want to behave as the rest, laughing, talking, but I am too spent and too overly self-conscious. Instead, I walk silently toward the door, trailing them. In the backstage area I remove my dancing shoes, fling them to the floor, the metal tips banging, slip into my espadrilles, avoiding the others' eyes.

Inez sweeps by and takes my arm. "Don't worry," she says. "The first rehearsal is always the hardest." One of the young men—the one called Jorge, with his slick black hair and close-set dark eyes—walks past whispering in a way I am surely meant to hear. "This is the star who danced for Franco?" His friend, Lope, snickers. I feel my face burn, look away.

"Don't listen to them," Inez coaxes. "Jealous, is all. Here, come with me. I can help." She guides me by the elbow into a small changing room, opens the dressing table drawer, rifles about, whipping out a scrap of paper and a pencil. Scrawls something across the sheet, whispering as she writes, reciting the form and steps of the dance . . . *Palmas, contra tiempo, subida* . . . Her brow furrows in concentration, the pencil dances across the page. She stops, holds the page up, eyes moving left to right over the marks she's made. This she thrusts into my hand. "Here," she says, clearly satisfied. "It's all there for you. You can study it. That's what I do." I stare at the page and back to Inez. She has already turned, is already bounding down the corridor, calling after the rest.

Thank goodness I do not need to explain that I can't read her marks. One more thing I cannot do. Still, as I watch her go I take the paper scrap, thrust it in my pocket beside the slip of paper with the Barcelona address. Perhaps I will dip it in water, place it in my mouth and chew until I can swallow the knowledge and make it a part of me. It is as good an idea as any.

We all head toward the hotel where the troupe is staying. I struggle to appear poised, confident. It is too much, this masquerade, so I slow my pace, hang back from the rest, soothing both my nerves and my tired feet. Several times Lola glances my way, but I avoid her eyes, longing for the privacy of my room. I watch them climb the steps and disappear inside, the double doors swallowing their carefree banter. Grateful for a slice of silence, I pause outside for a moment before I push through the doorway. Lola is waiting for me on the other side.

"A word with you," she says. She snaps her fingers and points toward the small bar off the lobby.

I follow her in. My heart pounds, wondering if she is going to send me away to Barcelona after just one rehearsal. Part of me thrills at the thought, and yet . . .

"Some advice." Her tone is curt, pointed.

"Yes," I say, bracing myself.

"I know you're feeling that you're in over your head. You're right to feel that way. There are some who, rightfully, feel as though you aren't quite up to snuff. Yet, if I could, I'd bet my last *peseta* that you'll prove them wrong. But I can't let anyone know that. In the meantime, you need to be humble. Show some deference."

I am at a loss. Is she suggesting that I'm arrogant? She must read the confusion on my face.

She points a manicured finger at me. "Aloof. You come across as aloof. Impatient. Refusing to join the group because, perhaps, you think you're better than the rest."

My face heats up in shame. "That is not how I feel. If anything, I . . ."

"I know," Lola says, "but they don't know that. Don't be so afraid to acknowledge your weakness. They'll respect you more. Accept you. Help you."

"I don't know the names of the steps. Don't know the patterns."

"So what? You will. That's why we rehearse."

I think of Marisol, what she'd said to me—"Remember! A thousand times—a thousand times is all it will take!" But it seems that a thousand times will take too long. Frustration presses tears behind my lids and I drop my eyes.

Señora Vega lifts my chin. "Spare me the tears. You're not some poor victim here. A hundred girls would jump at the opportunity that's been handed you." She levels me a hard look, her eyes holding mine. "Be your mother's daughter! Tomorrow's rehearsal I want to see a different Drina."

I open my mouth to answer, but she has already turned on her heel, leaving me there alone.

CHAPTER 45

Five more days of rehearsals, each as difficult as the day before. I work hard, try to fit in. Little by little I begin to anticipate the next move, and more often than before, name the desired steps and positions.

But then, just as my confidence begins to bud like a tiny flower, they thrust castanets into my hands! Oh, my *daj*—how can ten fingers be so stubborn? They fumble, they tangle, they freeze. I watch Luz and Inez, the small dark wooden disks gracefully cupped in their palms, each finger, from pinkie to pointer, rolling across, like the chatter of a field of crickets, chirping in time. But in my hands, I create the clumsy clatter of a dropped fork or spoon.

"The knot on the strap, Drina—it should face you." Señora Vega stops the group and demonstrates still again. Luz, who sits beside Alfonso, the guitarist, rolls her long-lashed eyes and sighs. She is beautiful in a thin, sharp kind of way—except for her fingers. She nibbles her nails almost to the quick. I notice the ragged cuticles as she covers her mouth with her hand to shield her not-so-secret words whispered to Alfonso. I hear my name—"Muentes"—and pretend to ignore them watching me struggle.

"Like this," Hernán says, grabbing my hand and adjusting the strap. "Remember? It needs to sit between the knuckle and the nail."

Señora Vega lifts her chin, gesturing toward the leather loop around my thumb. "Tighten. It's hanging too loose. No wonder you're lagging."

I want to take these dreaded clackers and throw them through the window, to free my hands, and then my soul. Perhaps I do not belong here—this is the thought that gnaws at my insides.

"Lunch," Lola announces. "Let's break." The group heads for the long table near the window where we gather to dine. I am too riled up, the vexation of the castanets continuing to try my patience. I stalk toward the *cuarto de baño*, prying the straps from my fingers, giving myself a slice of space and time to calm down before joining the others. I stride from the open dance hall into the narrow corridor, past the dressing rooms. Frustrated, I rid my fingers of the rattling gadgets—one, then the other—and the castanet in my right hand slips and clatters to the floor.

I crouch to swipe it up and allow myself the luxury of a long sigh.

As I rise, I see him coming through the back door.

"Ah, Señorita Drina! What perfect timing!" the Capitán exclaims, a sly smile parting his lips. My heart drops.

At that moment Oro appears.

"Salvador!" he cries, extending his hand, "What brings you back this afternoon?" The Capitán shakes Oro's hand, pulls him into a manly embrace, slaps him on the back.

They step apart and Salvador gestures toward me. "Oro, I want to bring an important friend here this evening to see this lovely one dance again. I'm sure you can arrange it. I can assure you, it will be the highlight of his evening—and of mine."

Oro smiles at me, revealing a glinting gold tooth on one side of his mouth. "*Si, si,*" he says, "I'm sure Señora Vega will agree. I'd love to see this one again myself." Like a pair of jackals the two of them eye me. Many words are poised on my tongue— You have found Boldo? I am not ready to perform! Will you stop looking at me as though I am something to devour?—but my lips remain sealed. I escape to the *baño* and listen for the retreat of their steps.

When I venture out, he is seated with the troupe at the lunch table, as I knew he would be, Oro setting out a tray of *tapas* and a pitcher of *sangria*. As I approach, the Capitán pulls out the chair to his right, indicating where I am to sit. Señora Vega is across from him, Luz to his left. "Come, Señorita Drina, we've been waiting for you," he calls. And to the group, "Our star has arrived, no? Franco's darling!"

My face reddens and I look down at the table.

"We are a troupe," Lola says. "There are no stars."

The Capitán ignores both Lola's correction and the troupe's obvious resentment. I sense he enjoys both. "Ah," he croons. "One lovely at my left, one across from me, another at my right . . . nothing I enjoy more than being a thorn among roses!" Jorge and Lope exchange a glance. Inez catches my eye, then looks away. Any progress I'd made with them, the Capitán has rolled back with his careless prattle. "Let's eat, shall we?" he exclaims, suddenly playing the host.

We dine quickly and quietly, everyone uncomfortable in the presence of the Capitán. He speaks loudly, looking from one of us to the other, commanding attention, a joke here, some teasing there. We respond with wooden smiles and waste no time getting back to rehearse. As Lola rises to join us, the Capitán places a hand on her shoulder, detaining her. From the dance floor I see his lips moving, chin nodding in my direction. She stands, hands on hips, head tipped. Runs a hand through her hair, considering. Oro joins the conversation, but he is even less subtle. He points toward me and I hear him mention my name. So does the rest of the troupe.

Somehow I muddle through the rehearsal, and the Capitán swaggers out of the dance hall, cocky with confidence. Lola dismisses the musicians and calls us together. "All right," she says, "Oro has invited us to perform this evening. I told him I didn't feel we were ready. But he insisted—said that on its worst day this troupe is better than many on their best! And since he affords us this rehearsal space, I feel we have a responsibility to oblige."

"Which dances will we perform?" This from Jorge, who is probably worrying about getting harnessed with me as his partner.

"I'll let you know. Some details for me to think about. Meet in the hotel lobby at 8:30, then we'll leave for the *peña*."

On the way out Lola takes me by the elbow. "Salvador has convinced Oro to have you dance this evening—solo. Apparently he is bringing someone who heard about your performance for Franco."

"But . . ."

"I've thought about it—the others will be offended for sure, at least at first." She nibbles the inside of her cheek, eyeing me closely. "But then I thought, if you can pull off what you did the night you danced for Franco, you'll earn their respect. They'll see what I saw—the raw talent. Your passion. Understand why I invited you."

I close my eyes. Wonder if I can conjure the dancer I was. We leave the *peña*, side by side, behind the rest. Walk in silence while the question looms large inside me. "The Capitán," I venture, "Is he . . . your beau?"

She throws her head back and laughs. "My beau? Oh, he's not beau material, my dear. He's a mouse who fancies himself a cat. Amusing while it lasts. But he is well-connected, powerful, in his way."

Cat or mouse, I cannot imagine her being pleased to know how he has been carrying on with me.

These thoughts plague me all the way to the hotel. I step ahead of her, push the door open.

"Drina!"

I turn.

"Forgetting something?"

I raise an eyebrow, distracted by thoughts of Boldo and second installments.

She throws a pair of castanets my way. I catch them midair—they snap sharply.

"Practice. All afternoon if you must." She breezes past me, casting one last look over her shoulder.

Evening comes quickly. I cannot focus my
attention, my brain flitting between many things—Boldo, the Capitán, Renato. Has he been counting the days, awaiting my return? Marisol. At the thought of my grandmother, something pulls at my heart. I picture her in Cadiz, sitting on the terrace, gazing out across the sea. Thinking of Felipe. Wondering about me? I push away the sadness rising in my throat. Pick up my bag and set out to meet the others. Lola holds court in the lobby, the troupe filling the small space with nervous energy and excitement.

"Lope and Luz—the *sevillanas*, you will be first. Jorge, Hernán, and Inez, the three of you will follow with a *solea*. As she speaks, their eyes shift my way. "Drina, you will be last. Oro has requested you appear alone as you did when you performed for the General. Perhaps a *petenera*."

They do not need to say a word for me to feel their anger. Lola presses on. "After that, we can improvise. Have a little fun with it. Come, let's get over there!" The seven of us join the musicians and walk the short blocks to the *peña*. Lola leads the way, the rest falling into pairs—Lope and Inez, Jorge and Hernán, leaving Luz with me. "The Capitán is your friend?"

she asks. She stretches the word "friend" so that it sounds like something sly and shameful. "I thought he was Lola's . . ."

"No, no," I stammer, "I mean, yes, he and Lola . . . I mean, I only met him once." Luz shrugs, picks up her pace, and leaves me behind. Up ahead she joins Alfonso, his guitar strapped across his back. They incline their heads and he glances back at me. I look down, walk the rest of the way in silence. If Lola notices the unspoken tension, she doesn't let on. I feel the troupe's resentment thicken into a wall between us. They will be watching me dance, waiting to pounce on every flaw.

Lola opens the back door to the *peña* and music, light, and laughter spill out into the night. As we enter I see the Capitán leaning against the inside door to the dance hall, smoking a cigarette. Lola nods hello and turns to us. "In costume by 9:20. 9:30 we go on. Find yourselves a dressing room—maybe women over here, gentlemen, there. Let's go!"

Quickly, I follow Luz and Inez into the last room on the right. In silence, clothes off, dress on, still damp under the arms from yesterday's washing. Hair, jewelry, *peineta* and comb, *manton*, and shoes. "I'll help with your buttons, and you mine?" I ask. The back of my dress gapes. Luz continues with her primping as though she hasn't heard. Inez shrugs and steps behind me, her fingers working their way up my back. "Thank you. Do you need me to—"

"No," she says, moving toward Luz.

I wrap my hair carelessly, reach for Marisol's comb that I hold in my hand for a moment before fixing it in the nest of my locks. The others begin to line up in the corridor. I hear them in the hallway, push myself to my feet and join them. Lope and Luz are first. I hear the strains of the *sevillanas* begin. Jorge, Hernán, and Inez wait in the wings with Lola. I stand just outside the dressing room door.

Suddenly, a hand on my shoulder. The Capitán takes me aside, inclines his face toward mine. His breath smells of mint and cigarettes. I am close enough to see the small brown fleck of tobacco on his lip. I inch back, and still he comes closer, places a hand on the wall over my shoulder, leans in. "Your hero will make an appearance here tonight," he whispers, "Just enough for you to see him. Then, he has strict instructions to leave. If we catch him nearby he'll be picked up and thrown back into prison." He smiles, straightens up. "So, dance up a storm for me, my lovely. First installment."

My hands shake as I nod—as close as I can come to a thank you. He squeezes my arm and moves inside. I hear the music announcing the trio of Jorge, Hernán, and Inez, rush back to the dressing room for a last look in the mirror, to check on who Boldo will see, if, in fact, he is here. Will he recognize me? Like a tightly coiled spring, I head down the corridor, every part of me tingling. The end of the hall—the doorway—the red velvet curtain. In my newly soled shoes my feet carry me.

I stop.

Breathe. Breathe.

Inch aside the curtain with my finger. Tip my head for a view of the room through the slit. Less crowded than the last time. Groups of men drinking. Couples at small tables. A line of patrons along the outside wall. My eyes scan their faces. There is the Capitán, some enlisted men on his right and left. And, oh my *daj*—in the middle of this group I see him. Unmistakable. Leaning against a column. Prominent brow, barrel chest, thinner, yes, but the same dark power. Clothes tattered but worn with pride. Eyes fixed on the stage.

For a moment, I do not hear the music that signals my entrance. But Lola's firm hand at the small of my back propels me forward, and the music does its magic. Seduces my body to forget and remember all at once. The *petenera* . . . Can it be the same mournful song my father first played for me on the gramophone?

Quisiera yo renegar . . . de este mundo entero volver de nuevo
a habitar el mar de mi corazón . . . I wish I could deny this
entire world, to once again inhabit the sea of my heart . . .

The *cantaora* wraps her soul around the melody—she could be Pastora Pavon Cruz herself. Her voice opens the wounds of my heart and I bleed into the dance.

When it is over, I bow, stare into the light. There, the Capitán and two of the enlisted men, applauding. But the space in front of the column is empty.

The music begins again—my cue to exit. My legs of jelly carry me past the troupe to the dressing room. Collapsing in the chair, I cover my face with my hands. For several minutes I stay like this. When I open my eyes I notice the rose on the dressing table. Brilliant gold with scarlet edges. The Capitán's calling card.

Air. I need air. Grab my fan, wave it in front of me, but this

301

is not sufficient. I stand, leave my room for the outside door. Shove it open. Fill my lungs to bursting.

A hand on my shoulder. I gasp. Spin. He covers my lips with his. Pulls my body into his for a long moment. Finally, we break apart.

"It was only the thought of you that sustained me."

His face, in all its intensity, steals my breath. "Boldo!"

"I never lost hope. Never!"

"You can't stay here! The Capitán . . ."

"I know. But I had to see you. I have a plan! Meet me tomorrow morning."

"But—Lola has a place for me in the troupe. My father—"

"Have you forgotten who you are, Drina? They're using you! Like they use all *Gitanos*. You don't owe them anything. In the end, they'll hurt you. Throw you away." He squeezes my upper arm. "Come home with me. Leave all this!"

There is a sound at the back door. He pulls me into the shadows. Whispers, "I'm going to leave *patrin*. Beginning here. It will lead you to me. Make certain you're not followed. Then we can go back where we belong. To our own people. Together, finally." He pulls me to him once more, kisses me on the mouth, then slips into the darkness.

"Drina!" The back door creaks open. "Are you out here? Drina?"

"Coming." With trembling hands I grab the railing, hoist the weighty *cola* of my dress, climb the stairs. I feel Boldo's eyes follow me every step of the way until the door closes between us.

ᴄHAPTER 46

The night is endless. When the dancing is through, we sit around tables passing food and drink. The Capitán plays host, buying rounds of drinks and platters of food. His is a generosity that is showy and full of itself. I pretend not to notice him watching me.

"Your *petenera* . . ." Inez says, with something close to respect in her eyes, "It was . . . I don't know . . . compelling. As though the dance began and you went someplace inside yourself. Mysterious. Moving." Jorge nods. "Well done. Really." Lola catches my eye and almost imperceptibly nods an affirmation. No one seems to notice Luz getting up and striding away from the table.

"True, true" the Capitán pipes in. "I saw one fellow in the back who couldn't take his eyes off of her. Did you notice him, Drina?"

Flustered, I nod my yes, but answer ,"No."

Lola laughs. "Don't get swept away in his gushing! Nice as it was, we're going to continue to sharpen the steps, hone the posture, improve the lines of your body, expand the arc of your arms, the alignment of your legs, spine, chin." She names my weaknesses as though reciting an endless list of chores. "Work on transitions between *llamadas.*" Perhaps she sees my face fall. With a sweeping motion of her hand she addresses the group. "You'd all agree that already we see improvement in the way you mark steps—*marcajes*—and how you use your weight—your *peso*—more dramatically. More and more we will build in the kind of control and restraint that will only strengthen your performance. I hope you've gotten a taste of how this will transform you into a real artist." The others nod encouragement.

I feel equal parts despair and hope. Hear the words, sense the truth in them—but hadn't Boldo's words rung true in another way? My insides churn. What is true? Who is right?

Lola stands. "Everyone's tired. Better get some sleep. Tomorrow—entire troupe—3:00. I likely won't see you until then. I have a round of appointments throughout the day."

Oro escorts us out. "Splendid job!" he exclaims. "I'll have the doors open all morning and afternoon, so come as you wish. Alfonso and Gaspar will be here if you want to practice." The guitarist and his brother, castanets in hand, wave their agreement.

"Thank you, Oro," Lola says. "Alfonso. Gaspar. Hope you'll have some takers." She looks directly at me. We collect our things and walk toward the door, Lola lingering behind in conversation with Oro. The Capitán sidles up to me, inclines his head, and whispers, "Indulge me. Let me watch you practice. Tomorrow, I'll come by with the car. 1:45? Or shall we say 1:30, to allow extra time?"

Is it my imagination that he emphasizes "extra time"?

"No, thank you," I mumble. "I should walk over with the rest."

"Ah, but you are different from the rest . . ."

"No, really . . ."

"As you like," he says, with a tight little smile, "another day then . . ."

Back in my room I fill the tub with hot water. Strip out of my clothes. Ease my blistered toes and aching calves into the bath. Crouch, sit, stretch out until my torso, arms, shoulders, and neck are submerged. Remember the first bath Carlita drew for me back in Jerez, how the *Gitano* taboo of reclining in still water wracked me with guilt. Now, I soak without a second thought. Boldo had asked, "Have you forgotten who you are?" Perhaps that is the problem. I get up, shiver, wipe myself dry. Turn back the bed and slip in, naked, between the cool sheets. Who am I without all the dressing, I wonder, as I fall into a deep, blank sleep.

I awaken to a white-sky day, sunny, but no hint of blue. Nine o'clock, by the look of it. The morning stretches before me. What to do? I think of Boldo, waiting at the end of his trail of *patrin*. Of Renato, waiting in Barcelona. My father, waiting for me to fulfill my mother's dream. Marisol waiting in Cadiz. Lola waiting for me to become an artist. The Capitán waiting for his next installment. For what and who am I waiting? "My *daj*," I whisper, "I must dance as I live and breathe. But where? With whom?"

Her voice caresses me from the inside out. *Swallows come and they go, according to the season.*

For a moment I recall the swallows flying across Spain to Africa and back, returning year after year to the places that sustain them. "*Daj*—what do you mean?" But like a gentle breeze, her presence has left me.

Restless, I pull on my clothes. Sit on the edge of the bed. One thought chasing the other like a game of tag. I get up. Pace. Sit back down. Nibble the inside of my cheek.

My bag stands against the armoire. It speaks to me. Tells me what I need to do to clear my head. Dance. Just dance.

I grab the valise, hoist the strap over my shoulder. Walk downstairs and leave word that I've gone to the *peña* to practice.

I squint into the brightness outside on the walk, turn north. One block, another, a third. There, the large clock and bell tower. I readjust the weight of my bag, hoist the strap farther back on my shoulder. Two more blocks. My feet click along the uneven surface. I walk past a café with outdoor tables. People hunch over small cups of black coffee. Sipping. Smoking. Noticing me hardly at all. And there, at last, the *peña*.

I pause a moment outside the door. Push. The stale air greets me, left over from last evening. I hear the musicians at the end of the hall talking, laughing, playing a refrain or two, killing time. Slowly I move along the hallway lined with photos.

Famous *cantaors* and *tacaors,* and then, the dancers. I stare at each dramatic pose, each perfect face, each splendid costume. "Make a name for yourself," my father said. If I did, would my picture hang here among these renowned faces? Who would I be then?

Alfonso steps out of the practice room. "Ah, our new star," he says, his voice cold and his eyes hard. "The latest to catch the good Capitán's eye." He leans back toward the doorway, calls inside. "Gaspar, hurry—Señorita Muentes has arrived!" His voice drips disdain. Then he looks back at me and lowers his voice to a near whisper. "Just because you're a *Muentes,* born with a silver spoon in your mouth and *flamenco* in your blood, doesn't mean you don't have to earn your place here like everybody else."

A flame of anger flickers and ignites. I step closer so that my face is inches from his. My heart pounds and I feel tears burn behind my eyes. "So that's what you think?" I shout. "That whatever I have has been handed to me?"

Alfonso takes a step back.

"You don't know anything about me!"

I throw my head back, turn on my heel. I will not let him see me cry. I stride along the corridor, staring down the photo gallery of anonymous eyes. Pull the door open, my bag still in hand. Step outside where the air is fresh. I wipe my tears with the back of my hand and stand very still for a moment.

Down the stairs, I see it.

A broken twig, the bark peeled back, nailed to the trunk of

a tree. The angle of its break forming an arrow, pointing west. Heart pounding, I am drawn by the ancient signs of my people.

There, a flapping scrap of bright blue calico, impaled on the finial of an iron fence. I reach up, lift it off the black, rusted spike. Finger the soft fabric. On . . . on . . . one foot in front of the other. The next block, two round stones in a row, sitting on a concrete wall, one small, one larger . . . Instinctively my eyes discover sign after runic sign, drawing me from neighborhood to neighborhood. Shoulder aching, I slip the strap of my bag down my arm and into my hand, moist with sweat. It bumps against my leg as I journey toward my past. The black feather of a magpie, its hollow shaft poking through a peeling, curled war poster, then another tied into a cascade of ivy against brick.

The sound of a deep, reedy whistle interrupts. I stop. Beyond, a wide avenue sprawls. Taxicabs and pedestrians line the street. Two buses are parked along the curb. People pass, lugging bags and valises. My eye travels to a large, long building.

Again, the whistle. I head in the direction of the hollow sound, toward the wide-open doorway. The train station. For a moment I am a stone in the river of people flowing around me.

"Barcelona, track five," the voice booms through static. My heart beats rapidly. I set off into the throng of travelers, then pause. Place my satchel on the floor, remove the white envelope lined with a neat stack of bills. Finger the luggage tag, where the paper my father pressed in my hand is safely tucked. This, the address where Renato waits, where my father prepares for me to return to him a star.

Jostled and nudged, I push on, looping back the way I came,

retracing my path to the sunlight. From the doorway I peer out into the busy plaza. Spy the black feather tucked in ivy, glide toward it. My fingers tremble as I pluck it from its place, as I weave it through the buttonhole of my blouse to remind me. Nearby, a bougainvillea climbs a wall, red blossoms tumbling over greenery. I collect a cluster of blooms, wrap the blue calico scrap around the stems, fold back the edges so that the bright azure frames the scarlet. This I carefully wedge into the spot where the feather had been placed. The colors shout against the ivy. It will do.

I turn my back on it, run.

Inside, people stream in many directions.

"Barcelona, leaving in two minutes. Track five."

I slip the paper my father gave me from the safety of my luggage tag. Another peeks beneath it. With a steady hand I ease it out, stare at the figures penned there:

C A D I Z.

I glance toward the sign above the next track. Check the marks, one to the other—first, the broken circle, next, the upward facing arrow, then the flattened ring, next, the pillar, and yes, finally, the lightening slash. My grandmother's *patrin*. Her runic signs. "Cadiz," I say, softly.

"You want Cadiz?" a woman responds, pointing. "Track four. Leaves after the Barcelona train. You have plenty of time."

Yes, I think. She is right. No need to rush. There will be plenty of time for so many things. Things I cannot yet imagine. A seedling of calm takes root and begins to sprout within me. My heart slows. It blossoms into something else, something new.

I pick up my bag, slip the strap over my shoulder. Inside my soul I hear the strains of a *Malagueña,* and it propels me, in time, along the concrete platform between the tracks. An old man sitting on a nearby bench tips his hat, smiles. A triangle of yellow light spills from the open door of the train, beckoning. Grasping the envelope, I cross the threshold into the long shiny car. Pause. Grasp a bar overhead to steady myself. Get my bearings.

I listen to the final call for the Barcelona train, watch it pull out of the station. Then, "Cadiz, track four, five minutes." An engine rumbles, the vibration traveling through my feet, into my body—a new kind of music and this becomes the accompaniment to my prayer for Boldo: *Forgive me, but I will not go back to being half of who I am.*

I find a seat beside the window, sit and gaze through the pane. But all I see in the glass are my eyes, the Muentes eyes, staring back at me. If I squint I can summon around them the faces of Felipe, of my father. My grandmother. Fingering the pendant at my throat, my thoughts fly to Marisol. "I am here," I whisper to her. "I am me. Not this or that. I am neither, and both."

But she always knew that.

I close my eyes at the powerful yearning I feel, melt into the ease of the welcome I know she will offer. Her words come to me suddenly: *Drina, what I want is for you to be a bird with the heart of a mountain. Grounded. Solid. Understanding you have a place that will always be there for you. Knowing that, you have the freedom to fly wherever your wings take you.*

The train whistle blows, a lonely, breathy sound. The

trainman, one gloved hand on the door, calls out across the station. "Last call, Cadiz!"

I jump to my feet, heart pounding, yank my valise from under the seat. The trainman draws the heavy door across the frame slicing my view of the platform outside.

"Wait!" I dash toward him, planting my foot in the space between portal and door.

"What are you doing, Señorita?"

"Out! Let me off please! Now!"

"Make up your mind," he mutters as he rolls back the door. I swoop from the compartment, the door swooshing closed behind me. After a moment of groaning and rumbling, the train accelerates and flies past in a colorful blur, the draft of air in its wake buffeting my face, ruffling my hair. The image comes to me again, of the brilliantly plumed birds that wing across Gibraltar, returning, year after year, to Cadiz. It calls to mind the words of my *daj*: *Swallows come and they go, according to the season.*

Can I not do the same? And what had my grandmother said? Be a bird with the heart of a mountain? Yes, Marisol will be there in Cadiz, waiting, like the Mountain of Tariq. This I know.

A wave of fear clutches me. Lola's rigid steps and tedious practice loom like a wall between me and my dance. I think of how her insistence on precision has blocked my spirit and chained my passion. And then there is the Capitán. But there have been other walls, other barricades I've struggled to cross. Has not all of it somehow enriched my dance and broadened my soul?

I stand before the empty place where the train had been. Yes, Marisol will be there, whether in Cadiz or Jerez, or perhaps someplace new. Hers is a home that abides in my heart. This I carry with me as surely as the valise in my hand, as the wrung-out paper scrap with CADIZ scrolled across it that I stash securely beneath my luggage tag.

I sling the strap of my satchel full of shoes and fan, castanets and shawl over my shoulder, make my way through the station and into the brightness outside. A phrase of the *petenera* I have come to think of as mine plays in my head as I travel back along the avenue . . . *a habitar el mar de mi corazón.* Yes. Once more I will inhabit the sea of my heart.

I quicken my steps. If I hurry, I will still arrive back at the *peña* ahead of the rest, to strap on the shoes of my *daj*—and dance.

HISTORICAL NOTE: THE GYPSIES

For more than 700 years, the Gypsy people have been mistreated and misunderstood. Even the name "Gypsy" was given to them because it was mistakenly thought that they had originally emigrated from Egypt when, in fact, they actually came from the Middle East and India.

Throughout history, Gypsies have been persecuted and excluded from society. Perhaps this is because they are a nomadic people, travelling from place to place in family groups, working as traders and trainers of animals, peddlers and tinkerers, fortune tellers and entertainers. Because they are always on the move, it's harder for others to know them. Gypsies have their own unique language, too—called Romany—which few outsiders understand. Because they have no organized religion, Gypsies were often thought of as heretics by strong supporters of the Catholic Church and other religious groups. But in fact, Gypsies are a deeply spiritual people who observe strict purity laws that govern the way they live.

In the 1500s, Gypsies moved into southern Spain, to the region called Andalusia. It was here that the music and dance of the Spaniards mingled with that of the Gypsies, resulting in a dramatic art form called *flamenco*. Though the Gypsies lived in Spain for many centuries, they never became a part of mainstream Spanish life. The situation for the Gypsy people in Spain worsened during the 1930s as Spain descended into the chaotic violence of the Spanish Civil War.

Spain in the 1930s was sharply divided into two broad political groups: the Republicans and the Nationalists. The Republic (also known as "The Popular Front") largely represented poor workers and peasants who slaved on the farms of the wealthy landowners. For the most part, this group was anti-Catholic, because the Catholic Church had aligned itself with those who were wealthy and in power. The Republicans were backed by the Russians and supported by international brigades of foreign volunteers. But even though the Gypsy people were poor and powerless too, they were still considered outsiders by Republicans.

The Nationalists represented the moneyed classes, the landowners, and the military elite. They supported the centralization of state power and the Catholic Church. The Nationalists were backed by Germany's Hitler and Italy's Mussolini, both fascist dictators. In 1938, the Nationalists won the Spanish Civil War under the leadership of another dictator, General Francisco Franco. Franco imprisoned almost 300,000 men and women and exiled half a million more from Spain, sending many to German concentration camps. Gypsies were distrusted by the Nationalists, too, and many were abused, tortured, or killed.

For all of Spain, the 1930s were a time of frightening divisions and choices that sometimes separated families: Stand with the Republic? With the Nationalists? But Gypsies, mistreated and misunderstood in the best of times, could only stand alone.

Bird With the Heart of a Mountain is set in this turbulent, violent time in Spain. It is here that Drina, part Gypsy, part Spanish, dreaming of a life of dance, must carve out an identity of her own.

GLOSSARY

Ajuntaora—an elder woman in the Gypsy clan responsible for the *pañuelo* ritual to ensure that a bride is a virgin

Alegrias—a form of Flamenco music and dance, originating in Cadiz, that follows a set 12 beat pattern

Baila—a Spanish phrase of encouragement shouted at a dancer, meaning: She/he dances!

Bandolier—the ruler of a Gypsy community

Bodega—a storeroom where sherry is aged and stored

Campagna—a group of Gypsy families traveling together

Cantaor—Spanish word for singer

Cola—the train of a long dress

Compass—a 12-count bar of music

Contra tiempo—opposing rhythms

Darro—a Gypsy word for dowry

Divano—a meeting of Gypsy elders to settle a dispute or solve a problem

Duende—a passionate mysterious quality or spirit that powerfully draws others in

El Yeli!—the words *"El Yeli!"* are sung at Gypsy weddings to celebrate the bride giving herself honorably to her husband.

Fandango—a lively Spanish dance

Feria—Spanish word for a fair

Floreo—hand movements in Flamenco dancing that mimic the blossoming of a flower.

Gadje—Romany word for a non-Gypsy

Gitano—Spanish word for Gypsy

Golpe—rhythmic effect produced when a Flamenco guitarist strikes the soundboard of the guitar

Jaleo—shouts of encouragement given to performers

Jamón—Spanish word for ham

Letra—the section of a dance that takes place as the cantaora is singing the lyrics

Llamada—the opening of a dance or a new section of the dance

Malagueña—a sad, mournful song, originating from Malaga

Mantilla—a lace veil worn on the head

Marcando—marking time

Palmas—rhythmic hand clapping that accompanies flamenco dancing

Pañuelo—a ritual in which a group of elder women of the Gypsy clan gather to witness the examination of the bride to make certain that she is a virgin. When finished, they sing *"El Yeli!"* and wave a cloth with three petals embroidered on it. The men have a tradition in which they tear their shirts while the bride is carried to her groom.

Paseos—Spanish word for an informal stroll or promenade. During the Spanish Civil war the word was used to describe the rounding up of citizens by informal brigades to be led to execution, usually by beating.

Patrin—grass, twigs, or other materials left behind by Gypsies for the purpose of marking a trail

Peineta—a decorative comb worn in the hair

Peña—a meeting place of musicians and dancers

Peseta—a silver coin

Plantas—a flamenco term for striking the floor with the ball of the foot

Pliashka—a Gypsy ceremony to mark an engagement

Rinkeni—a Romany word meaning pretty, attractive

Romany—a word used to refer to Gypsies and their language

Rondeña—a folk dance song originating in Serrania de Ronda, Spain

Sevillana—a type of folk song originating in Seville

Siguiriya—a deep, expressive style of Flamenco music

Soleá por bulerías—a hybrid form of Flamenco that has characteristics of both *soleares* and *bulerías*

Taconeo—flamenco footwork in which the heel rhythmically strikes the floor

Tocaor—Spanish word for someone who plays Flamenco guitar

Tsinvari—Romany word for evil spirits

Vardos—colorful horse-drawn wagons that travel in caravans, providing transportation, storage, and shelter to Gypsy people

ACKNOWLEDGEMENTS

Many thanks to my editor, Melanie Kroupa, for her diligence and vision, to Carlota Santana, director of *Flamenco Vivo*, and to dancer, Leslie Roybal, for sharing their expertise on the art of flamenco. Any inaccuracies in this regard are mine. Also, thanks to Virginia Weir for accompanying me to Jerez, and to the Gipsy Kings for inspiration. *Olé!*

ABOUT THE AUTHOR

Barbara Mariconda is the author of books for readers of all ages, including *The Voyage of Lucy P. Simmons* which *Kirkus Reviews* praised for its "dramatic and visually stunning" prose. In writing *Bird with the Heart of a Mountain* it was a haunting Gypsy melody that first captured the author's imagination, that drew her to Jerez, Spain, and into Drina's world. She serves on the Board of Directors of *Flamenco Vivo* in NYC, which promotes the art of flamenco to new audiences (www.flamenco-vivo.org) and she strives to empower the next generation of young authors through her company, Empowering Writers. You can visit her online at **www.barbaramariconda.com**